THE DANCING PRINCESSES

THE DANCING PRINCESSES

An Adaptation of the
Grimm Brothers' Fairy Tale
"The Twelve Dancing Princesses"

Jaclyn Su Harris

Library of Congress Control Number:		2021917448
ISBN:	Hardcover	978-1-6641-9161-7
	Softcover	978-1-6641-9160-0
	eBook	978-1-6641-9159-4

Print information available on the last page.

Rev. date: 08/23/2021

To order additional copies of this book, contact:
Xlibris
844-714-8691
www.Xlibris.com
Orders@Xlibris.com
832233

To my family for always believing in my talent and encouraging me to write. I hope this first book will satisfy them.

Author's Notes

I should note that my tale takes place in a fairy-tale equivalent of the early to midseventeenth-century Germany. As a result, one of my characters has a disorder that will today be diagnosed as Asperger's syndrome or an autistic spectrum disorder but back then would not have been diagnosed or recognized as such. There were people even in the time of Martin Luther who might have been autistic but weren't diagnosed as such because autistic spectrum disorders, including autism itself and Asperger's syndrome, weren't identified until the twentieth century. I myself wasn't diagnosed with Asperger's syndrome until sometime around 2000, about four years after I graduated from college.

While my novel is based on the fairy tale "The Twelve Dancing Princesses," there is a tale within the novel that is based on another fairy tale, "Little Snow White," also collected by the Grimm brothers. While we're very familiar with the Evil Queen, who persecuted Snow White as being her stepmother in the first edition of their fairy-tale collection, the Grimm brothers made the queen Snow White's *biological* mother and not her stepmother; the change came in later editions, possibly to tone down the story for children. The Snow White–based tale will have the queen be the birth mother and will provide an interesting explanation for her jealousy. Also, the gowns that the faeries provide for the princesses are based on the description of the gowns that the princess in the Grimm brothers' fairy tale *Allerleirauh* (All-Kinds-of-Fur) asks for to escape her widowed father's decision to marry her ostensibly because she is the only woman who is as beautiful as his deceased wife. Check that fairy tale out for a description of the gowns.

I looked to other sources for inspiration in my novel. One is a book by Robin McKinley titled *Beauty: A Retelling of the Story of Beauty and the Beast*. Beauty, the main character, is a bookworm, much like my character who has Asperger's syndrome; and while she is in the Beast's castle, he shows her his library, which contains books that haven't even been written at the time she saw them. Here, my faerie character also has a library that contains books that haven't been written by the time my novel takes place and shows it to the bookworm.

Another source is a ballad named *Heer Haelwijn*. This is a Dutch folk ballad that was actually published only in an anthology from the nineteenth century but actually dates back to the thirteenth century; also, the story itself is probably even older and has elements dating back to Carolingian times and even Germanic pre-Christian legends. According to Wikipedia, where I found the story, there are different versions of the *Heer Haelwijn* tale, with him being either an evil man, a magician, a demon, or a faerie lord who sings a magical song that compels any maiden who hears it to go to him in the forest, where he kills them. Some versions have him behead his maidens, others have him hang or drown them (or both), and still others have him turn them into stone with his magical stone.

Finally, a princess hears the song and is drawn into the forest to meet him. In some versions (like in the ballad), she knows of his reputation but has a plan; but in other versions, a white bird warns her. Either way, she meets him and goes with him to a field of gallows where he announces his intention to kill her but is impressed enough with her beauty to allow her to choose her own method of being killed. She chooses to be beheaded but urges him to take off his shirt so her blood won't stain him. He lays down his sword and proceeds to undress, and either the cloth muffles his magical song or prevents him from using a spellbinding gaze or he turns his back to the princess as he undresses. However it happens, the princess takes the sword and beheads him.

The ballad then mentions that Haelwijn's head continues to speak and urges the princess to rub a pot of ointment taken from beneath the gallows on his neck and then take his horn, go into a cornfield, and blow on it so that all his friends will hear. She refuses to do so because he is a murderer. She washes his head in a well before returning home.

While this is not mentioned in the ballad, on the way, she meets Haelwijn's mother; and when asked about Haelwijn, the princess reveals his fate. She then goes home, and there is a feast, with the head being put on the table. One of the reasons why Wikipedia notes that the tale might go back as far as Carolingian times is that, in the ballad, the princess asks her father, her mother, her sister, and finally her brother for permission to go to Haelwijn. Her brother agrees as long as she keeps her honor safe. In Carolingian times, it was a custom for a brother to watch over the honor of his sisters.

When I read the entry on *Heer Haelwijn* in Wikipedia, I found out that in Germanic pre-Christian legends, there was the idea of a nature spirit or a faerie using a magical song to lure people into his realm, usually the forest, where he causes their death. Also, given how sexual Haelwijn is, it is possible that he was once the deity of an ancient pagan fertility ritual and that his being a dangerous murderer came about after pagan folk rites were shunned by Christianity, especially sexual ones. Thus, I chose to have Haelwijn be a faerie lord who never actually killed the maidens whom he lured into his realm but instead kept them as concubines inside underground chambers and to have the princess be the one he intended to be his lady (i.e., wife). Therefore, in the ballad, as my bookworm character read in the faerie library, Haelwijn never tried to kill the princess but instead entered into sexual contact with her but began to undress only after lowering her down onto the ground; and when he pulled his upper clothing over his head, she awoke from his spell, remembered her father and brother's fears that Haelwijn would kill her, and thus used her sword to behead Haelwijn, only realizing her error when she met Haelwijn's mother and learned his true motives and thus never marrying as in the footnote in one version.

I took the name Aldana from one of the daughters of Charles Martel, who was the father of Pepin the Short, the first of the Carolingian rulers to become king of the Franks. The daughter's name was Auda, but she was also called Aldana.

A third source of inspiration, ironically enough, lies in the lives of people surrounding Henry VIII of England. One of my three princesses (not the bookworm one) is based, to a large extent, on Catherine Howard, the fifth wife of Henry VIII. Catherine was a vivacious and giggly girl who was most interested in music and dancing. Before coming to court and catching the eye of Henry VIII, she was raised by the dowager duchess of Norfolk, her step-grandmother. There, she was molested by a music teacher named Henry Mannock, who was the first inspiration of the music and dance teacher in my novel. Catherine and Henry had sexual contact, but it never proceeded to intercourse.

The other inspiration was Catherine's first real lover, Francis Dereham, a secretary to the dowager duchess, mainly in terms of the fate of Dereham inspiring that of the music and dance instructor in my novel. The final influence was that of Anne Boleyn, the second wife of Henry VIII, as I used her final speech when she was about to be beheaded as inspiration for a similar scene in my novel.

I also looked at Mercedes Lackey's book *The Black Swan* (which I have) for a few details here and there, at the Harry Potter books for the detail about the faeries moving in the pictures, and online at various websites (including Wikipedia) for inspiration in terms of gardening, fashion, and military tactics of the early to midseventeenth century. Moreover, the castle that the princesses go to every night is actually based on Neuschwanstein Castle, and I looked at architectural plans for it online to get some details. There are probably other sources that I used for inspiration that I have forgotten about or failed to mention.

CHAPTER 1

Today was the day the members of the royal court of the kingdom of Orgon were coming to Duke Thomas's manor as part of their intended royal progress. As a result, the estate had to look its absolute best. That included the gardens at the manor, especially the formal gardens at the front. Near the manor, there were low planting beds with closely clipped hedges, colored gravels, and even flowers. These beds were elaborate and created with low boxwood to resemble the patterns of a carpet. Farther away, the beds were simpler and contained fountains with sculptures and basins of water. Finally, carefully created groves of trees were the borders between the formal garden and the park, where there were masses of trees carefully tended by foresters.

There were four subdivisions of the gardens. The first and largest was the formal gardens. This tended to be the area where people could stroll, and there were spaces for festivities. The second was the private garden used by Duke Thomas and his family. It was surrounded by a high fence and was carefully locked, and the head gardener, a middle-aged man named Peter, went in there to take care of the trees and flowers in the garden, along with whoever stood guard in there at nights during warm weather. Whereas the formal gardens were in front of the manor, the private garden was at the rear.

The third subdivision was the vegetable garden. This was a small area that had a compost heap and several plots of land and was also located at the back of the manor but closer to the entrance than the private garden. This was where the vegetables that the people on the estate ate grew. And finally, there was the herb garden, also known as the witches' garden. This was where herbs were grown, and it was located in a small area on the opposite side of the vegetable garden. Some herbs were used to flavor food in cooking, but there were herbs that were used for medicinal purposes, and some were used for both.

Mark tended this garden. He was working under Peter, and his job was to cultivate the garden, making sure that the herbs got enough sunlight and water, keeping them safe from pests and plant diseases, and making sure that certain herbs, such as mint, didn't take over the whole garden. He had been doing this work for a little over a year, ever since the previous gardener, a middle-aged man, became ill and could no longer properly take care of the garden. The doctor at the manor diagnosed the gardener as having consumption. Mark's father, a baker who prepared bread for the nearby town and some of the people from the manor, heard about the need for a skilled gardener; and since Mark took care of the kitchen garden that his family used for vegetables, fruits, and even herbs, he went to the manor, and Peter hired him. He was eighteen years old at that time and was now nineteen.

Mark was tall, somewhat slim yet sturdy. He had jet-black hair and dark brown eyes and was tanned from the sun due to working all day in gardens. He was handsome, and quite a few peasant girls who worked at the manor had eyed him, but he wasn't especially attracted to any of them. He was also friendly and somewhat talkative when having leisure time but not usually very talkative when working in the garden as he was very focused on his work.

Today Mark was especially concerned about making sure the garden was well tended and free from pests and disease. King Robert had three daughters, and the eldest and heir apparent, Karen, might spend time in this garden collecting herbs for medicinal purposes. He didn't want Princess Karen collecting herbs that were pest ridden or diseased.

Mark remembered the first time Princess Karen had come to the herb garden. He'd only been working at Duke Thomas's estate for a couple of months, and he was working in the herb garden very hard. The head gardener had told him about the royal progress coming to Duke Thomas's manor and had informed Mark of Princess Karen's interest in herbs, so he was making sure it was properly taken care of.

When the royal party arrived, Mark was satisfied that the garden was in good order, so he chose to wait until the royal party arrived in the gardens. While he believed most of the royal party would not enter the herb garden and thus he would only see them at a distance, Princess Karen might come in; and if she was going to pick herbs, he wanted to assure her that the herbs were free of pests and disease.

It was late afternoon in May, sometime between four and five o'clock, if the position of the sun was accurate. There were no clocks in the house where Mark had grown up, so he learned quickly how to tell time by the position of the sun. The weather was warm, and if people came out of the back entrance to the manor, Mark could see them passing by the walk that led to the herb garden.

Then he thought he heard footsteps. Soon he saw an extremely lovely girl of about fourteen or fifteen standing in front of the herb garden area, accompanied by a young woman of about twenty and a page of about fourteen. The girl was possibly the most beautiful girl Mark had ever seen in his life—tall and willowy with golden red hair that was braided and tied into a sort of crown around her head, a heart-shaped face, a high forehead, large dark green eyes, an ivory complexion with a hint of rose in her cheekbones, a well-defined nose, and a small mouth with full pink lips. She wore brown gloves on her hands and had a silken canopy over her head that was carried by the page, presumably to avoid spoiling her complexion. And she was one of the princesses.

However, Mark didn't know this girl was one of the princesses from her dress since it was relatively simple, at least when compared with Mark's own ideas of how a princess might dress. The dress was emerald green in color, which in and of itself was expensive, but neither the bodice or the stomacher, a triangular pattern in the front opening of her bodice, was heavily embroidered or covered in gold or precious gems. The sleeves were fairly long but didn't hang down and weren't slashed, there weren't many layers of skirts, and she didn't have a long train that the other woman would have to carry. In fact, she didn't have a train at all since the dress only went down to her ankles. However, the girl wore a gold circlet on her forehead, and it was studded with pearls, so Mark was sure she was one of the princesses.

The twenty-year-old, young woman presumably was a lady-in-waiting to the princess. She wore a simple lavender-colored dress and was a pale blonde who wore her hair in a bun in the back, with a cluster of curls framing her face. She wore a lavender hat and a veil that covered her face. She was carrying a basket in one hand, and Mark wondered what it was for. If the redhead in green was Princess Karen, however, it was most likely for picking herbs. The page had brown hair and hazel eyes and wore a reddish brown doublet with matching hose and hat.

The princess looked somewhat surprised when she saw Mark and then gave a most lovely smile. "Hello," she said in perhaps the most musical voice that Mark had ever heard. "I haven't seen you here before."

"I only began working here a couple of months ago, shortly after my eighteenth birthday," Mark explained. "The guy previously in charge of the herb garden became very sick and had to stop working. You must be one of the princesses, judging by the circlet on your head."

The princess nodded. "I'm Karen," she said as she held out her gloved hand.

Mark took it and gently kissed it. "I'm Mark," he said. "I've heard that you spend a lot of time in the herb gardens, picking them for medicinal purposes."

Princess Karen nodded. "That's correct," she said. "I'm an herbalist. I collect, grow, dry, and store plants for medicinal purposes. I also sketch them, though I'm more interested in actually working with them than sketching them."

"I've always been more interested in herbs as part of cooking than as part of medicine," Mark admitted. "My mother raised a vegetable garden that consisted of vegetables, fruits, and even some herbs that were used for cooking food for our family. I took care of the garden for her."

"I got an interest in herbs from my mother as well," Princess Karen confided. "She was also an herbalist and actually wrote a book on the subject in the early days of her being queen. I heard that her knowledge of medicinal herbs actually helped save her life right after her final pregnancy ended in a stillbirth, and she got childbed fever since the birth was so difficult."

As she said all this, she took the basket that the lady-in-waiting offered her and entered the herb garden, accompanied by the page and the silken canopy. Mark tried to remember when the queen might have had her final pregnancy; given that he was three or four years older than Princess Karen, he may have been old enough to remember his parents talking about it. Of course, that depended on how old Princess Karen was at the time.

"Do you mind if I ask how old you were during your mother's final pregnancy?" Mark asked.

"I was six then," Princess Karen said. "My nurse was the one who told me the details. Apparently, my maternal grandmother died from childbed fever, and this inspired my own mother to study herbs. She hoped that the medicinal properties of herbs might save other women suffering from childbed fever. And she *was* able to find an herbal remedy that treated the symptoms and ultimately enabled the mother to recover, although in many cases the health of the mother was permanently broken, including that of my own mother. She lived for two more years before finally dying, but she was sick for much of that time. She gave me her herbal book on her deathbed."

Mark now had vague memories of his parents talking about the queen being ill a lot, and he remembered hearing of the late queen's death. He would have been about eleven then and going to grammar school, thanks to his father being well off and able to pay to send his sons there. Mark knew how to read and write, though his spelling wasn't very good, and he knew arithmetic. But his father was only wealthy enough to send one of his three sons off to university; Mark's elder brother was slated to take over his father's work, and Mark himself didn't really want an education beyond grammar school since he wanted to become a gardener. Also, he was less of a bookworm than his younger brother.

"So you became an herbalist because of your mother?" Mark asked.

"Not just because of her," Princess Karen said. "My youngest sister, Daria, is a bookworm. And between me and my other sister, Winnifred, I've always been the one that's been more interested in botany. Winnifred prefers music and dancing to botany, especially dancing. That's why Mother gave me her book. I was interested in botany by the time I was seven, so she knew I would take an interest in her herbal book. But the book *does* remind me of Mother."

As she said this, she bent down to begin picking herbs. For the rest of the time, Mark pointed out the best herbs for her to pick. Once she was finished, he asked her, "What herbal remedies do you know?"

"I know some good ones for calming people down and getting them to sleep, although I have to use wine with the herbal remedies to get people to fall asleep," Princess Karen admitted. "I'm great with those kinds of remedies. I also know some remedies for more terminal diseases, although I'm not sure how effective they are. I mean, they might alleviate the symptoms, but I'm not sure whether they'd effectively treat the cause."

"The fellow whom I replaced," Mark said, "he was diagnosed with consumption. Maybe you can help him."

"I'll have to check my herbal book to see if there is any way to successfully treat consumption," Princess Karen said. "If so, I'll ask my father and the dowager duchess if I can see the fellow and treat him."

She then headed back to where her attendant stood. Once she rejoined her attendants, she turned and said, "It's been nice meeting you, Mark. Farewell for now hopefully."

Mark bowed. "I agree," he said. "Farewell, Princess Karen."

The princess nodded, and then she and her lady-in-waiting were gone.

* * *

Princess Karen's herbal book had suggested using ginger tea to prevent nausea and thus prevent a loss of appetite and weight, as well as freshly crushed garlic in food or boiled in milk and black pepper roasted in clarified butter. It also suggested a combination of clean air, rest, and certain postures that could stimulate healing, something that the former gardener was already using since he had moved to a cottage on the very outskirts of the town along with his eldest son, who was taking care of him. Mark remembered that while the princess did not actually see the fellow who had consumption because the royal court would be leaving the next day, she managed to give garlic and a recipe for ginger tea and one for black pepper roasted with clarified butter to the dowager duchess, who was in charge of the estate while Duke Thomas was at court. The dowager duchess, in turn, would send them to the former gardener.

And even though Princess Karen and the rest of the royal court would leave the manor the next day to continue the royal progress through their land and thus would not be around to see if the advice would work, the herbal remedies along with the clean air, rest, and changes in posture *did* seem to have a beneficial effect on the former gardener. It seemed to clear his lungs and enable him to at least avoid losing any more weight, and it may have even served to drive the disease into remission, if the reports Mark heard the eldest son give to Peter were any indication.

Summer, fall, and winter passed, and now it was late May again. In early winter, the dowager duchess began showing signs of a serious, chronic illness. The doctor, however, did not diagnose consumption but cancer. As Duke Thomas had two sons who were of age, twenty-two-year-old Brian and twenty-year-old Otto, the plan was for Brian and his new wife, Irene, to take over running the estate once the royal progress arrived at his manor while the duke, the duchess Olivia, and Otto remained at court. It was a good thing as the dowager duchess's health quickly deteriorated, and by this time, she was practically bedridden.

Mark had accidentally overheard the dowager duchess discussing her grandchildren with her ladies-in-waiting while they walked past the herbal garden and knew that Otto had been betrothed to Princess Karen when they were both children and that, once the princess turned sixteen, Otto would marry her. But he also heard that Otto was a wild, reckless young man who had fallen in with a group of young men who gambled, drank, and ran around with prostitutes and barmaids. The dowager duchess hoped fervently that marriage to Princess Karen would straighten him out, but Mark had doubts about that. He wondered how Princess Karen felt about the whole thing, if indeed she even knew how wild and reckless Otto was.

CHAPTER 2

"Welcome to my estate," Duke Thomas said as he dismounted from his horse right outside the manor, with his two eldest sons right behind him.

Karen heard her father, King Robert, say, "It is an honor to be here, my lord, Duke."

The king dismounted from his horse, and menservants of the duke moved forward to help Karen and her younger sisters, Winnifred and Daria, dismount. "Thank you, sir," Karen said to the manservant who helped her. "How is the dowager duchess? I heard her health is poor."

"That is why she did not come out to greet you," the manservant replied. "She is almost bedridden and can only go out once a day for exercise. The doctor thinks it's some form of cancer, and it's only a matter of time before she dies."

"I'm sorry to hear that," Karen said.

"Me too," said Daria. "If it's cancer, I hope she's not in much pain." The youngest daughter of King Robert was twelve years old and was pretty with long naturally straight black hair that was curled up at the edges, subtle gray eyes, a creamy complexion, a straight nose, and a small mouth. However, her facial features in general were considered elflike, and Karen knew some people believed Daria might have been a changeling, a faerie baby who was a replacement for a real human child who had been stolen by the faeries. This was in part because Daria had a hard time socializing with others and often tended to retreat into reading books. She also had a very hard time showing empathy, although Karen knew she could feel it. Moreover, Daria had an unusually sophisticated vocabulary for someone her age, and she loved folklore about faeries. She would collect them and constantly talk about them to her ladies-in-waiting or to Karen and Winnifred. Winnifred was bored and often showed it, but Karen would listen. Of course, Karen had to teach Daria how to know when Karen wanted to change the subject to something else, but Karen did so. Karen herself was unsure whether Daria was a changeling as when Daria was about two and people first began speculating, there was an effort to confuse her by cooking in eggshells, but it didn't really work as she merely began crying, and her nanny had to comfort her. Fortunately, nobody tried to burn Daria in an oven, hit her, or whip her since she was a princess after all, and Karen was relieved about that.

Winnifred said, "I agree. I don't ever want to suffer." She looked more like the image of a princess in some ways. Her complexion was like wild rose petals and cream, somewhat like that of Karen herself. More importantly, her hair was golden blond and delightfully curly, and her eyes were as blue as a cloudless sky. That said, the rest of her face wasn't quite as lovely as that of Karen's since Winnifred's face was a little too angular to be considered beautiful by most people, she had a prominent nose, and her mouth was wide, although at least her lips were full. But Winnifred's figure made up for it, for already, she was beginning to show that she had the ability to attract men, thanks in part to being more buxom than either Karen or Daria, especially Daria, who had the slightest figure of the three sisters. Karen had already heard several of the more senior pages mention how attractive Winnifred was becoming.

She had also seen Winnifred eyeing the more attractive senior pages and even trying to flirt with them. And that was the problem with Winnifred. She had almost no common sense and tended to be reckless with little, if any, self-control. Winnifred was the least educated of the three princesses; Daria was always an intellectual, and Karen was the crown princess, so she had to have the kind of education needed to successfully rule the kingdom of Orgon. But Winnifred did know how to read and write, even if she didn't have the kind of education her sisters had. Winnifred also knew how to do fine needlework, but she took the most interest in music and especially dance lessons.

Over the winter, the music and dance instructor for the princesses had to retire as he was an older man and had come down with arthritis in his knees and hips. A twenty-six-year-old gentleman named Francis, the second son of a wealthy merchant who became a gentleman when he graduated from university, replaced him. From the moment he first arrived to teach the sisters music and dancing, Winnifred was taken with him, and Karen could see why. He was a very attractive man with fair hair that he curled, blue eyes, an aquiline nose, and a strong chin with a full beard. He also had an athletic figure presumably due to having learned how to dance to become a dance instructor. Karen just hoped Francis didn't try to take advantage of Winnifred since she was only fourteen and had such little common sense.

Karen knew that her father had ordered Winnifred's ladies-in-waiting to keep a close eye on her ever since Winnifred was a toddler, when she wandered into one of the ponds on the castle's formal gardens and almost drowned; and since Karen was the crown princess, her father often confided things to her. So Karen knew that Winnifred's ladies-in-waiting had told her father that Francis and Winnifred often had whispered conversations in front of them but out of earshot, and that was why Karen worried that Francis might try to take advantage of Winnifred.

Karen then heard Otto say, "Nobody wants to suffer, especially me." Karen frowned. While she agreed that nobody wanted to suffer, the second son of Duke Thomas's comments suggested a degree of self-centeredness that always annoyed her. Arguably, Otto was also very handsome. Like Francis, he was a blond, only his hair was more golden than Francis's. He, too, had blue eyes, an aquiline nose, and a strong chin; but unlike Francis, he had a small beard, although it might have been because he was a younger brother, as well as a slim figure.

Karen had been betrothed by proxy to Otto when they were children since his father, Duke Thomas, was one of her father's most fervent supporters. As a result, Karen had long known she'd marry

Otto when she was old enough; although she would have been old enough to get married when she turned fourteen, her father didn't want her to get married that young out of fear that she'd get pregnant too young and thus would have such a difficult birth that she'd never have children again, so the agreement was for the wedding to take place when she was sixteen, which would be in a couple of months.

But Karen had already begun to have misgivings about marrying Otto. While people tried to shield her from talk of Otto's activities, she *had* heard enough rumors to know that not long after Otto had turned fifteen, he had apparently fallen in with a wild crowd of young men at court who gambled, drank, and ran around with prostitutes and barmaids. Karen was a responsible sort of person, and while she wasn't totally averse to marrying a guy who was a bit wilder than her, she felt Otto was too irresponsible, especially given that the rumors were more about the wild parties Otto and his companions were involved with. That said, she *had* heard that Otto stopped running around with prostitutes after one of his companions spent time with a prostitute and came down with a disease a year and a half ago. Otto now tended to tumble various female servants at court, although she'd heard rumors that he occasionally spent time with barmaids when his companions were with them. Still, Karen remained concerned over Otto's behavior and his selfish comments.

Perhaps had Karen been madly in love with Otto or had she even cared for him, she would have ignored her misgivings. But she wasn't madly in love with Otto. In fact, she wasn't even in love with Otto; and despite being just fifteen, almost sixteen, she already knew she couldn't *ever* be in love with him. Nor did she feel she could really care for him. And whenever she spent time with Otto, he never gave her any sign that he loved her or that he viewed her as anything other than a way to a crown or perhaps a pretty trophy to hang on his arm.

She had told her misgivings to her father. However, her father was concerned about what Duke Thomas might say or do if he backed out of the whole thing, especially if the duke believed that Karen's misgivings were responsible for the breaking of the betrothal contract. Duke Thomas apparently prided himself on being too strong to be ordered about by a woman and looked down on men whom he felt were ordered about by women. Her father felt Duke Thomas would never respect the king if he backed out just because Karen didn't want to marry Otto.

So Karen pointed out that since Otto was a gambler as well as a drunkard, if he became her husband, he would become king consort when her father died, and his gambling habits might deplete the royal treasury and ruin the realm. Her father agreed to discuss the possibility with Duke Thomas, and she later heard that he did so. However, Duke Thomas refused to break the betrothal contract. Did he want to become the father of a king, even if it was just a king consort, and was that his reason for his refusal? Probably. But he might just have been one of those men whose word was his bond and thought that he should never break a contract he entered into, for any reason, even if the breaking was mutual on both sides and agreed to.

Karen had thought about running away, seeking sanctuary in another court, and trying to find a husband of *her* liking while she waited there. But every time the idea of running off crossed her mind, she ultimately rejected it. Had she been just a princess and not the crown princess, she might have done just that. But running away would be neglecting her duty not just to her father but also to the country she was about to rule. So at this point, she believed that she had to accept the marriage, despite her qualms.

That was when Karen heard Duke Thomas say, "Maybe the herbal recipes you have can help my mother."

"I'm afraid all the herbal recipes can do is alleviate the pain," Karen told him. "Cancer can't be cured, at least not by any herbs I know of. But I will try to alleviate the pain for her."

"Maybe the faerie realm has herbs that can cure your mother," Daria suggested, but Karen barely heard her. The mention of herbal recipes had brought her mind back to the time she met the young gardener who worked in the duke's herbal garden.

She had liked Mark almost from the start. He was very handsome but in a very different way from Otto or Francis. Whereas both men were blond and blue eyed, Mark had jet-black hair and dark brown eyes. And whereas they were fair skinned and spent little time in the sun, Mark was tanned from working in the sun all day. But he worked with herbs, and so did she. He may have been more interested in herbs as part of food and she in using herbs as part of medicine, but at least they both liked working with herbs, which was more than she could say for either Francis or Otto. Moreover, when she first looked up at him, a faint spark had stirred in her. Maybe not love but at least attraction or interest. She hadn't felt that way with Otto, although she knew him fairly well by the time she became old enough to be interested in guys, so maybe familiarity had blunted the sparks.

"Is the young man that was the gardener in the herbal gardens still working here?" she asked.

"He is," the manservant said.

"Maybe I'll visit him once I get changed into more appropriate garb," Karen said. "Besides, some of the herbs that can alleviate the dowager duchess's pain are in the garden here, and I can pick some to use."

"What is the plan while we are here?" her father said.

"Later tonight, once we have had dinner, we will have some dancing," Duke Thomas decided. Winnifred squealed in delight naturally since she loved dancing more than anything except music. Daria didn't mind it, but she often got bored and left the dancing early to go to the library. Karen would probably stay around until the dancing was over, however, as she liked to dance too—not as much as maybe she liked gardens, but she liked to dance.

"I will get some peasants to dance when the more formal dancing is over," Duke Thomas added. "And once the ladies have left the ballroom, we shall return to the great hall for, shall we say, less refined amusements."

"Very well, my lord, Duke," her father said as he led them all to the doors that led inside the manor.

*   *   *

Mark heard footsteps in the formal garden area. He turned to face the path that led past the gardens. There was Princess Karen, attired much as she had been a year ago, accompanied by the same lady-in-waiting and page who had been with her when they first met.

Mark bowed. "It is an honor to meet you again, Princess Karen," he said.

"I agree, Mark," Princess Karen said.

"I'm here to pick some herbs that I can use in herbal medicine that can hopefully alleviate the dowager duchess's suffering from cancer," she explained. "But I also wanted to pay you a visit and find out how you have been doing since I last saw you."

"I have been doing well," Mark replied, "as has my predecessor. His lungs cleared up, he regained some weight, and his disease is apparently in remission. Unfortunately, the same can't be said of the dowager duchess."

"I know," Princess Karen said sadly as she stepped into the herbal garden.

Mark looked closely at her and felt a faint stirring in his heart. While the only noticeable change in Princess Karen's appearance was that she had become a little more buxom and a little less willowy than when he last saw her, that was enough of a change to signal that she was now a very beautiful girl and would become a very beautiful young woman within a couple of years. "And how have you been doing, Your Highness?" Mark asked.

"I've been doing fine enough," Princess Karen said as she moved through the garden, examining the herbs. "But within a few months, I'm going to be married to Otto, the second son of Duke Thomas. I'm not sure I want to do so, however."

Had she heard the rumors about him? Mark wondered. *Is that why she's not interested in him?*

"Why not?" he asked.

"I've heard he tends to drink excessively, gamble, and run around with women," Princess Karen told him. "If I was madly in love with him or even if I had any real affection for him, I might be willing to go through with the marriage. But I don't even like him all that much, and I don't think I could ever be in love with him. Yet Duke Thomas really wants the match, and my father is unwilling to back out just because I have misgivings as Duke Thomas would feel that I am ordering my father about. And if I was not the crown princess, I would probably run away to some court to find sanctuary and try to get a husband whom *I* would prefer. But running away would not just affect my father but it would also affect the realm I'm to rule someday."

Mark said, "It's unfortunate that you don't like the man you're going to marry. What about your sisters? Are they betrothed as well?"

"Winnifred is betrothed to Henry, the king of Brangavia," Princess Karen said. "That's a neighboring kingdom of ours. He's apparently thirty and, last year, buried his wife of nine years, whom he married when he was twenty and she was fourteen. His queen apparently came down with childbed fever and died. Father won't marry off any of his daughters until they're sixteen, so Winnifred will be married after she turns sixteen. I've heard that he's a good man but very serious, so I don't know how well he and Winnifred will get along."

"Why is that?" Mark asked before realizing maybe he shouldn't be asking so many personal questions. "I hope I'm not being too inquisitive."

"Even if you are, I don't mind," Princess Karen reassured him. "Winnifred is a vivacious girl, *very* vivacious. She never liked it when I or Father asked her to be more serious. King Henry might like her because she's attractive and charming, but I don't think she'll get along well with someone who's very serious."

Mark had the odd feeling that Karen was downplaying the extent of Winnifred's liveliness, but it was possible that she just didn't think she should go into detail with a mere gardener like him. "And what about the princess Daria?" he asked.

"She's not betrothed to anyone," Princess Karen said, picking herbs the whole time.

Finally, she stood up and said, "These should do for creating an herbal remedy to alleviate the dowager duchess's pain."

At that point, they heard footsteps approaching. Mark and Princess Karen turned as did the lady-in-waiting and the page attending the princess. The head gardener, Peter, was approaching them.

The head gardener had curly brown hair, hazel eyes, and a full beard, unlike Mark, who only had a small beard. Peter was a little on the heavy side and had clothes that, although still suited for being in the gardens, were more fashionable than Mark's own reddish brown jerkin, open-collared white jacket, and long reddish brown breeches. Peter's white shirt was wider than Mark's, he had a fashionable linen falling band, and his breeches were fuller and gathered at the knee since Peter was wealthier by far than Mark.

"Hello, Princess Karen," Peter said, bowing to the princess, who curtsied to him.

After greeting Karen's lady-in-waiting and the page, Peter then turned to Mark. "I have some news for you, Mark," he said.

"What is it?" Mark asked.

"After the royal party, the duke and his family, and their attendants all finish dinner, there will be formal dancing," Peter explained. "After the aristocracy and royal party all dance the allemande, some of the peasants will be dancing for the royal party. You know how to dance, right?"

"I know how to avoid falling over my partner or my own feet," Mark said dryly, and he thought he heard a feminine giggle. Was it Princess Karen? "But court dances must be more graceful and intricate, and our dancing might bore our guests silly."

"There are no plans to have Maypole dancing, if that's what you're referring to," Peter said. While Mark learned how to dance by dancing around a Maypole and personally loved it, he was sure that the court would not take part in Maypole dancing; and if they couldn't, it would probably bore them to tears.

"Maypole dancing isn't something that the court does, so it would be terribly boring for me or for Daria," Princess Karen confirmed, "especially Daria. She prefers reading. Winnifred might like it, but if it's done badly, I doubt she would."

"All right then," Mark said. "I'll take part as long as it doesn't distract me from my duties."

"It won't," Peter assured him. "You can have your dinner before the dancing begins since the court dancing will involve four different dances. When the peasant dancing is over, the ladies will retire, so you may leave then. However, one servant has to be on duty tonight in the private garden. Tonight it's your turn to be on duty."

"So it's a tradition to have a servant on duty in the private garden here as well as back at court?" Princess Karen asked.

"Yes," Mark said. "At least a servant has to be on duty at night from May to October. In April, it depends on whether the night is rainy. There's little need for a servant to be in the private garden in March or November, and there's no need during the winter months. Too cold."

"I know," Princess Karen said. "Although princesses are supposed to be especially sheltered from country matters, as they say, I've heard Otto complaining several times about having a hard time finding a private corner with a girl he was pursuing in the dead of winter."

"Once you've finished your dinner, I'll hand you the key to the private garden," Peter informed Mark.

"Thank you," Mark said. "Is that it?"

"Yes," Peter said. "You may go back to conversing with the princess."

"I'm going to be heading back inside to work on preparing the herbs I picked for possible use in an herbal remedy for the dowager duchess," Princess Karen said. "I'll see you later tonight, Mark."

"Until tonight, Princess Karen," Mark said, bowing. She curtsied and left with her lady-in-waiting and the page.

CHAPTER 3

The court dancing was over. Now it was time for the peasant dancing to begin. Servants entered the ballroom where the dancing had taken place, bringing in chairs for the members of the royal court and the aristocratic people in the manor to sit on. Other servants brought good wine in for the royal family, the ducal family, and the women in the royal party and in the manor while beer was provided for the remaining men. There was concern that there would not be enough good wine for everyone in the manor to drink after the dancing, and it was probably better to have a good beer than a poor wine.

Karen sat down in the chair provided for her and glanced around her. Next to her on one side was Otto, who had been her partner for the court dancing, and on her other side was her father. On his other side were Daria, who had partnered with her father for the court dancing mainly because she was most comfortable dancing with him, and Winnifred and Francis, who had been Winnifred's partner.

Winnifred and Francis were currently sitting with their heads close together and whispering in a way that made Karen nervous. She really hoped they weren't planning some sort of escapade—or at least that Francis wasn't planning some escapade since Winnifred was probably the type of girl who would go along with any plans a handsome guy might make, and Francis was handsome. She needed to keep an eye on her sister.

Once they all settled into place and had their wine or beer, Karen heard her father say, "I hope the peasants who will be dancing are good, my lord, Duke. I hate having to see bad dancers stumble over their feet or their partners, even if they're trying to do a good job."

"Do not worry, Your Majesty," Duke Thomas said. "Before we came here, I had my steward find out which peasants and servants were the best dancers, and he had the twenty best dancers, male and female, informed that they would be dancing tonight."

Well, at least Mark is one of the best male dancers in the village. Otherwise, he wouldn't have been asked to dance, Karen thought with an inner sigh of relief.

It was then that the door leading outside to the gardens opened, and ten excited, bright-eyed red-cheeked girls who were blonde or had light brown hair trooped into the room, all dressed in what was probably their best black wool skirts, embroidered aprons, stayed bodices, and linen shifts. They were each accompanied by ten nervous, mostly red-faced young men in *their* best outfits. Mark was one of them.

Karen spotted a servant appear beside her father with a basket. Two by two, each pair made their bows, first to the king, then to the princesses, and finally to the duke. When Mark stepped forward with his partner, Karen could see that he was with a rather pretty blonde, something that made Karen frown, although she didn't know why she wasn't happy about seeing the pretty blonde standing beside Mark. After all, he was a gardener on the estate and thus a working man. Shouldn't he be with a girl of his own class?

As each couple rose from their bow to the king, the servant handed each partner a bunch of ribbons, which apparently delighted the girls and interested at least some of the boys. A flautist and a lute player came forward, introduced by the duke as part of his personal household; clearly, they were going to be the musicians for the dancers. Karen was relieved to see this as at least the musicians would be competent enough to provide a decent tempo or melody. The musicians spoke to the dancers for a few moments presumably to find out what tunes the dancers were familiar with. Once done, the dancers formed up in pairs, and the musicians began to play.

Karen watched the dancing with some interest. It was a kind of gliding dance where the peasants held each other very closely as they moved around the floor. She could see Mark's point about peasant dancing as it wasn't nearly as graceful or as intricate as the allemande, the courante, the saraband, or the gigue, but it was danced well enough that nobody fell over their own feet or those of their partners, including Mark.

After the first dance, all the guys stepped back and watched as the girls performed a second dance, this one having all the girls dance around and around in a circle. Karen occasionally glanced over at her sisters. Winnifred seemed fairly interested, while Daria was beginning to look a little bored. That wasn't a real surprise since Daria wasn't really interested in dancing and, in truth, often felt awkward while dancing in front of an audience. She didn't like to perform in front of others. At the end of the dancing, her father gave the girls more ribbons, only they were pierced with a silver coin, although Karen wasn't sure how much silver was actually *in* the coins. Nonetheless, peasants rarely saw silver coins and would view it either as a good bride price or as part of a dowry, and the girls were clearly delighted to have them.

The third dance had the boys doing a dance that generally involved a lot of leaping about with the occasional move. Karen thought Mark was one of the better dancers, and she may not have been the only one; she once glanced over and saw Winnifred eyeing Mark. This annoyed Karen, though fortunately Winnifred's attention was soon diverted to another boy, freeing Karen to look back at the boys. Once they were done, the duke called for some beer for the dancers, who drank it down gratefully.

The final dance had the boys and girls doing a sort of ribbon dance, which involved the boys taking the ribbon streamers and dancing around the girls while tying the ribbons around them and the girls dancing in a circle the whole time. It was interesting to Karen, if only because of the complexity of having the girls dancing while having ribbons tied around them, but she could clearly see that Daria was bored. Once the dancing was finally done, the king was the one who called for beer, claiming they must be thirsty after all that exercise.

Karen then began calling some of the girls over to look at the embroidery in their costumes. While noblewomen who attended Karen, Winnifred, and Daria would often be skilled in activities that noblewomen and royalty took part in, there was one area of skill that the princesses could employ peasant girls in as well as noblewomen, and that was embroidery. If these girls had enough skill with the needle, they might get a position as a weaver in Karen's personal household or Winnifred's or Daria's.

However, even before Karen began examining the embroidery, she caught a glimpse of Daria speaking quietly to her father. Soon afterward, she heard Daria excusing herself on account of a headache. More likely, Daria was just going to go to the library and do some reading, but she could well have had a genuine headache; she'd had them before, not often but enough times that it would be a plausible excuse.

Daria and her attendants departed as Karen continued to examine the embroidery on the girls' costumes. One of the girls was named Elke, and she was Mark's partner; Mark himself stood quietly to the side, possibly waiting for the rest of the women to retire. Elke had embroidered her own costume as had all the others, and she was the best of the seamstresses. Karen knew that one of the seamstresses in Daria's household was about fifty and was having a hard time embroidering due to her joints swelling up in the winter. Elke could be a good replacement for that seamstress, so Karen promised to recommend Elke for a position in Daria's household. Elke was delighted, of course.

Once all the girls were reunited with their partners, King Robert stood up and said, "Thank you all for giving us a fine performance."

Duke Thomas stood up and said, "Now if you will excuse us, it is time for the princesses to retire to their rooms while the men in the household and the royal party will return to the great hall to enjoy some amusements of our own, unless they want to take a stroll in the gardens with or without the ladies of the court since it's a very warm night."

As the members of the ducal household and the royal party prepared to depart, Karen stepped over to her father and quietly said to him, "I promised to recommend one of the dancers, a girl named Elke, for a position in Daria's household as a weaver."

"I heard," the king said. "I'll check with the duke, and if he agrees, tomorrow he'll send a page to invite Elke to the manor. There, Daria and I will examine her work. And if she's good enough, she'll probably get a position. Incidentally, I spoke with Duke Thomas concerning the bedrooms for the people who were part of our party, and the lesser-ranked men will be sleeping at the inn. I would have put Francis with them, except that he's your dance master."

"Maybe you should have put him with them," Karen said. "I heard him and Winnifred whispering, and I'm worried that he's plotting something with her."

King Robert thought for a moment and then said, "That *is* somewhat troubling. But just whispering together isn't proof that there's a plot going on. Anyway, you will have a guest chamber all to yourself, while Winnifred and Daria will sleep together tonight. The lesser-ranked women will get dormitories tonight. Your ladies-in-waiting will have a dormitory next to your room, and the same will go for the ladies-in-waiting for Winnifred and Daria."

"Thank you for telling me this," Karen said. "I'm going to check on Daria to make sure she really has a headache. If she does, I know a herbal remedy for it." Her father nodded and then headed out with the other men.

As a page escorted Karen and her ladies to their quarters, Karen's thoughts were on Winnifred and Francis. She really hoped they weren't plotting anything that would get them in big trouble.

*　　*　　*

23

"So you may get a position working in Princess Daria's household?" Mark asked Elke as the royalty and aristocrats prepared to leave.

"Yeah," Elke said excitedly. "And take a look at this silver coin I got. It would make a nice dowry, wouldn't it?"

"It would," Mark agreed, "for whoever might be interested in marrying you."

"What about you?" Elke said. "I know you had a bad experience with Sarah's father, but you're too handsome to avoid marriage altogether."

Mark smiled and said, "I'm not avoiding marriage altogether. I just haven't found a girl who interests me enough that I really want to marry her. And even though you have a good dowry now, I'm not so interested in you that I really want to marry you."

Elke sighed. "I was sort of hoping your disinterest in me stemmed from being afraid of not being able to provide a bridal price or being interested in a girl who didn't have a dowry," she admitted. "Do you think you'll find someone whom you would *really* want to marry?"

"Of course," Mark reassured her. "And I hope you find somebody who really wants to marry you whether you get a position in Princess Daria's household or not as long as Daria's willing to give up good workers if someone wants to marry them."

"True," Elke said, smiling. "What are you going to do now?"

"I'm going to get the key for the private garden from the head gardener, and then I'm going to go there and begin my guard," Mark said. "Thanks for dancing with me."

"You're welcome, Mark," Elke said as the two parted. Elke was led out by a page since she did not work in the manor but on her father's farm as a milkmaid, while Mark walked out the doorway that led to the gardens.

He stood on the back part of the house, which overlooked the vegetable garden, the herbal garden where he usually worked, the private garden, and a small chapel. Standing at the bottom of the stairway descending from the entryway to the gardens was Peter. Mark walked down the stairs and joined him.

"Here is the key to the private garden," Peter said, handing Mark a brass key. "Once you enter the private garden, you must lock the gate behind you. You will be on your own for the rest of the night. I trust you will do a fine job."

"I will," Mark promised as he took the key and headed down the path. Usually, he took the first right pathway, which led to the herbal gardens; but this time, he had to take the path that led straight until he reached a fountain with a marble sculpture. From there, there were two pathways, one that led to the private garden and another that led to the chapel. When he reached the fountain, he took the left path, which led to the private garden.

Soon he reached the gate. It was six feet high—high enough that, when locked, you'd have to be an active guy to jump over the gate and get inside. It was also surrounded by six-foot-high walls, which further suggested that you'd have to either be an active guy or get a ladder. Fortunately, Mark didn't need a ladder; and while he *was* active, he didn't need to be to get in. He simply unlocked the gate and entered, locking it once he got inside. Then he looked around.

The private garden was a lovely place, shaded by trees and filled with flowers. He could detect the sweet scents of various roses, which were cultivated separately from the roses that were in the formal gardens. He knew that the dowager duchess liked spending time in this garden, but she couldn't do so now because she was in such pain from cancer. In the middle of the garden, there were a bench and a cloak for the person who slept in there. Mark went over to the bench, took the cloak, and sat down, covering himself.

At this moment, Mark felt like the happiest young man in the world. He was content with working in gardens, and this was the loveliest part of the gardens on the estate. He was paid a decent wage, got good food, and had a comfortable room, even if he had to share it with a lot of other men. Other than perhaps a girl to share his life with, what else could he want?

CHAPTER 4

Murmurs and feminine giggling drifted through Mark's semiconscious state. Then he heard the unmistakable sound of someone trying to open a door. Mark's eyes flew open, and he looked up. He was lying down on the bench and could see the moon shining through the trees. It was so bright and full tonight, but Mark had little time for contemplation given the sounds he was hearing.

Mark silently sat up, pulling the cloak around him to protect himself from the cool night air. The sounds he had heard stopped, and then he heard a very low male voice complaining. The fellow, whoever he was, was speaking so low that Mark couldn't really understand what he was saying, but the tone of his voice made it quite clear that he was complaining about something, probably the fact that the gate was locked.

Mark then heard a feminine voice say, "Don't be upset, Francis. It's so warm out. There must be plenty of other places where we can find privacy." The voice was quite young, belonging to a girl in her early to midteens. She could be one of the girls who was fostered by the dowager duchess.

Francis? Mark thought. He quietly got off the bench and quietly crept toward the gate, doing his best to make sure he wasn't heard by whoever was in front of it. As he did so, he tried to think of any men named Francis whom he knew who lived or worked on the estate.

Or maybe this Francis *wasn't* somebody who lived on the estate. He might be a member of the royal party. After all, the people who lived and worked on the estate for at least a year would probably have known that the gate to the private garden was locked and that they should avoid the private garden. There were plenty of other places to find privacy after all, just as the girl had said. If that was the case, then the girl could be a member of the royal party as well.

Mark reached the gate just as he heard the male voice quietly but distinctly say, "You're right, Your Highness. Let's find another spot."

This stunned Mark. If he heard correctly, the girl wasn't just one of the girls fostered by the dowager duchess or even a girl who was part of the royal party. She was one of the princesses. But he was fairly sure that whoever the princess was, it wasn't Princess Karen. For one thing, Princess Karen knew the garden would be locked; so if she was having an escapade with this Francis fellow, she probably would have warned him about the garden being locked. For another thing, he'd heard Princess Karen speak before, and the feminine voice did not sound familiar to him. And finally, he had the distinct impression that Princess Karen was too responsible to get herself involved in an escapade that would get her in big trouble.

No, this wasn't Princess Karen. It was one of the other princesses, either Princess Winnifred or Princess Daria. He wasn't sure which one, however. But it didn't matter. Whichever princess it was, it was no doubt his duty to ensure that she didn't get into big trouble by engaging in some escapade.

He quietly peeked over the gate, standing on his tiptoes. The moonlight illuminated two figures moving away from the gate, one male and one female. Mark quietly put the key in the lock and turned it.

The gate opened almost soundlessly, given that Mark was being very quiet about opening it. Mark emerged, quietly turned around to lock the gate behind him, and then followed the two figures, wondering which princess would be dumb enough to get involved in some escapade.

*   *   *

Karen was suddenly woken up by a pounding on the door to her bedroom. She got up, pulled the curtains from her bedchamber open, lit a candle, and went to the door, throwing a dressing robe over her green shift. Daria stood just outside the door. She wore a red dressing robe over her own nightdress, and her dark hair was mussed up from sleep.

"What is it?" Karen asked.

"Winnifred," Daria said. "She's gone."

"What?" Karen asked, hardly able to believe her ears. "She's not in the room you were sharing?"

"No," Daria said. "I woke up about a minute ago, needing to go and get a drink of water. And when I glanced over to check on Winnifred, there was no trace of her. Also, the door was wide open, with the key used to lock us in, in the lock. She must have slipped out when I was fast asleep."

"We've got to find her," Karen said. She glanced over and saw that the ladies-in-waiting for herself and her sisters were outside their chambers as well. She began giving instructions to them, advising them to search all the areas of the manor. Daria and one of her ladies-in-waiting had to go find the king and tell him what happened.

"What if she isn't inside the castle?" Daria asked.

"Then we'll have to search the gardens," Karen said. "Also, somebody needs to find Francis. If nobody can find him, he's probably with Winnifred. I saw them whispering together some time ago, and I suspect they made plans to slip out somewhere."

"What?" Daria cried out. "We've been told too many times to stay in our rooms after we retired to them!"

"And you're very obedient," Karen added. "But you know that Winnifred isn't the brightest star in the sky. I suspect that if she and Francis slipped out to find a private corner, he talked her into it. But we must begin searching."

*   *   *

Mark saw Francis and the princess slip into the small chapel that served as the minister's quarters. He sometimes performed the sacrament of confession here, though whenever Mark had gone to confession before receiving the Eucharist, he had done so in the chancel in the manor. He had heard that the minister only performed the sacrament to the dowager duchess and her attendants in this chapel.

The door was unlocked, so Mark slipped in after Francis and the princess. During the time Mark had trailed them, he had been able to figure out that both Francis and the princess were blondes since their hair was very light in the moonlight, lighter than Karen's hair would have been since she had red hair. He wondered which princess was a blonde—Daria or Winnifred.

Mark waited for his eyes to adjust to the darkness. As he did so, he heard feminine giggling and then Francis's voice. He couldn't hear the words, but the tone suggested that he was reproving the princess. When Mark's eyes adjusted to the darkness, he saw Francis and the princess standing at the altar rail. Neither one saw him.

Francis then took the princess into his arms and began kissing her. This was bad enough, but then Mark saw the princess put her arms around Francis's neck. Mark knew he had to stop this. Whichever princess was with Francis, she was being extremely imprudent—at the very least—in not only slipping out with a guy but also having an amorous meeting with him. Mark had to protect her by dragging Francis before the duke and the king.

So Mark quietly crept forward. As he did so, he thought he saw Francis start touching the princess's bosom. Then he heard the princess moan.

This drove Mark to action. He rushed forward and grabbed hold of Francis, pulling him away from the princess. At the same time, he loudly called for the minister to wake up and come out. He then took hold of Francis's arms, pushing the guy in front of him while waiting for the minister to come.

After a couple of minutes, Mark heard footsteps, and then the minister appeared in the entryway, yawning. "What is happening?" the minister asked.

Mark said, "Francis and one of the princesses—not Princess Karen—tried to enter the private garden but then came here. Francis then began kissing the princess and then touching her bosom before I broke things up." He glanced over and saw the blond princess leaning against the altar rail, looking as white as a ghost.

The minister looked over and saw the princess. "Princess Winnifred?" he asked, thus possibly identifying the princess. She looked terrified as she looked at the minister and then at Mark.

"I don't know which princess it was other than the fact that it wasn't the princess Karen because she knew the private garden was locked," Mark explained. "She was with me when the head gardener assigned me in charge of the private garden. What hair color does Princess Winnifred have?"

"Blond," the minister said. "Princess Daria has dark brown hair, and Princess Karen has golden red hair."

"I know the princess Karen has golden red hair. Then it was Princess Winnifred whom Francis was with," Mark said. "I don't think Francis works here either because he would have known the private garden was locked during warm, dry weather."

"I'm the dance and music instructor for the princesses," Francis sputtered.

"Anyway, I have to bring Francis to the duke and the king for questioning," Mark explained, "possibly Princess Winnifred as well."

"I'll take the princess," the minister said, approaching the frightened princess Winnifred. "You go on ahead, and I'll follow."

"Thanks," Mark said, pushing Francis along out of the church and through the pathway to the back of the manor. As he did so, he wondered just what Princess Winnifred and Francis were thinking when they decided to have this amorous meeting. While he knew that ladies and fostered girls weren't likely to get into escapades here, even if the dowager duchess's sickness made it a little bit easier for the bolder and more easily influenced girls to do so, he was sure it was even harder for ladies at the royal court to get into escapades. And having an escapade with a *princess* was tantamount to suicide in Mark's eyes. The risk wasn't worth it for him. So why did Francis take such a risk? And why would Princess Winnifred go along with the whole thing?

*   *   *

Back inside the manor, King Robert had been informed of Winnifred's disappearance by an alarmed Daria and one of her ladies-in-waiting. The first thing the king did was to send a servant to wake up Duke Thomas and inform him about the situation and to tell the duke to meet him in the great hall. There, the two would wait for news about Winnifred.

Afterward, he urged Daria to rejoin Karen and have the two of them inform him if Winnifred had been found. He then sent two of his attendants to look for Francis and make sure he was in the dormitories. If not, then they were to start searching as well.

King Robert and the remainder of his attendants then proceeded to the great hall, with torches lighting the way. The great hall was deserted at this time of night and practically unlit except for two torches at either side of the entrance and a flickering fire in the hearth that was going out. Accordingly, one of the king's attendants got some wood that was stacked next to the hearth, put the wood in the hearth, and used a torch from the entrance to light the fire. He then used the torch to light more torches in the great hall so as to provide some light for the king and the duke.

As King Robert and his attendants entered, he looked around. The torches illuminated battle flags of soldiers long gone, which hung from the beams above the huge hall, as well as tapestries displaying intricate landscapes full of fantastic beasts. White plaster coated the stone walls, helping keep cold drafts out and insulating the room from the damp that came after rainy days. Wooden chairs were arrayed along the walls, and the king's attendants all sat down on them while Robert moved down the carpet toward the chairs that the dowager duchess apparently used for manorial courts, where she would have presided over the administration of justice. Since the dowager duchess was now bedridden, her eldest grandson, Brian, and his wife, Irene, would take over her manorial court duties once the royal court party departed. But tonight Duke Thomas would have to sit beside King Robert.

King Robert sat down on the bigger of the two chairs since he was the king and waited for Duke Thomas to come. After a few minutes, he heard footsteps and saw the duke enter the great hall, followed by some of his servants. The duke, looking like he had just been roused from sleep, joined the king, sitting down in the smaller of the chairs. "I hear one of the princesses has gone missing?" he asked.

"Winnifred," the king said. He sighed. "My daughter Karen thinks she is with Francis, the man who teaches my daughters music and dancing."

"Why?" asked the duke.

"According to my daughter Daria, Karen thinks that the two made plans to slip out somewhere," the king explained.

"You mean for an amorous meeting?" asked the duke. The king nodded.

That was when they heard more footsteps, several in fact. Karen appeared in the entryway, along with Daria. "Has Winnifred been found?" King Robert asked.

"Yes, Father," Karen said. "She's alive and unhurt but looks like she's on the verge of hysterics. The minister is with her. The herbal gardener, Mark, is with them, and he's holding Francis in front of him."

"Send them in," the king said.

As Karen and Daria went out, he turned to the duke and said, "I have a bad feeling about this situation."

The duke nodded in agreement, and then Francis appeared in the doorway, held tightly by a tall young dark-haired, dark-eyed man of about nineteen years of age, presumably Mark. They were followed by the minister, with Winnifred holding on to his arm and looking as white as a ghost.

"Bring Francis and Winnifred forward and explain how you found them," the duke ordered the minister and the young dark-haired man.

The foursome moved down the carpet until they stood before the king and the duke. The young man roughly threw Francis to the ground before bowing, while the minister gave a small bow since Winnifred was still clinging to his arm.

The tall young man explained, "I was asleep in the private garden when I heard what sounded like murmurs and feminine giggling. Then somebody, possibly Francis, tried to open the gate to the garden. I woke up and overheard complaining, followed by Winnifred reassuring him that there would be other places where they could find privacy. Of course, I didn't know that it was Winnifred talking or even that Francis was with one of the princesses until I heard him address his companion as Her Highness. I slipped out of the garden and followed them to the chapel where the minister resided, and then I saw Francis kiss Winnifred and then touch her bosom. That was when I grabbed hold of Francis, pulled him away from her, and called for the minister."

"I was woken up by shouting," the minister added. "When I came into the rectory, that was where I found the trio. Mark explained the situation to me, and I decided to take Winnifred to you while Mark brought Francis."

King Robert nodded and then noticed that Winnifred seemed about ready to faint. He said, "Karen, Daria, please take Winnifred to her room. I won't question her today. I'll wait until tomorrow."

"I'm sure Winnifred will be happy with this," Karen said. "And I'll give her something to give her a good night's sleep."

Robert waited until Karen escorted Winnifred out, accompanied by Daria, and then turned to Francis, who had his head lowered and was on his knees. "Well, Francis, I would like to know what you were doing with my daughter Winnifred and *what you were thinking*!" he suddenly shouted. Francis looked up, and he looked terrified, causing the king to grin evilly.

*　　*　　*

Karen led a very pale Winnifred to her bedroom, with Daria following her. Karen turned to Daria and said, "Please watch over Winnifred while I create a remedy to calm her down and help her sleep."

Daria nodded as Karen headed to the storeroom in the cellars to get the chamomile. Once she did so, she went to the kitchen to prepare an herbal tea for Winnifred to drink. As she prepared the tea, she urged the servant who had accompanied her to fetch a cup of wine for Winnifred.

The server returned with the cup and followed Karen through the halls to the bedroom doorway. Winnifred was now weeping hysterically; Daria was trying to comfort her, but Karen could tell that she wasn't very successful. Well, maybe this would help.

"Here, Winnifred," Karen said, handing her blond sister the cup of herbal tea.

Winnifred accepted it and drank the cup of tea. Once she was finished, Karen led her into the bedroom she shared with Daria and handed her the cup of wine. Winnifred sipped it slowly as Daria entered.

Once Winnifred was finished with the wine, the ladies who served her and Daria came forward and helped her shed the folds of her pale blue gown. Underneath, she wore a wispy blue chemise of a slightly darker shade.

The ladies then turned the bedcovers back and helped Winnifred into it. They then closed the bed-curtains as Karen led Daria out into the hallway. "Let's allow her to go to sleep before you enter the bedchamber," Karen whispered to Daria, who nodded in agreement.

"I hope Father won't punish her severely," Daria whispered back. "She may be foolish, but I don't want her locked up in a dungeon."

"I seriously doubt Father would lock her up in a dungeon," Karen reassured her. "In her room maybe, but a dungeon? No. Francis will get *that* kind of punishment."

Daria sighed in relief. "Maybe we should tell Winnifred that she won't be locked up in a dungeon. That might calm her down even more."

"When you go back inside, if she's awake, you can tell her that," Karen said.

"I'll head back in now," Daria said. "I need to go back to bed myself."

"I'll get dressed and go to the herbal garden," Karen said. "That always helps calm me down."

"Very well," Daria said as she turned to go back into the bedroom.

Karen and the ladies accompanying her returned to the princess's bedroom. There, Karen put on her simplest green dress, brushed her red-gold hair, and turned to her ladies. "Lily, please come with me," she told one of them. Lily was her personal lady-in-waiting, a pale blonde who was twenty-one years old and was her closest attendant. "The rest of you, please go back to bed." The ladies obeyed, and Lily followed Karen out to the back exit of the manor. Karen pushed open the door and went outside, followed by Lily.

The moon was high in the sky, and its light illuminated the paths. Karen took the path that led to the herbal garden. The scents of the herbal plants filled the air, especially the scent of chamomile. That was why Karen went to the herbal garden whenever she was upset since her mother's herbal book said that chamomile was effective in treating anxiety.

Karen took deep breaths, filling her body with the scents. Gradually, she began feeling calm. And as she calmed down, she thought about what she had told Daria.

Their father would no doubt be very angry with Winnifred, but Karen didn't think he'd lock Winnifred up in a dungeon. True, the history books she'd read had noted that two princesses who were wives to the eldest sons of the king were locked up after being convicted of adultery, and Winnifred *was* betrothed; but unless Francis actually slept with Winnifred, the middle princess probably wasn't guilty of adultery. Besides, everybody who knew Winnifred well knew that she had no common sense where a handsome face was concerned. Their father would probably put the blame on Francis and punish him severely, maybe even have him executed, while Winnifred would most likely be put under house arrest and confined to her quarters.

A few moments later, she heard footsteps heading her way. Karen turned to face the entrance and see who was coming. Soon she saw Mark come to the entrance to the garden. And he looked angry.

*   *   *

The instant Mark saw Princess Karen, the anger in his expression faded away, and he smiled nervously before bowing. "Hello, Your Highness," he said. "May I come in?"

"Of course," Princess Karen said.

Mark stepped inside the gate, closing it behind him, and walked up toward Princess Karen and her lady-in-waiting. "I was surprised when I brought Francis and the minister brought Princess Winnifred back to the castle to see that you and your other sister were awake," he said.

"Daria woke me up when she found out Winnifred was gone," Princess Karen said. "That's also why Father and the duke were awake. Daria alerted Father, and he had the duke alerted."

"I see," Mark said. He had been relieved when he returned to the castle to find out that he didn't need to wake the king and the duke up, but he *had* been rather surprised to find out that the other two princesses and the king were already awake.

"How are your sisters?" Mark then asked.

"I had to give Winnifred some chamomile tea and then have her sip some wine before having her go back to bed," Princess Karen told him. "Daria's gone to bed as well."

Mark was relieved but then shook his head as he was reminded of the sheer stupidity of Princess Winnifred by the mention of her. "I can't believe Princess Winnifred would be so stupid as to sneak out of her bed in the middle of the night to have an amorous escapade," he said. "What was she thinking?"

"I can believe it," Princess Karen said. "Winnifred never had a lot of common sense, and she has none where a handsome face is concerned. She'd go along with anything that a handsome fellow asked her to do. I'm more shocked that Francis would even *think* of having an amorous escapade with Winnifred. She'd tried to flirt with some of the more attractive senior pages before, but they all refused to flirt back. They knew they'd be in big trouble if they were caught alone with her. Francis should have known it as well."

"He may have known it, but he persuaded her to go somewhere alone with him anyway," Mark said. "And before I left, I learned why."

"Why?" Princess Karen said.

"He blurted out that he hoped that when the Princess Winnifred went to Brangavia to marry King Henry, he might have gained enough favor with her to come along and become both her personal dance teacher and her lover," Mark revealed. "I think he was hoping to gain influence over her and use it to gain favor at King Henry's court. That's when I left."

He turned away as he said it, the memory of what Francis had blurted out making him very angry all over again. But he wasn't just angry over Francis's being such a social climber. Rather, Francis's social ambitions triggered other more painful memories for Mark.

He heard Princess Karen say, "I knew Francis was at least somewhat socially ambitious. When he came to court, he told Father about his background. His father was a merchant and was wealthy enough to send his sons to school and even at least one of them to university. While his father was content with his position in life, Francis wanted to be a gentleman, so that's why he went to university. He also always took great care over his appearance, more than Daria or even Winnifred, and I would take over ours. But I never thought he'd be *that* ambitious."

Mark took a deep breath and turned around to face Princess Karen and her lady-in-waiting. "Had I met Francis before today, I might have figured out that he was a social climber," he admitted. "I have enough experience with them to recognize the type."

"Because you work at the duke's estate?" Princess Karen asked.

"More than that," Mark said. "When I was growing up, I knew a number of girls who lived in the town near the estate. One of them was named Sarah, and she was my age, maybe a couple of months younger. She was very pretty with strawberry blond hair and blue eyes. When I became old enough to be interested in girls, I became attracted to her, and she was attracted to me as well, even before I became attracted to her. This was when I was about sixteen."

Princess Karen looked thoughtful for a moment. She then said, "One of Winnifred's ladies-in-waiting has that name, and I know of another lady in court with that name, but the lady-in-waiting is a brunette and the other lady is blond."

She then frowned as she thought of something. "Wait, I may have heard of a girl with strawberry blond hair who has that name," she said. "She works as a chambermaid, but I heard a couple of rumors that her father was trying to get sons of landed knights who weren't going into the church interested in her. And she came to court from the town near the duke's estate."

Mark was relieved that it was night since, hopefully, Princess Karen wouldn't see his face darken. "I think that's the same girl," he said. "Her father is a tailor, and when I was growing up, I heard my father complain about how ambitious Sarah's father was. Her father wanted to be the tailor to the dowager duchess or to the gentlemen and ladies who lived on her estate and constantly sucked up to the dowager duchess so he could do so. But as he grew older, his social ambitions extended to his desire to be the tailor to the royal court or, if he couldn't do so, to at least getting his children married to people who were at the court."

Princess Karen looked like she comprehended what happened. "So he ended your relationship with Sarah?" she asked sympathetically.

"Yes," Mark admitted, sighing. "He left his eldest son in charge of the tailoring business here, took his other children, and moved to the royal court. I heard he did it after Sarah refused to stop seeing me. He knew I wanted to be a gardener, and he didn't want any of his daughters marrying mere gardeners."

Princess Karen then came forward. When she got close enough, she reached up to touch his shoulder in a gesture of sympathy. "I'm sorry," she said. "You didn't deserve what happened to you."

Suddenly, Mark felt somewhat better. "Thanks," he said, smiling and raising a hand to cover Princess Karen's. Her hand felt warm and soft under his own. But was it trembling slightly? Or was it his *own* hand that was trembling? He wasn't sure.

"So that's why you left when you learned what Francis's goals were?" Princess Karen continued. "Because you were reminded of Sarah's father being so ambitious and of how he ruined your chance at love and marriage with Sarah?"

"Yeah," Mark admitted. "I was tempted to slap him at least, and I didn't want your father to get angry at me if I lost my temper and not only slapped Francis but actually also attacked him. I *hate* social climbers."

"I can understand why," Princess Karen said. "And I don't think many people like social climbers anyway, unless they're tyrants."

"And I don't think your father is a tyrant," Mark said, "not from what little I've seen of him at least. But I'm sure he's angry at both Francis and your sister Winnifred. I hope he won't hurt your sister— for your sake at least. She *is* betrothed after all, and having sexual contact with another man, even if it never proceeded to intercourse, might well be construed as adultery if the woman is betrothed to another man."

Princess Karen sighed at that. She withdrew her hand and turned away. Finally, she said, "I don't think Father will execute or even imprison Winnifred beyond confining her to her quarters. She has such little common sense that Francis will most likely get all the blame for the affair and be severely punished. But that doesn't mean Father *won't* imprison Winnifred in some cell, and I *have* heard stories of adulterous wives of princes who were heirs to the throne being locked up for a time. Father might well do so, even if I don't think he will."

Princess Karen then apparently hugged herself. At that point, she looked so vulnerable that Mark was strongly tempted to comfort her. For one moment, he fought against it. He was a *gardener* after all, and an act that would have been appropriate with a country girl or a servant on the estate would probably be improper with a young woman of noble blood, let alone a *princess*.

But the next moment, he thought, *Hang propriety! She's upset, and she needs comforting. Even princesses need comforting.* Stepping closer until he was right behind her, Mark put his hands around Princess Karen's shoulders, turned her around so she could face him, and then gently drew her into his arms.

Princess Karen responded by throwing her arms around his neck, resting her head against his shoulder and hugging him tightly. Mark gently rested his cheek against her hair, hugging her as well. He could feel her trembling, so he stroked her long golden red hair, which tumbled down past her shoulders.

After a few moments of his stroking her hair, Mark felt Princess Karen stop trembling and then move her head from his shoulder. "Feeling better now?" Mark asked softly, lifting his head to look down at her. The instant he actually looked at her, however, Mark knew he'd made a huge mistake.

Karen's green eyes seemed huge in the moonlight, revealing depths that Mark had never seen before in a young woman's eyes. He was spellbound, unable to look away, unable to pull back. Even though a part of his mind was yelling at him to look away, to move away, his muscles just wouldn't obey. And what was more, he had the odd feeling she was feeling the same way about *him*, like she couldn't pull back or look away, even if she wanted to.

After what seemed like an eternity just staring at each other, Mark heard Karen say, "Y-yes. Thank you, Mark."

"You're welcome, Karen," Mark said softly—then the spell was broken as he realized what he had said, how he had addressed her. Shocked, Mark pulled back and turned his face away so he wouldn't have to look at Karen—no, *Princess* Karen. After all, she was still a princess. And he was merely a gardener.

"What's wrong, Mark?" he heard Karen—*Princess* Karen—ask.

Mark waited until he was far enough away from her before he turned to face her. "I called you Karen," he said. "I forgot to add your title. And I shouldn't have done so. I shouldn't have even hugged you."

For now, Mark recognized a horrible truth—a truth that he had never wanted. He was in love with Karen. And this was the last thing he'd ever wanted to happen to him. After all, Francis was probably going to be executed just for having intimate contact with Princess Winnifred, and Francis probably merely lusted after that princess, along with wanting to use her for social advancement. Actually *falling in love* with a princess was even worse.

Karen looked confused for a minute, and then her own eyes seemed to widen as if she was catching on to what he meant. "Maybe you are right," she said at last. "Maybe you should have just not embraced me but instead tried to comfort me verbally."

Mark nodded in agreement but then sighed and said, "But it's too late—for me at least."

"And maybe for me as well," Karen added with an odd tone in her voice that made Mark wonder briefly if she was feeling the same way toward him that he now felt toward her.

But the next moment, he shook the thought away and said, "I have to return to the private garden. And you need to go to bed, Your Highness."

"He's right," the lady-in-waiting attending Karen said. "Come along, Princess Karen."

Karen allowed her lady-in-waiting to take her arm and lead her away from Mark and the herbal garden. At the exit, Karen turned and said, "Good night, Mark."

"Good night, Princess Karen," Mark said and watched until she was gone.

Mark returned to the private garden, and once he was inside and the gate was safely locked, he tried to go to sleep. But already, he knew that whether he liked it or not, things had irrevocably changed, and he would never be the same person again.

CHAPTER 5

The next morning, having been dressed by her ladies-in-waiting, Karen emerged from her bedroom to find that Daria was standing outside the bedroom that she and Winnifred shared. "How is Winnifred?" asked Karen.

"She managed to get some sleep, but she's still terrified," Daria said. "And I had a hard time falling asleep myself. I actually had to go to the library to calm myself down by reading before I was finally able to fall asleep."

"I'm not sure I can blame you," Karen said. "Father's going to interrogate her today since she wasn't in any state to be questioned last night. I want to be there to have her be calm enough to answer questions. And I had a hard time falling asleep myself last night."

Karen was telling the truth. She *did* have a hard time falling asleep but not because she was worried for Winnifred. It was because of Mark.

Until last night, she related to him mostly as a princess would to a gardener, albeit one who shared her interest in botany. She was friendly enough but aware that her social status forbade intimate conversation with him. But then they bonded over a mutual dislike of Francis due to his being a social climber and concern over Winnifred. And then Mark, in an effort to comfort her, drew her into his arms, and she embraced him, accepting the comfort he offered.

That turned out to be a huge error, for once she stopped trembling and moved her head from his shoulder, she looked up at him when he asked her if she felt better now, and he looked down at her. And in that instant, time seemed to stop for her as she found herself getting lost in Mark's dark eyes. She couldn't move away, couldn't look away, even if she wanted to. And she didn't really want to.

And it took her long—a few minutes? a few hours?—before she remembered Mark's question to her and replied to it. Then he called her Karen. For one brief moment, she was delighted that Mark had stopped addressing her by her title and just called her "Karen." Then she saw the look of horror on his face before he quickly pulled away and turned his head so he wasn't looking at her anymore. That was why she asked him what was wrong.

When Mark explained why he pulled away to her and blamed himself for embracing her, it took a moment, but then she understood. And with that, the terrible truth dawned on her. She had fallen in love with Mark. And nothing could come of this love. She didn't know if her father would allow her to marry Mark since he was a gardener, and even if he *was* willing, she wasn't absolutely sure Mark reciprocated her feelings, although she suspected he did. And even if she was right, Mark would never confess his feelings. He always kept her at a distance in their interactions before this moment after all.

But it was too late to turn back time and have Mark just verbally comfort her without any physical contact. All she could do was move forward and try to return to a more distant relationship with Mark, hiding her heartache as much as possible.

It was at that point that their father arrived. "Is Winnifred up to being interrogated?" he asked.

"Well, she calmed down last night, but she's still terrified," Daria said.

"I can get her some chamomile tea so that she will be calm enough to answer your questions," Karen volunteered. "Just don't be too hard on her, Father."

"Very well," Father said, and Karen headed off with Lily.

On the way to the kitchen, Lily suddenly asked, "Did you really have a hard time getting to sleep last night, Your Highness?"

"I really did," Karen said. "I wasn't lying."

"But I doubt you had such a hard time getting to sleep because you were worried about Winnifred," Lily said.

Karen sighed. Lily had been there when Mark had joined her in the garden after all. *She* had seen what happened and probably suspected the truth. "I'm never going to be with Mark," she confessed. "I don't know if Father will accept him as a potential husband for me, even though Mark saved Winnifred from being taken advantage of by Francis. And even if he did, it's possible Mark doesn't reciprocate my feelings."

"I think he does," Lily said. "I saw the look on his face when he looked down at you."

"I think he does too," Karen admitted. "But I'm sure he'll never *confess* to being in love with me. He may even think he doesn't have a chance with me. How many princesses marry gardeners?"

Lily chuckled at that. "I have to admit, I have yet to hear of a princess who married a gardener," she said.

"Nor have I," said Karen. "He knows that princesses don't marry gardeners or anybody who's a servant in a manor or in a castle. He'll do his best to keep me at a distance, so I'll have to return to a more distant relationship, even if doing so hurts."

They said nothing more while they walked to the kitchen. Once there, Karen prepared a cup of chamomile tea; and once it was done, she and Lily returned to Winnifred's bedroom. Daria opened the door to the bedroom, and she, Karen, their father, and Lily all entered.

Winnifred was sitting on the bed that she and Daria shared, and she still looked white, her light blue eyes showing the fear she still felt. She wore a sky blue dress with flowers embroidered on the hem, and while she normally looked fine in sky blue colors, her pallor made her look bleached and faded this time.

"I've got some chamomile tea for you, Winnifred," Karen said, coming forward with the tea. Winnifred looked up, smiled wanly, and then took the cup, drinking all the tea down. Once she finished, Winnifred handed the cup back to Karen as their father came forward. A servant pulled up a chair, and he sat down in front of the bed.

"You need to be completely honest with me," the king told Winnifred. "It's the only way you can possibly avoid imprisonment." Winnifred nodded, still looking white as a ghost but seemingly calmer, thanks to the tea.

"Was this the first time you and Francis secretly met alone?" the king asked.

"Y-yes," Winnifred said. "We had no real chance of meeting in secret back home sooner because he had come to court over the winter." What she didn't say but Karen knew was that, in winter, there were very few opportunities for any amorous couples to meet in secret due to the cold weather and the lack of privacy. It would have been even harder for a princess to meet a lover in secret because she was carefully surrounded by ladies-in-waiting. March would still have been too cold, and April would probably have been too rainy. This was probably the first chance Francis could find to meet Winnifred secretly, and he took it.

"So you never had the chance to consummate a relationship with Francis?" the king asked.

"No, I didn't," Winnifred said, "especially since last night was the first time I could spend time alone with him—before that *boy* ruined things for us."

"My ladies-in-waiting informed me that Francis was seen whispering to you out of earshot of them, and Karen told me last night that she saw the two of you whispering together," the king continued. "If this is true, what was the subject of the conversations?"

Gradually with some coaxing, Winnifred spilled the whole story. Francis apparently met her when she was walking with her attendants and asked her for a moment of her time, claiming it had something to do with her dancing skills. But once she was out of earshot of them, he flattered her about her dancing skills, telling her that she was the best dancer among her, Karen, and Daria. Gradually, he told her that she was someone special, someone who deserved better than a marriage with an older guy who was too serious to please a beautiful young woman like Winnifred. She was so flattered that when he suggested that he be the one to show her what pleasure she could have if she spent time alone with him, she rapidly agreed.

However, by the time he gained her consent to the plan, people were preparing for the royal progress, so Francis decided it would be best to wait for an opportunity to spend time alone at the first manor they went to. The whispers between Francis and Winnifred when Karen saw them was them making plans to have Winnifred sneak out by getting hold of the key used to lock her and Daria in from the inside, meet up with Francis, and then go to the private garden since the formal gardens, even in the dead of night, might not afford enough privacy.

Karen, Daria, and the king all listened as Winnifred told the whole story. Finally, the king stood up and said, "Thank you for telling me this. Daria, stay with her and make sure she doesn't try to harm herself. Karen, please come with me. For now, we will stay here while I send a messenger back to the palace to tell them that I will be canceling the royal progress and returning home in about a week's time. During this time, I will question Francis further."

Karen followed her father outside. Once outside, Karen said, "What will happen to her?"

"During the week that we stay here, I will convene my royal council and take advice concerning her fate," the king said. "But for now, she will be confined to the quarters that were prepared for her and Daria and only be able to go outside once a day. At night, the door will be barred from the outside by a heavy beam. Once we get home, I'm not so sure what will happen. But most likely, she will not be thrown into a dungeon or even taken to the tower where high-status prisoners often reside, who can get better treatment. Francis might go there, although it's just as likely he'll be thrown into a dungeon. Instead, she will probably be confined to her quarters and continue to go outside only once a day while I try to hasten marriage plans so that she's safely wed to King Henry."

Karen sighed in relief. "I'm glad about that," she said. "I don't care if you throw Francis in a dungeon, especially since it seems he was only pursuing my sister out of a desire for social advancement."

She hastened to explain, "The gardener who found them, Mark, left right after Francis blurted it out. And when he went the back way, he saw Lily and me in the herbal garden and told me that."

"He's a good young man," the king said. "I'm grateful to him for saving my daughter Winnifred from a possible predator. I wish to reward him. But exactly *how* should I reward him?"

"Why don't you talk to the duke or his elder son, Brian, about it?" Karen suggested. "Mark works on the duke's estate after all."

"That's a great idea," said the king. "I'll go locate them and ask them for advice right now. What about you?"

"I don't know whether I'll go to the gardens or just stay in my quarters," Karen said. However, she did know that if she *did* go to the gardens, she would probably *not* go to the herbal garden. Instead, she'd probably go to the private garden or more likely go to the formal ones. After what had happened between her and Mark, she might feel too awkward about facing him again this soon. And she was fairly sure Mark would try his hardest to get things back on a more formal footing between them. And the formal gardens weren't private enough for any amorous couples to do more than share a kiss anyway.

"I thought you'd be heading off to the gardens right away," the king said. "You're the botanist in the family, and the gardens often seem to be a soothing experience for you."

"Since you reminded me of this, I'll go to the formal gardens," Karen decided.

"Why not the herbal one?" the king asked.

"I was there last night," Karen said simply. She didn't want to reveal the full reason since she knew she and Mark could never be together. Why rub salt in the wound by admitting the truth?

But that was when Lily said, "It has to do with . . . a boy." Karen looked at Lily in shock. What was she trying to do, make matters worse?

That was when her father gave Karen a penetrating look that made Karen want to get out of there as fast as possible. Finally, the king nodded and said, "You may go to the formal gardens. I doubt Mark will be there."

Karen gave her father a grateful look as she quickly left with Lily right behind her.

*   *   *

King Robert waited for the duke to arrive in the great hall. As he did so, he thought about what his daughter's personal lady-in-waiting said about the reason why Karen had been so reluctant to go to the herbal garden. *It has to do with . . . a boy.*

If the king wasn't mistaken, this meant that Karen was actively avoiding a fellow. And the only fellow who spent a long amount of time in or near the herbal garden, as far as he knew, was Mark. But why would Karen want to avoid Mark? Had he made advances to her? Possible but highly unlikely. After all, Mark had dragged Francis to the king and the duke once he caught sight of Francis making advances toward Winnifred. Mark, of all people, would probably avoid making advances to a princess since he wasn't even a gentleman but a common gardener.

Then the truth struck the king. *His daughter was in love with Mark. That* was probably why she was actively avoiding him—she knew that the difference in class meant that she could never be with Mark. Or could she?

The king's thoughts were disturbed by the appearance of Duke Thomas, accompanied by his attendants. "Please sit down beside me," the king said. Duke Thomas bowed and approached the smaller throne, sitting down beside the king.

"What is your pleasure, Your Majesty?" Duke Thomas asked.

"I wish to honor the young man who saved my daughter Winnifred from a social climber who was taking advantage of her," the king began.

"Mark?" the duke asked. "That is a very good idea. He should be honored. How do you wish to honor him? Perhaps transfer him to the royal gardens so he can be the herbal gardener there? I hear they could use a good herbal gardener there. Or make him the chief gardener here once my current chief gardener retires?"

Those were good ideas, but ever since the king had concluded that Karen was actually in love with Mark and was avoiding him because she believed she could never be with Mark, he had begun thinking that maybe he should make Mark a gentleman. While being a gentleman might not make Mark a suitable candidate for being a royal consort, it would at least be a start. Moreover, thanks to Francis's reprehensible behavior, the king had every intention of executing the guy, so it would be a good move to also give Mark Francis's coat of arms since Francis would have no need of it.

"Actually, I was thinking of making Mark a gentleman," the king said. "Moreover, I was thinking of giving him Francis's coat of arms as well. Francis will have no need of it, not after what he did with my daughter Winnifred."

"You're going to execute Francis?" asked the duke.

"Of course," the king said.

"Well, you are right in pointing out that it would be a good way to punish Francis's effrontery by rewarding the guy who saved your daughter," Duke Thomas said. "I agree. Shall I have Mark sent here so you can reward him yourself?"

"That would be a very good idea," said the king. "Send for him right away."

"Of course," the duke said and turned to a page to give the necessary instructions.

*   *   *

Mark was surprised at first when one of the duke's pages told him that the king requested his presence in the great hall. But then he thought about the possible reasons why the king might want him to come there. Given the circumstances, Mark could only think of two possible reasons. The first and most logical one was that the king wished to reward him for his saving Princess Winnifred from Francis. But the *second* reason, though less likely, was still possible, and that troubled Mark. It was possible that the king had somehow learned that Mark had fallen in love with Karen. And the thought terrified Mark since he was sure the king would not take too kindly to the idea.

But there was only one way to find out why the king requested his presence. So Mark left the herbal garden and went into the manor, following the page to the great hall. There sat the king and the duke, much as they had sat last night when Mark dragged Francis in to face them.

Mark walked toward them, and once he stood in front of them, he knelt down. "You requested my presence?" he asked.

"I did," said the king. "Please stand up."

Once Mark did so, the king said, "I am truly grateful to you for saving my daughter Winnifred from a social climber who was taking advantage of her lack of sense. I wish to honor you for your service."

Well, at least he doesn't seem to suspect that I'd fallen in love with Karen, Mark thought in relief.

"I'm merely happy that I was able to protect your daughter," he said.

"I believe you, but I feel that you need a more substantial reward," the king said. "Therefore, with the agreement of Duke Thomas, I have decided to make you a gentleman."

Mark stared in shock, hardly able to believe his ears. "What?" he asked.

"I have decided to make you a gentleman and grant you a coat of arms," the king explained. "In fact, I have decided to give you the coat of arms that once belonged to Francis. He will no longer need one since I plan on executing him for the crime of high treason."

Mark was in a state of total disbelief. He had never ever expected to get this sort of reward. The most he had hoped for was perhaps an advancement in rank among the gardeners. "Wh-why are you honoring me this way?" he said.

"I wanted to punish Francis for his effrontery," the king said. "But there is another more important reason. I have reason to believe that my eldest daughter, Karen, really likes you."

Mark nearly panicked at that. "She can't like me!" he protested. "Not in a romantic way. I'm a gardener. She's a princess!"

"Do you like my daughter?" the king asked. The duke looked at the king in a somewhat surprised way.

Mark insisted, "Even if I did, she's still a princess. And even if you make me a gentleman, I'm still not of suitable birth."

"But it would be a beginning," the king explained. "And if you prove yourself further—"

Mark interrupted, "I'm honored by your decision to reward me for protecting your daughter Winnifred, and I will accept the advancement in rank," he said. "But even as a gentleman, I'm too lowly in birth to be a suitable consort for your daughter Karen, even if I *am* in love with her."

"Very well," the king said. "While I am staying here, I will send heralds across the countryside to announce that I am going to raise your rank to that of a gentleman and will be granting you Francis's coat of arms as a royal reward for your service to the king."

"Thank you, Your Majesty," Mark said evenly. "But if you are going to raise me to the rank of a gentleman, it appears I won't be able to continue working in the manorial gardens."

"No, you won't," Duke Thomas said. "I will have to hire somebody else to replace you. Or my son Brian will have to do so. You will have to follow us to court and learn the traditions of being a gentleman."

Mark nodded since he realized that he had no choice but to obey the orders of the duke and the king. But he had to ask, "Sire, why did you believe that the princess Karen really likes me?"

"After interrogating my daughter Winnifred, Karen decided to go to the formal gardens," the king explained. "I was surprised since I know how much she loves herbal gardens, and her personal lady-in-waiting, Lily, told me that it had to do with a boy. The only fellow I could think of whom she would spend enough time here and would want to avoid is you. And when I wondered why, that was when I concluded that she was in love with you and thought she couldn't be with you because of the difference in class."

"She would have been right," Mark said. "I'm not saying that I'm in love with Karen, but if I was, she's too far above me in class for me to have any chance. I'm sorry, but this is the truth."

"I understand," the duke said suddenly. "For now, you may continue your duties while my son Brian or I look for a replacement for you in the herbal gardens. We have a week to do so since the king will be staying here that long. In the meantime, I will have my tailor create new clothes for you since your current clothes are hardly suitable for your new career as a gentleman. You will have to have a linen shirt, a doublet, breeches, and long cloaks for inclement weather or winter. You will also have to get new shoes and not just for winter. The king will be seriously displeased if a gentleman he has so rewarded isn't well shod or well clothed."

Mark nodded in resignation. This wasn't really what he had dreamed of—or wanted. But he had to adapt, so he would do so. "May I depart now?" he asked.

"You may," the king said. "And thank you for rescuing my daughter Winnifred."

"You're welcome, Your Majesty," Mark said as he took his leave. And as he returned to the herbal garden, he sorely wished he could turn back time and have chosen to comfort Karen with words and not by embracing her. Then maybe he wouldn't be in such a predicament.

But it was too late. He was now a gentleman—and he would still never have the chance to be with Karen.

* * *

Alberich waved a hand, and the image in the magic mirror he used to spy on the human realm disappeared, replaced by his own reflection. Alberich had always been interested in the world of mortals and had a magic mirror constructed solely for the purpose of watching them. The antics of the mortals often amused him. Moreover, after he was born, an ancestor of his informed his parents via a magic painting that Alberich would marry a mortal woman. However, the ancestor didn't identify her since, while faeries who went behind the Golden Curtain were able to predict the future, their ability was limited compared with the Creator, God, who knew everything and saw everything.

Although Alberich did not know the identity of the mortal woman whom he would marry, he had seen the daughters of Robert, king of Orgon, and knew that the eldest daughter, Karen, was a botanist who loved working with medicinal herbs and had some skill with them. Since the faerie realm had medicinal herbs that were far more powerful than the herbs in the mortal world, Alberich had sometimes thought that Princess Karen was the mortal woman whom he was meant to marry. Other times, he thought it was Princess Daria as, even though he knew she was really born mortal, her faerielike appearance along with her interest in faeries made him think she might be compatible with him.

But then he saw the whole scene with Princess Karen and Mark the previous night. He saw that the two had fallen in love. Moreover, the next morning—this morning—he consulted the portrait of his ancestor, and that was when he learned that Mark was meant to be with Princess Karen. So Alberich decided that if he wasn't meant to be with Princess Karen, he should help her be with the guy she was *meant* to be with—Mark.

Alberich then watched King Robert honor Mark for saving the princess Winnifred by making Mark a gentleman in part because the king realized that Princess Karen was in love with Mark and wanted to help her out. Alberich respected King Robert for this since most mortal kings would probably prefer that their heirs marry somebody of royal or even noble descent, even if the prospective marriage partners turned out to be self-centered and selfish. That King Robert would consider a commoner who was a nice fellow a possible candidate for the husband of one of his daughters, especially the crown princess, spoke volumes about the king's concern for his daughter's happiness in Alberich's opinion.

Unfortunately, both Princess Karen and Mark were all too aware of the difference in rank between them, especially Mark. And Mark was so convinced that his lowly rank would be a barrier to being with Karen that he'd never reveal his feelings to anyone. But what good was faerie magic if one couldn't use it to get past differences in rank or age or past the choices of others? Alberich had the power to get the two past that point, and he was going to use it.

And there were other problems that King Robert had beyond the problem of a princess and a gardener being in love, worse problems. The first was Princess Winnifred. The incident with Francis had made the king determined to wed her to King Harry of Brangavia as soon as possible. But Alberich was confident, if not entirely sure, that if Winnifred was married to King Henry, she'd probably commit adultery, and the king would find out about it sooner or later and probably have her executed. Alberich had to consult with the paintings of his ancestors to make sure that this would be Winnifred's future if she married King Henry, but if it was, the only chance she would have to avoid execution would be to have her stay in the faerie realm for the rest of her life.

The second problem was the king of Vindicia. While King Robert did not know of it yet, the king of Vindicia had his eye on King Robert's land and was now planning a series of expeditions to conquer Orgon or at least wrest some territory from King Robert since Vindicia also bordered Orgon's lands, and the king was very power hungry. Alberich knew this, but this problem was one that King Robert would probably have to deal with on his own. While Alberich's magic could solve a lot of problems, this wasn't really one of them.

Alberich went to consult the paintings of his ancestors who had gone beyond the Golden Curtain so he could learn what would happen to Princess Winnifred if she married King Henry since this would help him make his plans for both her and Princess Karen. He might have to recruit them to cooperate with him once he formalized his plans, but that probably would not be a problem, especially where Winnifred was concerned.

CHAPTER 6

The castle was now in sight. Karen rode near the head of the royal procession behind her father. Winnifred and Daria rode alongside her.

It had been a very interesting week since Francis had been caught trying to take advantage of Winnifred. Francis had been questioned several more times by her father, the king, with the councilors being present as well as Karen. Winnifred's ladies-in-waiting had also been questioned by the king and councilors.

Francis confirmed Winnifred's account of how he partially seduced her and also denied that they had any amorous meetings before that night. He also said that while he had contemplated trying to bribe one of her ladies-in-waiting so as to gain access to Winnifred during the winter months and March, he did not do so. The ladies-in-waiting also denied that Francis had tried to bribe any one of them. Since Winnifred, like her sisters, was always attended when she left her quarters (and even sometimes while in her quarters), it was quickly concluded that the relationship between the social climber and the princess had never been consummated; thus, even though Winnifred was betrothed to another man, she was not guilty of adultery as she never went far enough to risk the possibility of consummating her illicit relationship with Francis.

Nonetheless, there were going to be consequences for both Francis and Winnifred. Karen had been present with her father all week as the council deliberated on the best way to punish them. It was quickly decided that once they returned to court, Winnifred would merely be confined to her rooms and only allowed to leave her rooms once a day to get some fresh air. What was more, whereas the princesses all had their own rooms at the castle, one of the other princesses would have to room with Winnifred at night to ensure that she did not get into any more escapades, and the doors to her rooms would be barred every night. And they decided that Karen would be the one to room with Winnifred.

There were two reasons for this. The first was that Winnifred and Daria were far less close to each other than either one was to Karen. Winnifred loved to dance and was quite good at it; Daria, while being decent with dancing, wasn't as comfortable with it—at least not in courtly situations. Winnifred was merry, lively, and vivacious; Daria was a quiet bookworm more comfortable in a library than in social situations. And Daria was highly intelligent and had more common sense than Winnifred. Karen was afraid that Winnifred and Daria would quarrel constantly, especially if they spent more than one night together. The second reason was that the council believed Karen could restrain Winnifred more effectively than Daria could.

Deliberating Francis's immediate fate took longer. The council was unsure if they should throw Francis into a dungeon once they returned home to the palace or if he should be housed in the tower, given that he previously had a good position as music and dance instructor to the princesses. However, both Karen and her father supported the idea of throwing Francis in a dungeon because both were outraged at Francis's effrontery in attempting to increase his social standing by seducing a princess who would be married to a foreign king. In the end, the council agreed that Francis's former good position should not protect him from being severely punished, and they agreed to have Francis thrown into a dungeon once they returned to the palace.

Karen had been very surprised when she learned that Mark was going to be made a gentleman because he had saved Princess Winnifred and had asked her father why this was the case. That was when she learned that her father actually was *not* against the idea of Mark marrying her as long as the young man was decent and returned her affections. Karen told him that she thought Mark returned her love but also that she thought Mark would never reveal his true feelings as she believed he was totally convinced that she'd never marry him. Her father confirmed her suspicions of this.

The plan was that once Duke Thomas and his eldest son found an appropriate replacement for Mark, he would go to the castle and begin learning the arts of being a gentleman, and the hope was for them to find one before the royal party left the ducal manor. Meanwhile, the duke's tailors and shoemakers were put to work making new clothes and good shoes for Mark to wear once he left the ducal manor and went to the castle since he had to look the part. Karen did not have many conversations with Mark during this time in part because of the council meetings that she had to attend, and when she *did* have conversations with him, they were rather awkward. Mark insisted on being as formal with Karen as he possibly could and refused to even consider the possibility that he might be a more suitable consort for Karen now that he had been made a gentleman.

Also, Duke Thomas wasn't entirely pleased with the king's support of a match between Karen and Mark as, a couple of times, she inadvertently overheard huge arguments between her father and Duke Thomas. From what she heard, it seemed Duke Thomas was less against the idea of such a match because he wanted to get Karen and Otto together and more against it because, even though Mark had been made a gentleman, he was still born a commoner while Karen was born a princess.

The day before the royal party was scheduled to return to the castle, Duke Thomas and his eldest son managed to find a suitable replacement for Mark, and he was told he could have one more day working in the gardens; but on the day that the royal party was scheduled to depart, he was to go with them. So now Mark was part of the royal party, and when Karen glanced back from time to time, she could see him riding on a horse, looking ill at ease. He looked more handsome now that he didn't have to wear working clothes, which often were fairly drab due to the earthy colors peasant clothing had. He wore a red doublet with a white linen shirt underneath, breeches of a darker red color, and a short red cloak of a lighter shade. He wore tan riding boots, and boothose to protect his stockings from wear and tear. His outfit wasn't as fashionable as those of some of the other men, especially that of Otto, but given that he was once a working man, that was perhaps to be expected.

Karen then glanced back toward Otto. He was wearing a blue doublet, also with a white linen shirt underneath, breeches of a lighter blue color, and a short darker blue cloak, as well as tan riding boots and boothose. The main difference between his outfit and Mark's, other than color, was the presence or lack of lace. Otto's collar and boothose had plenty of lace on them, whereas Mark's had none. Otto had always been something of a dandy, while Karen was more modest, another reason why she had been reluctant to marry him. Now, of course, all the prior motives for reluctance paled compared with the very important fact that she was in love with someone else.

But would she have to marry him anyway? The vast majority of aristocratic and royal marriages were arranged after all. They were all about uniting two families in aristocratic marriages and oftentimes two *countries* in royal ones. And while she knew her father wanted her to be happy, individual happiness wasn't the main goal in such marriages and indeed often was a low priority. Still, what she overheard in the arguments that her father and Duke Thomas had suggested that the duke might be more open to ending the betrothal between her and Otto if a candidate who was of high birth *and* whom she could eventually feel affection toward, if not love, could be found for her.

Suddenly, Karen heard her father call for her to come forward and ride with him. She urged her horse forward and caught up to the king. "What is it, Father?" she asked.

"You already know that my plan was to hasten arrangements for your sister Winnifred to be wed to King Henry of Brangavia," the king began. Karen nodded. "Well, it will have to be postponed until I can find a more suitable candidate for your hand in marriage."

The statement stunned Karen. Was he really ending her betrothal to Otto? And what about Duke Thomas? "Is my betrothal to Otto over?" she asked.

"I've been talking things over with Duke Thomas," her father explained. "He is convinced that a princess should not be wed to a young man who was born into a rank lower than that of aristocracy, specifically the younger son of a duke. However, I have told him that you are not in love with Otto and pointed out all the reasons why you don't want to marry him other than the fact that you are in love with Mark, of course. Also, the original contract betrothing you and Otto was meant to bind Duke Thomas closely to our family as an ally, and this is not as necessary now as it was back then. So we came to a compromise that ended the betrothal on the condition that I find some other suitable young man whom you *could* fall in love with, or at least feel affection toward, and arrange a marriage between you and this other young man."

Karen sighed in relief. "Thank you, Father," she said. While she wasn't totally happy with the news—Mark was still off-limits after all—at least she was no longer betrothed to Otto. And since her father was concerned enough about her happiness to end the betrothal, she could trust her father to find a young man of suitable rank whom she *could* at least feel affection toward. At least that was what she hoped would happen. Still, she wished Mark was of suitable birth so that she could be free to marry him.

* * *

As the royal party rode up a hill, Mark got his first good look at the castle where the king and his family usually lived. The castle apparently was located on a spur projecting from the hill it was built on and was surrounded on three sides by steep hillsides overlooking a river that flowed around the spur in a large bow. The only way in was over a man-made ditch that served as a moat, with a drawbridge that currently was lowered so the royal party could enter the castle safely. From what Mark was told by some of the courtiers, while most of the neighboring kingdoms were at peace with the kingdom of Orgon, the kingdom of Vindicia was still a threat, so the royal seat had to be located in a place that was hard to attack.

As Mark rode with the rest of the royal party over the drawbridge and into the castle area itself, he looked around. From the outside, the royal castle was very big, twice as big as the manor he lived in and with three multistoried towers rising above the main building. A large number of servants and grooms formed a double line of torches on either side of the courtyard, cheering the arrival of the king, the princesses, and the rest of the royal court. He heard music playing to welcome the royal party and saw what were presumably squires come forward and help the princesses and the other female members of the royal court dismount from their horses. Other squires simply held the horses while the men dismounted. Mark saw one man dismount and then pull Francis, who had been put in chains since his arrest and had ridden in front of the other courtier, off the horse both had been riding on.

"Welcome back, Your Majesty," one squire said. "We are both honored and surprised by your presence here, so soon after leaving on your royal progress."

"You know full well why I have returned so early," Mark heard the king say. "But it is good to be back home. Has the castle had a proper airing?"

"Of course," a servant said. "Once we learned you were going to return early, we made sure that the castle had a good scrubbing and cleaning. And we managed to prepare enough food that would be ready for you by the time you arrived home."

"That is a relief," the king said. "Guard!"

A guardsman stepped forward. The king said, "Take Francis to the dungeons."

Another guardsman came forward, and together, they grabbed hold of Francis, dragging him away. Mark almost felt pity for the fellow. Francis looked defeated; his blond hair and his beard were disheveled, and his fashionable clothing had been replaced with a simple dirty white shirt and black breeches. And now he was going to be thrown into a dungeon and eventually executed. Still, Francis had brought his fate on himself.

As Francis was dragged into the castle, the king turned to the other servants and courtiers and said, "We shall settle ourselves in, and later tonight, we shall have a dinner to celebrate our return home."

It was then that they heard a trumpet blast. Mark wondered what that was for. He looked toward the sound of the blast and saw a man standing on top of a battlement, pointing in the direction that they had just come by when they entered the castle area. "What is it?" Mark heard the king ask.

"I see a rider coming this way!" the man on top of the battlement, presumably a watchman, called out.

"Is he a native or a foreigner?" asked the king.

"I think he's a native," the watchman replied. "And he's alone. I see no signs of anybody else with him."

"Leave the drawbridge down," the king ordered. "It looks like we'll have to postpone entering the castle for now." The royal party, the servants, the squires, and the grooms stood around, waiting. Soon the rider came galloping into the courtyard.

The horse was dark brown in color with black legs, a black mane, and a black tail. The rider appeared to be a commoner much like Mark himself had once been. He wore an earthy brown shirt, brown breeches, and brown riding boots. "Your Majesty," the man said, "I have terrible news."

"What is it?" asked the king.

"Soldiers from the kingdom of Vindicia just crossed over the border between Vindicia and Orgon," the man said. "They have seized my hometown and are preparing to use it to proceed farther into Orgon and conquer it."

"It looks like the banquet to celebrate our return home will have to be postponed," the king said. "Before dinner, the members of my council and I will have to create a strategy to stop the king of Vindicia from conquering our land, and tomorrow we shall have to mobilize our troops to go into battle. I would rather not have to go fight the enemy so far from here, but if I have to, then I will."

In that instant, Mark knew what he was going to do. He was going to join the king's troops and go into battle himself. He was no longer a gardener but now a gentleman, and he really had nothing concrete to do. More importantly, being part of the king's troops and going to the border between Orgon and Vindicia meant that he could get away from the court—and from Karen. If there was a chance he could marry Karen, he'd stay; but of course, there was no chance. And he didn't want to stay around a place where he had no chance of winning the one woman who had his heart.

But that was for tomorrow. For now, he'd settle in since he probably wouldn't take part in council deliberations and would just spend the rest of the night ensuring that if he and Karen met, they'd meet in some place where there would be little risk of scandal.

*   *   *

The deliberations did not take long. It was agreed that the king would organize and head an army, some of them being mercenaries who were from friendly countries. The rest would be natives of Orgon, led by aristocrats who often spent time at court. They would rely on scouts to find out the position of the enemy and eventually challenge the enemy on terrain that would prove beneficial to the soldiers of Orgon rather than those of Vindicia.

The mood at dinner was relatively somber. The fact that people would be going to war weighed heavily on the minds of the people who were present. At the end of dinner, the king stood up and said, "You know that the king of Vindicia, that bloodthirsty tyrant, has decided to invade our lands with the purpose of conquest of Orgon. Tomorrow morning, the aristocrats should begin calling up people from their estates to fight for their sovereign lord and king."

It was then that Mark stood up and said, "With your permission, Your Highness, I wish to enlist in your army."

King Robert was surprised, and he heard Karen gasp in shock or maybe alarm. He had planned to have Mark stay at the castle and learn all the arts of being a gentleman, including learning how to dance courtly dances. He did *not* intend for Mark to go into battle, especially considering his daughter Karen's feelings for him. Even if the difference in birth was an obstacle, the king didn't want a guy whom Karen was in love with and who had been responsible for rescuing his daughter Winnifred to go to war and possibly be killed.

"Why do you wish to join my army?" King Robert asked.

"I am no longer a gardener," Mark explained. "I am not used to living the life of a gentleman, and I have nothing concrete to do. I wish to have something to do that is concrete and not a product of idleness."

"Is that you're only reason?" King Robert asked, looking intently at Mark. He was suspicious that Mark wanted to get away from Karen because he didn't want to see her every day and be reminded of the difference in birth between the two.

"No," Mark admitted. "But it is the only reason I can truly give you."

The king sighed and said, "I wish to discuss this with Duke Thomas as you once worked for him, and he would be considered your lord even now that you are a gentleman. If he agrees, then I will permit you to join our army."

"Thank you, Your Majesty," Mark said, bowing as he sat down.

King Robert and the rest of the court listened as a minstrel sang a ballad of a knight who fell in love with his lord's wife. From time to time, King Robert thought he saw Karen glancing at Mark in concern and fear. He was sure Karen didn't want Mark to go to the wars, and he could understand why. He didn't want Mark to go there either since there was a chance he might be killed. On the other hand, being in a war situation would give Mark something to do and keep him from falling prey to melancholy.

Eventually, the king stood up and signaled to Duke Thomas to join him. Duke Thomas stood up, as did Karen, and they all left the great hall together. They all went up the stairs to the royal tower and walked out onto the battlements.

"I really don't want Mark to go to war," Karen said. "He could be killed!"

"It is up to Duke Thomas," the king insisted. "Mark would be a gentleman in his service since he had once worked on the duke's estate, so he would have the final word. I don't want him killed either, but if he stays here, he could fall prey to melancholy since he seems to be convinced that he can never be with you."

"I think we should let Mark go into the army," said the duke. "But since he isn't really trained for warfare, we should put him in the infantry and teach him how to fire a musket. And we'll keep him as safe as we possibly can, given what he apparently means to you, Your Highness."

"I agree with the idea of putting Mark in the infantry and teaching him how to fire a musket," the king said. "As you said, he isn't trained for warfare, and learning how to fire a musket is probably easier than learning how to fight with a sword."

Karen looked concerned but nodded, and with that, the trio went down the stairs to the great hall. The king signaled to his household, including his younger daughters, and they all stood up and prepared to leave the great hall. At a signal from the king, Duke Thomas went to get Mark so that the king could reveal his decision privately.

Daria and her ladies-in-waiting left, most likely for the library given that it was where Daria most often spent her free time. Winnifred and her ladies-in-waiting, as well as Karen's, joined Karen, and they all left for the private rooms that Karen and Winnifred would be sharing since Karen was to keep a close eye on Winnifred, especially after dinner.

Duke Thomas and Mark joined the king. "Duke Thomas has decided to allow you to join my army," the king announced. "But since you are not trained in warfare and since learning how to fight with a sword will take a long time, you shall be put in the infantry and learn how to fire a musket. And since Princess Karen is concerned for your safety, we shall try to keep you as safe as possible."

"Thank you, my lord," Mark said, bowing to the king. "I am relieved to be allowed to do something useful, even if it's also quite dangerous."

"You may now join the others, or if you prefer, you may go to the gardens," the king said, dismissing the young man.

Mark left, leaving the king with Duke Thomas. "I hope Mark isn't killed in the war," the king said. "He saved my daughter Winnifred from scandal, and Karen will be heartbroken if he is killed."

"I think that, besides trying to keep him as safe as we possibly can, we should pray for his safety," Duke Thomas suggested, "or at least for his survival."

The king agreed, and the two men entered the great hall, where the men were engaging in arm wrestling and bouts of unarmed combat.

*   *   *

Mark stood in the courtyard with the other men from the court who were going off to fight against the troops from Vindicia. As Mark was the only man in that group who had little military training, the plan was for him to go off with Duke Thomas to the special camp for new recruits. There, he would learn how to fire a musket and how to use a pike. The other men, including the duke's second son, would go off to the main campsite, which would be close to the location of the troops from Vindicia. Once Mark and the other new recruits had sufficient training, they would join the soldiers at the main campsite.

Ladies from the court were present to see the men go off to war, including the princesses. Mark glanced at the three princesses, beginning with the one who must have been Princess Daria since she had dark hair. Princess Daria seemed very anxious, although it could just have been because the king would be leading the troops to the main campsite, and she was afraid she might never see him again. Princess Winnifred looked more interested in the spectacle than concerned, and he wondered if she understood that some of the men might never return.

Finally, he glanced toward Princess Karen, only to see her head over toward him, accompanied by some of her ladies-in-waiting. Wearing a beautiful green dress finely embroidered with petal patterns and with her red-gold hair shining in the sunlight of the early afternoon, she looked more beautiful than ever to Mark, who had to try to keep his heartbeat from racing and remain calm.

Princess Karen reached Mark and stood in front of him. Her lovely green eyes were beginning to fill with tears, stirring powerful emotions in him that he had to contain. He briefly glanced away so he could regain his composure before facing Karen again.

"I have to go," he told her. "I can't stay here, living a life of idleness. I am not used to such a life."

Karen simply nodded and then stepped closer to him. Mark became nervous. What did she want?

She stood close to him for one moment and then surprised and alarmed him by suddenly embracing him, throwing her arms around his neck and holding on to him tightly. Mark's arms involuntarily closed around Karen's shaking body, holding her close. His heart felt like it was tearing in two at the thought of leaving her, yet he knew he had to leave for her sake and for his own.

"It may seem unladylike, but I might never see you again," Karen whispered. "And if I never see you again . . . I want you to know that I love you. And I need to know if you feel the same way about me."

"Are you trying to torture me?" Mark asked in shock and alarm. "You know I am not a suitable choice since you are a princess, and I am a commoner elevated to gentility."

"Maybe you aren't a suitable choice socially, but Francis was already a gentleman, and he was using my sister for social advancement," Karen reminded him.

"He wasn't a gentleman by birth either," Mark pointed out.

"Maybe not, but there are probably others like him among aristocracy or royalty," Karen noted. "Rank has little connection to a person's character, and I saw that when you saved my sister. Besides, if we never see each other again, hiding your feelings for me might not be necessary."

She has a point, Mark thought. And the fact that Karen basically threw herself into his arms all but said out loud that she loved him while the fact that he had involuntarily embraced her as well might well have stated that he returned her feelings. In that case, what was there to hide?

Despite this, Mark couldn't say the words in front of everyone. But he *could* whisper them to Karen. So he whispered back, "I wish I hadn't fallen in love with you. But I did. And you probably know that's why I'm leaving."

He felt Karen nod, and then he heard her whisper, "Then since we may never see each other again, please . . . kiss me goodbye."

Mark couldn't kiss her, not on the lips. But he *could* kiss her somewhere more intimate than her hand. So he lifted his head and gently kissed her on the forehead. Mark looked down at Karen then, and he could see the tears forming in her green eyes again. He could hardly look at her as he whispered, "Farewell, Your Highness."

"Farewell, Mark," he heard Princess Karen whisper back before she stepped away from him and returned to her sisters. When Mark glanced at them, he could see an expression of confusion on Daria's face and an expression of annoyance on Winnifred's.

Other women said farewell to some of the men as well, and the king said farewell to his daughters, all of whom were very unhappy to see him go, even the princess Winnifred. The prime minister assured the king that Francis would be put on trial, probably convicted of treason, and executed. Mark was happy to hear that since he believed Francis needed to be punished severely for taking advantage of a princess, even if Francis didn't get very far.

Then the men began to mount their horses, including Mark, who mounted a bay horse. As Mark sat in the saddle, waiting for the signal to depart with Duke Thomas for the camp where the recruits would be trained, he took one last look at the princesses. Princess Daria seemed more focused on her father than on anybody else. Princess Winnifred didn't seem as focused on her father as her younger sister did, but she, too, seemed focused on him more than on most of the other men. And when Mark looked at Karen, she seemed to alternate between looking at her father and looking at *him*.

He heard the herald sound the call, and then he trotted away, following Duke Thomas. He didn't dare look back at the princesses. He had to look ahead.

CHAPTER 7

"You really like that guy whom you said goodbye to, don't you?" Princess Daria asked after her eldest sister, Karen, and Karen's ladies-in-waiting entered the private garden, where Daria was taking a walk with her ladies-in-waiting and a musician.

It was the day after their father, the courtiers, and the trained soldiers departed. Daria had spent almost all her time since waking up getting dressed, having her late morning meal in the privacy of her own quarters, and reading books in the library. Her ladies-in-waiting, however, were concerned about her getting a headache due to eyestrain from constant reading, so Daria agreed to take a walk in the garden to refresh herself.

The sun was shining, the grass in the gardens was green, and the flowers were in full bloom. It was an incredibly lovely day, even if their father was away at the main campsite, where the soldiers would be preparing for combat with the troops of Vindicia. She had been afraid he would be killed and naturally begged him to stay behind once she first learned of his plans to lead his men into battle. But the king was convinced that he had to lead his men in defense of Orgon. Moreover, he was sure that the king of Vindicia would be leading his men or at least would be nearby, possibly on the other side of the border between Orgon and Vindicia.

But spending time in the garden, listening to the musician sing ballads about love, helped relax Daria and make her forget her fears and concerns. That was when Karen and her ladies-in-waiting entered the garden. Karen had a look of nearly total misery on her face, and that was why Daria blurted out her question about the guy—Mark, wasn't it?—whom Karen had said goodbye to.

Daria hadn't really thought much about Karen's approaching Mark when she first saw her sister do so. Daria was too upset about her father leaving. But then she saw Karen practically throw her arms around his neck and hug him tightly. Daria knew Karen well enough to know that Karen would never do such a thing in public with a guy—any guy—other than maybe her father, not unless she felt something for him, something like love. And when she saw Mark kiss Karen on the forehead, she realized something was apparently going on between the two, something that she had missed or not seen while they were at Duke Thomas's manor together.

Daria had wanted to ask Karen about it, but she wasn't sure when she should do so. After the supper that evening, Karen and her ladies-in-waiting had gone to the herbal garden to pick some herbs, and Daria thought about going with them, but she felt a headache coming on, so she went to her bedroom instead. Although Karen had come in to give Daria herbal tea, Daria was unsure of whether this was the right moment to ask Karen, so she didn't say anything then. And Daria had had no chance to speak to Karen until now. But now they were together, and now was as good a time as any.

Karen looked startled when Daria asked her the question, and then she sighed. "Is it that obvious?" she asked.

"I think even someone like me who has bad social skills can see that when a beloved elder sister suddenly hugs a guy before he is to leave and then lets him kiss her on the forehead, she is probably in love with him," Daria noted, smiling a little.

Karen sighed again. "No, I really don't *like* Mark," she said, causing Daria's eyes to widen. "I really *love* him."

Daria then asked a little awkwardly, "And does he reciprocate your feelings?"

"Yes," Karen said, sighing again. "That's why he chose to go to war—he was sure we could never be together. And he's right too. Duke Thomas, for one, thought that since Mark was born a commoner, he's not a suitable candidate for my hand in marriage, even though he was willing to end my betrothal to Otto."

Daria blinked. "I didn't know he'd done that," she confessed.

"Father told me yesterday when we were near home," Karen explained. "The prime minister is going to look at suitable candidates for my hand in marriage, *royal* candidates."

Daria felt sorry for Karen. She was in love with a guy whom she could never be with, unless . . . "Maybe the faeries can help," she suggested.

"The question is whether the faeries can be bothered to help a mortal woman, even if she's a princess," Karen noted. "You know as well as I do, maybe even better than I do, that faeries have their ways, and we have ours. And at best, they'd interact with us without thinking much about the consequences to their actions. Of course, most royalty and nobility might treat commoners the same way, if not worse."

Daria had to agree with her sister's assessment. The stories she'd read of the faeries almost never portrayed them as being genuinely kind toward human beings. The best ones really *did* tend to interact with humans without giving any thought about the consequences to their actions. Most were just tricksters who delighted in the messes that they made in the lives of humans. The *worst*, however, were otherworldly horrors who'd kidnap humans as mere playthings. And even the best ones were well known for punishing humans severely for even the slightest infractions, such as claiming that a human woman was more beautiful than any of the faerie women.

That was when Daria remembered accidentally overhearing something that the ambassador from Brangavia said while he and her father were arranging the planned union between the king of Brangavia and Princess Winnifred, something about the king's great-great-grandfather marrying the princess Vera, who was from the kingdom of Vindicia. They later had a daughter and a son, but as the daughter grew up, the now-queen Vera became bitterly envious of her own daughter's beauty and decided to have her abandoned in a forested area, hoping that either wild animals or robbers would murder her. But instead, she was taken in by miners from a nearby mining town, some of whom were child laborers. When Queen Vera found out her daughter had lived, her envy ultimately became so bad that she apparently consulted a witch for poison, supposedly for rats.

However, according to the story, the witch realized whom Queen Vera really planned to poison, so she secretly made a potion that had to be administered in three doses. The first two would only weaken her, but the third would put the princess in a deep coma, from which she could be awakened if somebody had the antidote for the potion. Queen Vera was led to believe that the third dose would kill her daughter and took it, using the disguise of a beggar to trick the princess into taking the potion. Ultimately, the princess fell into a deep coma and was placed in a glass casket. A couple of months after the princess fell into a coma, a prince from a different kingdom was on a hunting expedition when the witch contrived to meet him, told him about the princess, and provided him with the antidote. As the prince revived the princess, the witch revealed the treacherous poisoning to the king, who had Queen Vera executed. The princess wound up married to her prince, and they had a happy marriage.

But the reason why Daria remembered the story was that the queen had supposedly brought her troubles on herself, first by claiming that she was more beautiful than the faeries underneath Vindicia and thus having the faeries secretly give her a gift of a magic mirror when she married King Henry's great-great-grandfather. Then she got into further trouble by wanting the magic mirror to claim that she was not just more beautiful than any *mortal* woman in the kingdom but also more beautiful than *any* woman in the kingdom, faerie women included. The faeries underneath the kingdom of Brangavia were supposed to have punished Vera by making her daughter more beautiful than Vera herself and thus driving Vera to a bitter envy that led to attempted murder and her own death. Daria wasn't sure if the story was true or not, but if it was, Queen Vera had been an utter fool to make such claims.

But Daria knew that Karen wasn't such a fool. Even if Karen wasn't as familiar with fairy tales as Daria was, Karen knew better than to claim that she was more beautiful than any of the faerie women, especially since no human was really more beautiful than the least beautiful of the faeries. Winnifred might be dumb enough to claim such a thing, however. While Winnifred hadn't actually claimed she was more beautiful than any faerie woman, the possibility existed, and Daria hoped either Karen, their father, or Winnifred's nurse had enabled Winnifred to understand that making such a claim was tantamount to suicide, at least in Daria's eyes.

"Is there something you're thinking of?" Karen asked Daria. Apparently, she had seen something in Daria's expression that caused Karen to realize Daria was in deep thought.

"I was just thinking about something concerning the great-great-grandmother of King Henry of Brangavia that I overheard a couple of years ago," Daria explained, "that the faeries punished Queen Vera for saying that she was more beautiful than any faerie woman by having her be jealous of her own daughter. I'm not sure if this Queen Vera *was* such a fool as to actually claim such a thing, however."

"She might have been so," Karen said. "This Queen Vera was rumored to be extremely vain, which might explain the rumors that she actually *was* foolish enough to make such a claim."

"I hope Winnifred isn't foolish enough to say such a thing," Daria said. "You know how little common sense she has."

"I think Winnifred's nurse actually did her best to convince Winnifred that making such a claim was tantamount to suicide," Karen said. "I hope she did as Winnifred's in enough trouble already."

That was when Princess Winnifred and her ladies-in-waiting entered the private garden, embroidery in hand. Daria and Karen quickly turned the conversation toward other matters.

*　　*　　*

It was the third day since her father, Mark, and the rest of the younger courtiers had left the court to either take part in training or be part of the army. And Karen was doing everything she could to avoid indulging in grief or worry since such indulgence might not only lead to melancholy but actually make her ill as well. So Karen spent as much of her time as she could taking her father's place in greeting people who had petitions for the king, taking part in council meetings, going to the herbal garden in the company of her ladies-in-waiting to gather medicinal herbs, or spending time with her sisters and their ladies-in-waiting in the private garden. In Winnifred's case, she'd spend time with her only when the princess went to the garden as part of her being allowed to leave her rooms once a day for fresh air.

Greeting people who had petitions and taking part in council meetings provided welcome distractions for Karen since she could hardly grieve over Mark being gone from her life, possibly for good; nor could she really worry about her father when she had more important things to think about. But going to the herbal garden proved to be harder than it had been before she fell in love with Mark, especially since he had worked there. And whenever she picked herbs, she would often have a mental image of Mark helping her.

Spending time with her sisters in the private garden didn't really help matters either. Both Winnifred and Daria knew that Karen was in love with Mark, and while Daria was sympathetic, Winnifred was rather derisive, asking why Karen had to fall in love with a gardener who had ruined what Winnifred believed was just a good time with Francis. Karen tried to remind Winnifred that Francis was taking advantage of her and that Francis was about to be tried and probably convicted and executed for his actions, but Winnifred had a hard time understanding that Francis was just using her.

But that wasn't the only problem with Winnifred, Karen reflected as she, Winnifred, and their ladies-in-waiting returned to their rooms after they had supper on the third evening. Winnifred had begun complaining about her future husband, King Henry, stating that the king was too serious and that she deserved someone more lighthearted and fun loving. This annoyed Karen, especially since she had met King Henry a couple of times and saw that the king, while certainly a serious guy, seemed like a nice guy once you got past his seriousness and was dedicated to being a good ruler, something Karen approved of. But Winnifred wasn't wise enough to see Henry's virtues. Instead, she wished for a husband who was a lot of fun, to the exclusion of any other qualities.

Perhaps the sheer frustration of dealing with someone who had such little common sense was the reason why Karen was beginning to develop headaches, something she hadn't really gotten until this point. She loved Winnifred, but the girl could be very frustrating. Or maybe her headaches were related to the fact that she was trying very hard to distract herself from grief over being separated from Mark and concern for his and her father's safety. Either way, she had another headache, and that was why before returning directly to the rooms she shared with Winnifred, she went to the storeroom, got some medicinal herbs, and concocted an herbal remedy that would alleviate the headache. After drinking it, she and the ladies-in-waiting who accompanied her returned to her rooms.

Once they arrived, the ladies-in-waiting who attended Winnifred gathered around and said, "Princess Winnifred is ready for bed, Your Highness."

"I'm ready for bed as well," Karen said. "I took an herbal remedy for a headache, and I just want to go to sleep."

She went to the bedroom that she and Winnifred shared now, and the ladies-in-waiting gathered around, helping both girls shed the folds of their regular gowns and bringing them their night shifts. Whereas Winnifred's shift was blue in color, Karen's was green. The bed was tall enough to have a couple of steps from it to the floor, so both girls literally climbed into bed and the ladies-in-waiting closed the curtains around them, cutting off the last rays of the setting sun. Then the ladies-in-waiting left the two girls alone.

"Do you really have a headache?" Winnifred whispered to Karen.

"Yeah," Karen replied softly. "It could be due to frustration. Or I might be trying to distract myself a little too hard."

"What is it about that boy that makes you like him so much?" Winnifred asked.

"He's a very nice guy, and we have some things in common," Karen explained, "like gardening. And he was really helpful to me the night you got into trouble."

"I hate being reminded of that," Winnifred complained. "Do you always have to remind me of it?"

"I'm sorry," Karen said, trying to make peace so that she could get to sleep.

"Thanks," Winnifred said. "I just hate being cooped up and not being able to do as much dancing as I used to."

"Maybe I can help with that," said a voice that Karen had never heard before, a male voice.

Karen reacted quickly. She opened the heavy linen bed-curtains and saw a tall young man standing at the foot of the steps. He held up a hand and then gave her a gesture to be silent.

Karen glanced over at Winnifred, who had crawled over to see who had spoken, and Karen could see her sister look like she had stars in her eyes. So Karen glanced back at the young man, still standing there.

Karen could see why Winnifred looked like she had stars in her eyes, for this young man was most impressive. Enormous blue eyes looked out of a face with a broad white brow, chiseled cheekbones, a firm and grave mouth, and a strong yet beardless chin. And the face was framed by a mane of snow-white hair that fell down to a place just above his shoulders. His clothes, which covered a slim, athletic frame, were even more impressive. His short cape, slung artistically over his left shoulder, was a deep blue velvet with a creamy lining. His doublet was the same creamy color of the lining in his cape, also velvet and nearly smothered with diamonds, sapphires, and rubies. The slashing of the doublet and its open front allowed Karen to see that the shirt was of the finest white silk and embroidered in a very subtle design. His deep blue breeches were also velvet and fastened with buckles of the finest gold. And his low-heeled boots were made of the finest tan leather, soft enough that it could have been used as material for gloves.

Not only were his clothes sumptuous but he also wore around his neck what seemed to be a silvery chain intricately linked, with a huge pendant made of enameled gold in the shape of an eagle resting on his chest, as well as rings on every finger. And finally, on his head was a small golden crown with diamonds and pearls set in an intricate pattern. Whoever this young man was, he had a small fortune on him.

Karen signaled to Winnifred to stay behind the curtains before slowly climbing out of bed. She really needed to grab a dressing gown to cover her shift. The strange man extended one hand, and there was a bright green dressing gown in it. Warily, Karen took the dressing gown from him and slipped it on.

"Who are you?" she asked quietly. "And how did you get into my and my sister's bedchamber? No man is allowed inside this bedchamber, not even my father."

The young man went down on one knee and said, "Forgive me, Your Highness. My name is Alberich, and I am crown prince of a court of faerie."

Karen stiffened slightly at that, and her green eyes became even warier than before. While this *did* explain how he got so easily into her bedchamber, she still wasn't sure whether this faerie's appearance was a good thing or a bad one.

The stranger seemed aware of Karen's wariness, for he smirked and said, "You seem to be wary of me."

She probably should be tactful when explaining herself. Karen took a deep breath and said, "My sister Daria is an expert on faerie lore, and I learned quite a bit about it from her. I think that when dealing with a being that might kidnap a hapless human to use as a plaything and subject that human to all sorts of horrors that I don't really want to think about, caution is definitely advised. Don't you?"

The stranger laughed and said, "True, very true. But some faeries may be quite friendly to humans. Or at least they'll leave humans alone as long as humans do the same. We may be as diverse in that regard as you humans are. And in your case, I have no intention of kidnapping you or your sister and mistreating you. I have a more benevolent goal in mind."

Now standing at the bottom of the stairs that led to the bed that she and Winnifred shared, Karen glanced back briefly and saw Winnifred's blond head peeking out of the curtains. Satisfied that she was going to remain quiet, Karen turned back to the faerie. "Why are you here?" she asked quietly.

Alberich explained, "I am aware that you are in love with the young gardener who saved your sister from a human who was just as bad as some of the faeries that you are worried about, although less powerful. I am also aware that while your father is approving of a match between you and this Mark, others aren't so approving because Mark is a commoner. But there is a way for you and Mark to be together."

Before she could stop herself, Karen asked, "How?"

"Every night you can go down through a trapdoor that will be located underneath the bed that you and your sister share, pass through three groves of trees till you arrive at a clear underground lake where a boat will be waiting, and then take the boat to the other side, where my castle stands. Then you can dance until your shoes are worn out," Alberich explained.

"And how will that help me be with Mark?" Karen asked cautiously.

"I know through magical means that when people begin noticing that your shoes are worn out, your father will return and promise the hand of one of his daughters to any man who discovers the reason for the shoes being worn out," Alberich explained. "And if the man who solves the mystery isn't of royal or aristocratic blood but is a commoner, he'll still be able to marry one of you."

Karen was intrigued. This *would* enable her to marry Mark as she wanted. But she was still too wary to agree outright to the deal. So she asked, "Why do you want to help me?"

"Because while I am apparently fated to marry a mortal woman, I have learned that I am *not* fated to marry you," Alberich explained. "Your love for Mark is the real thing. Thus, I am willing to help you be with him. I am also willing to invite your sister to join you in nightly dancing."

"You are?" Winnifred suddenly asked. Karen turned and saw Winnifred pull open the curtains and prepare to climb out of bed.

"Wait there until I get a night-robe for you," Karen said. She turned, only to see that Alberich had a blue night-robe in his hand.

"Thanks," Karen said as she took it from him and gave it to Winnifred. Winnifred put it on and climbed down to join Karen.

"You're willing to let me and my sister dance at your castle every night?" Winnifred asked eagerly.

"Yes," he said. "But my reason for having you dance there is different from my reason for having Karen do so. Whereas I am prepared to let Karen remain in the mortal realm once the truth is revealed—hopefully by Mark—I wish you to remain in my realm forever."

This alarmed Karen. The last thing Karen wanted was to have Winnifred at the mercy of horrors who might do who-knows-what to her. "I can't let you hurt my sister!" she protested.

Alberich smiled and said, "Who said anything about hurting your sister? If I wished to hurt her, I wouldn't just say that I wished her to remain in my realm forever. I'd kidnap her here and now and not bother with letting you know and having you act like an overprotective big sister."

He had a point. Still, she had to ask, "Then why do you wish my sister to remain in your realm forever?"

"Because I have learned that if she marries King Henry, she will commit adultery with some other guy. The king will find out, of course, and he will have her beheaded. If she remains in the faerie realm, she will be safe from the harm that will come from her own foolishness," explained Alberich.

"So you really *are* concerned for my sister's welfare and for my own?" asked Karen.

"As much as a faerie like me can be, yes," Alberich reassured her.

Karen was going to think it over, but Winnifred made the decision for her. "I'd be happy to go to your castle," Winnifred said delightedly. "Let's do so tonight."

"No," Alberich said, "tomorrow night. I will need time to make the magic connection from my realm to yours through a trapdoor under your bed."

"Then I will go too," Karen said. "I wish to keep a close eye on my sister and make sure she'll be all right until I am ready to trust you. And if going to your castle every night, dancing, and watching my sister will enable me to marry Mark, then I'm happy to accept your deal."

"Thank you," Alberich said, bowing on his knee yet again. "Once the trapdoor is created, all you have to do is knock on your bed three times, and it will sink into the floor, enabling the two of you to go down into my realm. Also, new gowns will be ready for you to wear tomorrow night. The gowns that faerie women wear for our dances are extremely fancy, and you especially seem to prefer wearing simple, if opulent, dresses, Princess Karen. Your normal dancing gown *is* more opulent than that of your sister, Princess Winnifred, but it's not quite opulent enough for dancing at my castle."

"Very well," Karen said. "And if all works out, thank you for your assistance, Alberich."

"It will all work out," Alberich said. "And don't worry about Mark being killed. I'm going to make sure he'll survive long enough to return and marry you. Until tomorrow night."

He bowed and disappeared. Winnifred squealed, "Isn't this exciting?"

"And a little scary," Karen admitted. She wasn't fully trusting of Alberich, but she wanted to protect her sister, and this might be the only real shot she had at marrying Mark. She had to take the chance that it would work out.

CHAPTER 8

"Your sister is exceptionally happy today," one of Winnifred's ladies-in-waiting informed Karen the next evening as the princesses were going to the great hall to have their evening meal. "Do you have any idea why she's so happy?"

Karen sighed inwardly but outwardly retained her composure. This was the reason why she had decided last night, after Prince Alberich had left and she and Winnifred returned to bed, that she would stay close to her sister and not leave her, even to pick herbs for herbal remedies. Winnifred's lack of common sense meant that she might blurt the truth out to the other ladies-in-waiting, and that was the *last* thing Karen wanted at this point.

So from the moment both girls woke up and their ladies-in-waiting, who were waiting outside the bedchamber for the first signs that the princesses were awake, entered the room, Karen had kept a very close eye on Winnifred and, whenever she was able to, whispered to her that she should *not* give anything away about their plans for the night and for many nights afterward until Mark returned, and she could use the opportunity to have him find out the secret and marry her as his reward. Winnifred understood enough to not say a word, but her excitement was too strong for her to contain. Apparently, being deprived of the chance to dance had tortured Winnifred more than Karen knew, for the prospect of being able to dance every night at Alberich's castle seemingly exhilarated Winnifred so much that the women surrounding her could tell she was delighted. Several of the ladies-in-waiting had remarked on Winnifred's evident excitement, but fortunately for Karen, none of them had seemed willing to ask either Winnifred or Karen about it—until now.

"I'm afraid not," Karen lied. "I believe she's up to something, but she hasn't told me what it is." *That* was the truth technically. Winnifred *hadn't* told Karen what she was going to do, but she didn't need to—Karen was already in on the plan.

The lady-in-waiting frowned but didn't say anything else. She probably expected Karen not to know what Winnifred was up to—after all, Winnifred hadn't told Karen or anybody else of her planned escapade with Francis earlier.

They then entered the great hall, and Karen and Winnifred joined Daria and moved toward the head table, along with the more nobly born of their ladies-in-waiting. The ladies-in-waiting who weren't nobly born, including Elke, who had joined Daria's household while the royal party was at Duke Thomas's manor, moved to one of the lower tables. There, they wouldn't eat the delicacies that more nobly born ladies-in-waiting, even those who were impoverished relatives of aristocrats, might have, such as pies of lark's tongue.

Karen made a slight face at that. She never really liked those kinds of delicacies. Delicacies made of fruits were fine for her, but delicacies made from animals? Not really her favorite delicacies. She didn't know why. Daria shared her dislike of them, but Winnifred loved them. But at least Karen and Daria didn't often have those kinds of desserts, so there weren't many larks that had to be slaughtered to provide pies for women.

The evening meal went without incident. Winnifred behaved very well throughout, much to Karen's relief. Court musicians played and sang for the amusement of the princesses, singing ballads of chivalrous knights and purehearted ladies. When the final course of desserts was served, Karen took several oranges sweetened with honey and ate them. She saw Winnifred have a pie made of lark's tongue, while Daria took sweetened apples.

Once a final ballad was sung, it was the end of the formal part of the evening meal, and it was time for her and her sisters to retire for the night. Karen rose as did Winnifred, Daria, and the people attached to their households. Everyone stood and bowed as the princesses and their ladies exited the great hall.

"What do you plan to do tonight?" Karen asked Daria once they were outside the great hall.

"I'll be heading to the library and read until I become sleepy," Daria said.

"I hope you don't have any headaches from eyestrain," Karen said. "Winnifred, what do you plan to do tonight? Go to the gardens?"

"No," Winnifred said. "I'm ready to go to bed."

"Then we'll be going to our rooms and go to sleep," Karen informed Daria. "Good night."

"Good night," Daria said as she and her ladies left for the library.

Karen and Winnifred proceeded to their rooms and entered their bedchamber, accompanied by their ladies. Once there, their ladies helped them undress and gave them their usual bedtime shifts, which the princesses put on. Then they climbed into bed and waited for the ladies to depart the bedchamber.

Once their ladies-in-waiting left the bedchamber, Karen signaled to Winnifred to wait a few minutes. Eventually, when Karen deemed it safe, she nodded, and they both climbed out of bed and headed toward the wardrobe where the grand dresses that they usually wore for dancing and for great occasions at court, such as the departure of her father to war, were stored. Karen opened the wardrobe and realized that Alberich hadn't been joking when he said that he was going to provide them with more opulent dresses for dancing. The emerald green gown that Karen normally wore for dancing at her father's court was fairly grand as it was embroidered all over in a pattern of flowers and had emeralds in place of the whorls, which in regular flowers were used for pollination. It had a draped skirt with a long train, a moderate neckline trimmed with lace, and long hanging lace-trimmed sleeves. Winnifred's pale blue dress was slightly more opulent with an embroidered design of swirls instead of flowers, a lower neckline, a bodice encrusted with sapphires and ribbons, and lace on the sleeves. There were more jewels on Winnifred's dress than on Karen's as well.

But the gown Karen found herself looking at was much grander. In fact, she had a hard time actually *looking* at the gown. There were no jewels, ribbons, lace, or any other fancy decorations in the dress. It didn't *need* the fancy decorations, for the gown was golden in color and as bright as the sun when it shone in the sky. The gown had very short sleeves while the neckline was wide and ran horizontally across her collarbone, almost to her shoulders, and was lower than the necklines in the gown she wore for dancing at her father's court. Beside it was an underdress of golden silk, and beside that were three golden silk petticoats. Finally, below the gown, Karen saw dancing shoes that were almost as bright as the gown itself.

She heard Winnifred gasp in delight and then turned to see what her sister had found. On the other side of the golden dress was a silvery dress that looked like it was made of moonbeams and also had no jewels, ribbons, lace, or any other fancy decorations on it. And like the golden dress, the silvery one didn't need fancy decorations. Unlike the golden dress, however, the silvery one had no sleeves whatsoever, and the neckline was low and square, revealing a *lot* more of her cleavage than the golden dress did. Beside the silvery gown was an underdress of silvery silk, and beside that were three silvery silk petticoats. And below that gown were silvery dancing shoes.

We're going to have to help each other get into our gowns, Karen thought but didn't say.

"Wow! Aren't the gowns gorgeous?" Winnifred cried out in delight.

"They *are* quite lovely," Karen said in a quieter tone. "But we're going to have to help each other get into our gowns. After all, our ladies aren't here to put the petticoats, underdress, and gown on."

Winnifred nodded. But the next moment, Karen felt a strong tingle running over her body as if thousands of wings were beating frantically against it. She looked down and gasped as she saw her body being enveloped in a golden swirl. When the swirl finally settled, she saw that the golden gown that was as bright as the sun was on her in place of her sleeping shift. The golden silk underdress and three golden silk petticoats had also been put on, and she could feel the golden shoes on her feet.

"Well, that's helpful," Karen said dryly and heard a gasp from Winnifred. Karen looked and saw a silvery swirl enveloping Winnifred's body so that only her face could be seen. Her hair had been pulled up and was being braided and twined with what looked like blue sapphires. Seeing it, Karen put her hand up to her head and glanced in a nearby mirror. She saw that her hair had also been pulled up and had been braided and twined with emeralds. She then looked back at Winnifred and saw the silvery swirl settle into the folds of her silvery gown and saw the silvery shoes on her feet.

"Wow, this is cool!" Winnifred squealed.

"Yes, but please keep quiet," Karen whispered as she moved to the bed. As she did so, she saw that the sleeping shifts that she and her sister normally wore were on the bed. "I don't want our ladies-in-waiting to come in and see us leaving."

Karen then clapped her hands three times. Immediately, the bed sank into the floor, with the shifts being lifted away as it did. A trapdoor flew open. Karen glanced at Winnifred, who was now behind her; nodded; and proceeded to the open trapdoor.

Once there, she descended down a staircase that led from her bedroom to an underground passageway that was sparkling with gems. Karen waited until her sister joined her and then led the way through the passageway. Eventually, the two sisters emerged in the most amazing grove of trees that Karen had ever seen. The leaves were all silvery, glittering, and sparkling beautifully in the dim light.

"Wow!" Winnifred squealed. "Isn't this great?"

"It is," Karen agreed as they made their way along a pathway through the grove of silvery trees. Karen looked around in amazement at the silvery leaves. Eventually, the trees thinned, and they found themselves in another grove of trees. However, the leaves of *these* trees were golden in color. Karen reached out and touched one of the leaves, and she could tell it was pure gold. Pure gold was reddish yellow, dense, and soft to the touch, and this leaf was reddish yellow and felt very soft.

"This is even more amazing!" Winnifred squealed.

"I agree," Karen said as she led the way through the grove of golden trees. Finally, they reached a third grove of trees, and the leaves were the brightest diamonds she had ever seen. It was such a lovely place.

"If this is what I have to go through every night just to go dancing, let me go through here forever!" Winnifred exclaimed.

"You probably will, until someone finds out our secret," Karen said. "Then you'll stay in this realm for the rest of your life."

"It's a good thing you reminded me that I'll be staying here," Winnifred said. "Otherwise, I'd be telling you that I want nobody to find out."

Karen led the way through the grove of diamond-leafed trees, looking around in wonder as she did so. The faerie realm had many wonders. How many more wonders would they find before they got to their destination?

Eventually, the grove of trees thinned, and Karen and Winnifred emerged to find themselves facing a clear blue lake that stretched out to the horizon. At the side of the lake were two little boats, and two men who were presumably faeries stepped out of them. "Welcome, Your Highnesses," one of the men said, bowing. "Crown Prince Alberich has sent us to meet you and to take you to the other side of the lake, where his castle stands."

"Thank you," Karen said. "We appreciate his thoughtfulness."

"I sure do," Winnifred said, squealing in delight.

The man who spoke took Karen's hand while his partner took Winnifred's before leading the two girls to the boats. Karen got into the first boat, and the man who escorted her got in behind her. She saw him take a pole and push the boat away from the shore before using a rowing oar to scull the way to the other side and the faerie castle.

Karen looked out over the vast expanse of water and felt the last trace of nerves that she'd experienced while preparing to leave her room and while going down through the trapdoor fall away. This was such a lovely place. As long as the faeries weren't going to hand Winnifred over to devils as part of a tithe to keep the faeries from going to hell, her sister would be happy here. She *had* heard tales from Daria about how some faeries had to hand over someone to hell as a tithe, but she wasn't sure if the faeries from Alberich's court had to do so or not.

Eventually, the boats neared the other side of the lake, and Karen saw the faerie castle. And what a castle it was! It was much bigger than her father's and shone like a brilliant diamond. From what Karen could see, there were numerous towers, turrets, and gables on the building. The castle was set high on a hill, and three terraces descended from the top of the hill, where the castle stood, to the base. And at the edge of the lake stood the dock from which boats would travel across the lake.

"What are the terraces used for?" Karen asked her boatman.

"They're the formal gardens," the boatman explained. "In the back of the palace, there are more terraced gardens, but one is a private one, only used by faerie royalty. A second is the vegetable garden, where vegetables for faerie consumption are grown, and the last is the herbal garden. I hear you have an interest in herbal gardens."

"I do," Princess Karen said excitedly. "I'm an herbalist, and I make a lot of herbal remedies, though I can't really treat stuff such as cancer with them. All I can do is alleviate the pain."

"We have herbs that are much stronger than the ones where you live," the boatman said. "I believe there are herbs that can even cure this cancer of which you speak and other diseases that are incurable where you live."

Gradually, the boats approached the other side of the lake. Finally, the boats arrived at the dock. The faeries jumped off the boats and reached for the hands of the princesses to help them off.

Once the group left the dock, Karen saw a stairway leading up the hill to the castle. Holding her escort's arm with one hand and the train of her gown with the other, she walked up the hill to the castle. As she walked, she gazed at the gardens on either side of her with undisguised awe.

On both sides of the lower garden were fountains that looked like natural rock fountains, complete with grottoes and niches. On the left side of the lower garden, she saw beds of roses as far as the eye could see. On the other side, she saw common rhododendrons and lovely azaleas. And in the middle was a circular alley of cypress trees, providing shade for visitors such as Karen and Winnifred.

The group made their way up the stairway till they reached the second terrace level, where Karen saw more fountains, along with numerous citrus trees that stretched out as far as the eye could see. And in the middle of this terrace level, there was a beautiful large fishpond with numerous brightly colored fish swimming in the depths and fed by monumental fountains.

"There are other fishponds, one on the left side of the garden and one on the right side," Karen's escort said, seeing the awe in her eyes as she looked at the fishpond. "The ducks come to the pond on the left side, and swans come to the one on the right."

"Do the ducks, swans, or fish wind up as food?" Karen heard Winnifred ask.

"The fish often do," Winnifred's escort said. "The ducks and swans are less rarely food for the royal court."

Finally, they reached the last terrace, and Karen saw that the garden on this level had three fountains as well, along with beds of violets on one side and forget-me-nots on the other. Behind the central fountain was what appeared to be a stately large gatehouse flanked by two stair towers. Karen, Winnifred, and their escorts passed through the gatehouse, looking around in awe at the magnificent furnishings. Finally, they reached the end of the passageway and entered the courtyard.

The courtyard also had two levels to it. The lower one, where they currently stood, was surrounded on one side by a rectangular tower. The other side was open, and if Karen chose to look out, she could probably get a good view of the hill on which the castle stood. In the lower courtyard was a statue of a dragon, glaring at them.

They passed through the lower courtyard and took a stairway to the upper one, which was surrounded on both sides by two more buildings.

"The building on the left is where the gentlemen of the court reside," Karen's escort explained. "The one on the right is where the ladies of the court reside."

Finally, in front of them stood a huge building bigger than the other three. This no doubt was where Crown Prince Alberich and his parents and any siblings he might have had resided and where they held their festivities. As the foursome approached the main building, the shining doors opened, revealing Prince Alberich dressed magnificently in a doublet encrusted with sapphires and amethysts and wearing a lovely blue cape with matching breeches. "Welcome to my realm, Princess Karen and Princess Winnifred," he said, bowing as they approached. "It is an honor to have you come visit us."

"As long as you don't hurt us, it is an honor to be here," Karen said cautiously. "This is a magnificent place."

"I agree," Winnifred said, squealing in delight.

Alberich approached the princesses and glanced at the man holding Karen's arm. The man stepped back, and Alberich took Karen's arm. "Shall we go into the ballroom?" he asked.

Before Karen could reply, Winnifred squealed, "Oh yes!"

"That would be fine," Karen said.

Alberich led the way into the main palace building, which shone like a diamond from the inside as well as from the outside. As they walked, Karen said, "The gowns you gave us are magnificent."

"You like them?" Alberich said.

"We *love* them," Winnifred said in delight.

Alberich laughed. "Princess Karen, your gown was actually made of sunlight woven into a golden fabric. Winnifred's was made of moonbeams woven into a silvery fabric. If Princess Daria joins you, we'll have a gown made for her, which will be made of starlight," he explained.

"Winnifred's the one more interested in fancy gowns. I prefer simpler but still opulent ones," Karen said. "However, even I can admit our gowns are probably worthy for dancing at a faerie court."

"Thank you," Alberich said, stopping in front of a shining set of doors. "This leads into the ballroom. The rest of the faerie court is there, expecting you." And with that, he led them to the doors, which opened at his approach with a flourish of trumpets and a huge cheer coming from inside.

Karen gasped as she got a glimpse of the magnificent ballroom and crowd of faeries. Now she understood why Alberich had believed that the gowns Karen and Winnifred usually wore weren't opulent enough for dancing at the faerie court, for the crowd of faeries was dressed more magnificently than any lady or gentleman in her father's court ever was, with gowns and doublets almost *smothered* with dazzling gems of all kinds. And the ballroom itself was equally magnificent. The walls also shone like a diamond while chandeliers hanging from the ceiling seemed to be silver in color. And at one end of the ballroom stood a harpsichord that was either golden in color or made of pure gold. A musician as magnificently dressed as the other faeries stood beside it.

"I wish to welcome the Orgonian princesses from the world above to this court," Alberich began. "Welcome, Princess Karen and Princess Winnifred!"

The crowd of faeries applauded as Karen and Winnifred made their best court curtsies.

"And now let the dancing begin!" Alberich announced. The musician bowed, sat down in front of the harpsichord, and began playing an unfamiliar tune. The male faeries in the crowd approached the female ones, took their hands, and began dancing.

However, the dancing was unlike anything that Karen had ever seen or done before. Whenever she, Winnifred, and Daria danced with men, they always were at arm's length from the men. This had suited Karen fine enough, for she had never been in love with any of them, and she knew it had suited Daria fine as well. Winnifred sometimes didn't mind dancing at arm's length, but other times she did. However, when these men took the hands of the women, they put their free arms around the women, drew them in close to their body, and began whirling the women around the dance floor, turning as they danced.

"What kind of dance is this?" Karen asked Alberich a little nervously.

"You may call it a waltz," Alberich said. "I know your sister loves to dance. Maybe she'd enjoy dancing this type of dance."

"Yes!" Winnifred squealed, and the faerie man escorting her took her hand and led her into the crowd of dancers.

"I don't know how to dance this dance!" Karen protested. "I know how to dance the allemande, the courante, the saraband, and the gigue, but this is totally new to me!"

"I'll teach you how to dance it," Alberich told her kindly. "Then once your young man hopefully gets into this realm, you can help *him* learn how to dance it. But it may not be too hard for him—there are peasant dances that glide and slide much like this one."

And with that, he took Karen's hand and led her into the crowd of dancers. Once they got into the crowd, Alberich put his free arm around Karen's waist and drew her close enough that her gown brushed against his legs. Then he led her into the dance.

Everything seemed to be turning around Karen—the golden lamps, the silver furnishings, and the crystalline walls. It would have actually been exhilarating had Karen not needed to focus on dancing in triple time. She also felt that her steps were rather awkward. But it was her first time dancing this dance after all.

From time to time, she thought she saw her sister Winnifred waltzing along. She looked like she was having the time of her life. Karen smiled at that. And her partner didn't seem to be about to hurt her.

Alberich saw that Karen was looking at Winnifred and said, "You can be reassured that she will be safe here once you and your young man are together at last. Nobody here will hurt her. I'll make sure of it."

"That's a relief," Karen said, sighing as she did so. "I have heard that some faeries had to hand over humans as a tithe to keep from going to hell."

"The worst faerie courts have to do so, I think," Alberich said. "My parents don't have to hand over humans as a tithe to keep from going to hell, and I don't think I'll be handing over any humans myself, unless they insult me in some way."

"Well, I'll remind Winnifred not to insult you," Karen said. "She's not a bad person. However, she's just very foolish."

"I know," Alberich said. "But she's a fine dancer for someone who's never done the waltz. And so are you."

Karen smiled and said, "I am honored, Your Highness."

*   *   *

Karen danced six more waltzes, gaining more confidence and grace with every dance. However, after the seventh waltz, she told Alberich she was going to rest her feet, saying that they must be tired from all the dancing. That was when Alberich informed her that her shoes and those of Winnifred were going to be comfortable no matter how often they danced.

Karen then said that she was still going to sit out the rest of the dancing to prevent her shoes from being worn to pieces, unless they were also enchanted to prevent wear and tear. Alberich admitted that the shoes would develop holes eventually but added that, every night, new shoes would take the place of those that were totally worn out. He also added that they should let Winnifred dance as the holes in the shoes and the new gowns would eventually help lead to Mark being united with Karen.

So Karen sat down on a silver setter by the wall and watched Winnifred dancing with various male faeries. She noticed that not just Winnifred but also every other woman in the ballroom danced with a different male faerie, and she asked a servant who came with a golden goblet of clear water about it. He informed her that unlike mortals, who made a great deal about the honor of mortal females, especially aristocratic or royal mortal females, while condoning the amorous activities of mortal males, just about all faeries have open relationships with one another, and nobody minded. However, the faeries didn't approve of deceit or dishonesty in a relationship.

Karen thought quite a bit about what she had learned while drinking the water and afterward. She knew that the honor (by which virginity was meant) of gentlewomen, noblewomen, and especially princesses was very important because their higher status meant that they had value basically as living pawns for political arrangements. Townswomen and peasant women were freer in that regard than women like herself since women from the lower classes didn't have to make royal babies or cement alliances with potentially dangerous rivals. But she also knew that noblemen such as Otto had no problems pursuing peasant women or female servants because they didn't view the women as really important, which probably wasn't such a good thing.

Winnifred would probably be much better off in this sort of setting, Karen concluded. She was naturally more physically attractive than Karen was, and Karen had seen all too well how something that might not be so bad in a peasant girl was dangerous in a princess, if only because of the princess's higher status. So Winnifred needed to be in a place where her natural attractiveness wouldn't be a huge problem. And this clearly was such a place.

Time passed as Karen watched Winnifred to see at what point her shoes would be totally worn out. Finally, sometime close to three in the morning, Winnifred was finished with a dance when she looked down at her shoes. Karen was nearby and saw a hole in the shoe Winnifred held up clear as day.

At that point, the dancing ended, and Alberich announced that Karen and Winnifred had to go back to their home. Alberich signaled to the two male escorts for Karen and Winnifred earlier, and they took the arms of the princesses and led them out of the ballroom as the other faeries expressed their hope that the two princesses would return. Karen and Winnifred both promised that they'd return the next night.

The faerie escorts led Karen and Winnifred back to the boats. As they did so, Winnifred babbled about what a great time she had. Karen couldn't help but smile at Winnifred's delight even as she asked solicitously, "Are you tired? We stayed up very late."

"Not yet," Winnifred said.

"At least we can sleep in," Karen said, beginning to yawn. She *was* tired.

"I suppose the prime minister will have to conduct court business without me," she added. "At least he can conduct the morning court business without me. I'll join him after taking the midday meal."

"It's a good thing *I* don't have to bother with court business," Winnifred said.

"It *is* a good thing," Karen agreed. "While not all the aspects of court business are tedious, I know you well enough to know that it would still bore you silly."

They said nothing more for the rest of the trek to the boats. The faerie escorts helped the princesses into the boats and then rowed them back across the lake. Karen looked back at the faerie castle, shining like a diamond in the moonlight.

It was such a lovely place, far lovelier than the castle she lived in. And at least the faeries here were decent. Or they seemed to be so. She knew through Daria of cases where faerie courts were attractive but menacing in a way that no attractiveness could truly conceal. And the gardens, at least those that she'd seen, were quite lovely. She'd like to spend time in the herbal garden, but she'd probably have to get some overshoes to cover her dancing shoes.

Finally, they reached the other side, and the faerie escorts helped Karen and Winnifred off the boats before taking their leave. The faerie escorts began rowing back across the lake, and Karen and Winnifred turned to go back through the groves. They walked through the grove of diamond trees in silence, but once they got to the grove of golden trees, Karen heard Winnifred say, "You're right, I *am* tired. And my feet are beginning to hurt."

"You wore your shoes out, that's probably why," Karen pointed out. Karen's own shoes were still intact, and her feet felt almost as comfortable now as they had when she first went down through the secret passageway and through the groves. "Even shoes magically enchanted to feel comfortable when dancing aren't going to be so comfortable if you wear your shoes out. At least it won't be too much farther."

They continued through the grove of golden trees into that of silvery ones. Finally, they reached what Karen now saw as an opening in crystalline rock and passed through it, walking down the secret passageway until they reached the staircase underneath the trapdoor. Karen and Winnifred went up the staircase and emerged from the trapdoor, which closed.

The bed they shared emerged from the floor, and Karen noticed a silvery cloud swirl around Winnifred, covering her. Once the cloud lifted, Winnifred was back in her sleeping shift. Then Karen felt the same tingle running through her body, and a golden cloud swirled around *her*. Once the cloud was gone, Karen looked down and saw that she was back in her sleeping shift.

Winnifred was stumbling toward the bed, and Karen followed her. Once they climbed into bed, Karen's exhaustion took over, and she fell instantly asleep.

CHAPTER 9

"Welcome home, Your Majesty," the prime minister said as King Robert entered the castle courtyard.

"It is good to be home," King Robert said as he looked around. Not much had changed since he had left a little over a month before. A number of the court officials stood behind the prime minister, and so did some of the court ladies. But three ladies whom he did *not* see were his own daughters. This reminded King Robert of the missive sent by the prime minister urging the king to come home and suggesting that there was something wrong with his daughters.

"How were things in the month since you were gone?" the prime minister asked.

"Well, there was a skirmish between some of our troops and some of the ones belonging to the crown prince of Vindicia," King Robert said. "The troops that belonged to Vindicia were trying to gain territory. Our troops were able to cause theirs to retreat."

"I am glad to hear that," said the prime minister.

"I have left my field marshal in charge of the troops," King Robert said. "He is our best military leader and strategist, and he will make sure no troops from Vindicia will get anywhere near this castle. Now tell me about my daughters. Is there something wrong with them?"

"Not with Princess Daria," the prime minister said. "But there is something odd about Princess Karen and Princess Winnifred. I have noticed that, for about a month, Princess Karen has been more tired than usual, sleeping late into the day and waking up around noon. The same goes for Princess Winnifred. Also, their ladies-in-waiting have noticed the presence of impossibly beautiful gowns in place of their normal dancing gowns, along with dancing shoes that are just as beautiful as the gowns. Finally, the new dancing shoes of Princess Winnifred were totally worn through as if they had been danced in all night."

"What about Princess Karen's new dancing shoes?" asked King Robert in concern.

"They haven't been danced in as much," the prime minister said. "They have shown signs of being danced in but nowhere near as much as those of her sister Winnifred. I have asked them both about the new gowns and the shoes, but neither one explained how they got them nor how Princess Winnifred's shoes got so worn out."

"Maybe they will confess if I ask them," King Robert said.

"I hoped they would," the prime minister said. "That's why I asked you to come home and interrogate them."

"Where are the two princesses?" asked King Robert.

Lily, Princess Karen's lady-in-waiting, stepped forward from among the circle of court ladies. "They're in the private garden," she told him.

"Please bring me to them," King Robert said. Lily nodded and led the way past the prime minister, court officials, and servants.

It took a few moments for the pair to travel through the castle and then down the path that led to the private garden. Eventually, they reached the wall that encircled the private garden and the door, which was closed. Lily pushed it open. There, beneath some trees, were the two princesses and their ladies-in-waiting, all doing embroidery work. They looked up as King Robert and Lily entered, and then they all curtsied.

"I would like to speak to the princesses alone," King Robert said.

The ladies, including Lily, all bowed and quietly moved to leave. But before they left, the king added, "And return to the castle and wait for me to join you before you can return here."

Once the ladies left, Karen said in a dry tone, "You apparently don't want them listening in."

"No, I don't," the king said.

He continued in a stern tone, "I have learned from the prime minister that you have both been sleeping late, that you have new gowns and new dancing shoes, and that Winnifred's shoes have been continually and mysteriously replaced due to being worn through as if she has been dancing all night long. I must know why this is happening and, if you are going somewhere and dancing, where you are going."

"I'm sorry, Father, but I'm not in a position to explain why this is happening," Karen said evenly.

"And even if I could tell you where we are going, I wouldn't," Winnifred added defiantly.

King Robert kept trying to get his daughters to explain, but the only useful information that he got was Karen's reassurance that whatever was happening was no threat to his kingdom. Finally, defeated, the king left his two daughters inside the garden and returned to the castle. The ladies-in-waiting returned to the private garden while the prime minister joined the king.

"Did you succeed?" asked the prime minister.

"No," the king said. "Princess Karen said that she wasn't in a position to explain what was happening, and Princess Winnifred is openly defiant."

"Do you think this is a threat to Orgon?" asked the prime minister.

"Princess Karen insisted that it wasn't the case, and I tend to believe her," the king said. "It could be a spell, but if it is, I don't think faeries are involved. Most people believe that consumption occurs when faeries force men and women to dance in midnight revels, exhausting them and causing them to waste away. Yet Winnifred doesn't seem to be wasting away, and Karen certainly isn't either."

"Even if this isn't a threat to the safety of the kingdom, I still believe you should stay here and solve the mystery," the prime minister suggested.

"I agree," the king said. "While my daughters don't seem to be in any danger, they might be, and I want to protect them, especially Winnifred, given how much little sense she has."

"What are you going to do about this situation?" asked the prime minister. The king had to think about it for a moment. After all, this was a serious situation, even if it wasn't a life-threatening one. He had trusted Princess Karen to protect her sister by putting the two together in the same room, and it didn't seem to be working out so well. But if one princess couldn't do the job, then two might.

"I may have to have an additional bed made and placed in the bedroom that Karen and Winnifred currently share and put Daria in there with them," the king decided. "This might help stop whatever is going on."

"And if it doesn't?" the prime minister asked.

"Then I'll have to come up with a solution to solve the mystery," the king said grimly. "For now, I'll have a bed constructed and then placed in the bedroom that Karen and Winnifred currently share. Once that is done, I'll move Daria into the bedroom and hope that this stops the apparent nightly dancing."

The king decided to change the subject then, so he said, "Has Francis been arraigned for the crime of high treason?"

"He has," said the prime minister. "And he has been found guilty and will be hanged, drawn, and quartered."

"And Karen's sixteenth birthday is coming up soon," the king said.

"Indeed," said the prime minister. "And she was actually present when he was arraigned. She was most happy when Francis was found guilty and sentenced for execution."

"In that case, I will have the execution scheduled for Karen's birthday," the king decided. "I think Karen will be quite happy to see the guy who tried to molest her sister executed."

"I agree that she will," the prime minister said. "And your orders will be carried out."

*   *   *

99

Karen rode behind her father, glancing back from time to time at Francis, who was being transported to the place of execution in a wicker hurdle that was tied to a horse. This was the standard means of transportation of a criminal convicted of high treason instead of being tied directly to the horse and dragged to the place of execution, which was in the city square. Karen smiled grimly when she saw how bedraggled, weary, and resigned Francis looked.

Karen had been pleased when she learned that her father had scheduled Francis's execution on the day of her birthday. Normally, this wouldn't be something she would want to see on her birthday, but Francis had tried to molest her sister, so she wanted to see him punished severely for his effrontery.

Winnifred didn't attend the execution. Her father feared that she might become hysterical if she saw Francis executed, and Karen had agreed. Daria also wasn't present for the execution, though that was mostly because she was more interested in reading in the library than in attending a public execution. Also, Daria wasn't the crown princess, so there was less of a need for her to attend.

Karen knew that once Francis ascended the scaffold and made his speech, he would be hanged, cut down when he was barely alive, disemboweled, beheaded, and finally quartered, or chopped into four pieces. It was a gruesome way to die and thus reserved only for cases of high treason. The royal party, with the condemned man in its midst, reached the city square, having traveled down from the castle and into the capital city on the way. Karen saw that the gallows had been erected and waited for its victim.

Francis was taken off the hurdle and led to the scaffold. Once there, the king's commission was read, and the crowd was asked to move back from the scaffold so that Francis could address them. Karen remained on her horse as did her father.

Francis looked resigned as he began his speech. "Good people, I have come here to die since the law has rightly judged me guilty of high treason, and so I will not rail against my fate, nor will I try to escape it. My sentence is worthy and just, for I have been guilty of ambition, which led me to my treasonous act. I will not accuse my lord, the king. Instead, I ask that he have a long and happy reign, for he is a worthy and just ruler and a just and loving parent. All I ask is that you pray for mercy for my soul. And now I bid you all farewell. May God have mercy on my soul."

Karen watched as Francis was stripped to his shirt in preparation for the execution. Suddenly, she heard a voice say, "So this is an execution of a mortal man. I have to admit, he may well make a good end."

Karen looked around and saw, sitting on a white horse, Alberich, crown prince of the faeries. She then looked around and saw that nobody else was present. Alberich smiled at her amazement and said, "I just wanted to have a conversation with you concerning the fact that your father is planning to move your sister Daria in with you and Winnifred in a couple of days."

"Yes, and that concerns me quite a bit," Karen said. "Daria is only thirteen, and I feel she is too young to marry anyone."

"You are probably right," Alberich agreed. "But I never said anything about either courting her myself or having one of my gentlemen court her."

"Then what *do* you think should be done about this situation?" Karen asked. "I don't want to drug Daria, but she is a very bad liar. I fear she might blurt out the truth of the situation if she is allowed to join Winnifred and me in the faerie realm."

"I can take care of that with a potion slipped into some water that will prevent her from saying anything coherent if asked about where she had been," said Alberich. "Also, I plan on showing my library to Daria."

"You have a library?" asked Karen, more eager now.

"A much larger library than that of your father," Alberich confirmed, "with lots of tales about faeries from our point of view as well as those of the mortals we have had contact with."

"So you think it would be best for Daria to join Winnifred and me in the faerie realm," Karen concluded.

"I do," Alberich said. "I have watched her as well as you and your sister over the years, and I know Daria isn't really comfortable in social situations in your world. She may be more comfortable in my realm."

"Yes, Daria is socially awkward," Karen agreed. "And your ways aren't really ours. Then she can come with us, but I plan on keeping an eye on her until she becomes comfortable enough not to require watching."

"A protective big sister," Alberich concluded. "I approve. And if watching your sister means you have to stop watching Winnifred, you don't have to worry about her safety. I'll make sure nobody in my court molests her since you won't take it too well if that happens."

Karen sighed in relief. "Thank you, Prince Alberich," she said.

"I have no problems with a sister trying to protect a sister. If I did, I'd turn you into an ass," Alberich said, smiling. "Soon the execution will be over."

Karen grimaced. "I might return to the castle once they start quartering Francis's body," she said. "The remains will probably reek, and even though I came to watch the guy who tried to molest my sister be justly punished, I'm not sure I can stand the foul smell of the remains."

"You probably need to watch a few more executions," Alberich said somewhat dryly. "Anyway, I will leave now, and you can return to watching."

And with that, he was gone. And Karen now saw that while she'd been talking with Alberich, Francis's body had been taken down and presumably had been disemboweled, for now the executioner had an ax in his hand. Part of Karen hoped that the executioner was skilled as being beheaded by an inexperienced executioner was apparently horrible. On the other hand, the part of her that was still angry at Francis for what he did hoped that Francis would suffer even more by being beheaded by an unskilled executioner.

However, the executioner proved to be skilled, for his head was chopped off cleanly with one stroke. She saw the executioner hold up Francis's head with one hand and smiled grimly. Justice had been served.

She turned to her father. "My lord and father," she said, "I wish to return to the castle now. I believe the executioner will begin quartering Francis's body, and the remains will no doubt reek."

"And you may not have the stomach to stand it," the king said. "Very well, I will have two of my attendants escort you back to the castle."

Karen sighed in relief and, with her father's chosen attendants in tow, left the city square and returned to the castle. The men in question were older, married, and wise enough to avoid messing with the crown princess, especially since the king had made a severe example of Francis for molesting Princess Winnifred. She was relieved about that.

Along the way home, Karen thought about what Alberich had said about Daria. It was true that Daria was socially awkward, particularly around people she didn't know. She also had a definite interest in faerie lore. Alberich might well have been right in thinking that Daria would be better off in the faerie realm than married to someone in the mortal world.

But to make certain that he was right, Daria would have to join her sisters in the faerie realm. And Karen knew she would have to watch over her youngest sister. She was relieved that Alberich understood her desire to protect her sisters since she didn't want to get a faerie mad at her, not unless she had a good reason.

In a couple of days, Daria would move into the room that Karen and Winnifred shared. And that was when Daria would be exposed to the faerie realm. Karen hoped it would be a good experience for Daria.

CHAPTER 10

Daria was rather nervous as the ladies-in-waiting exited the bedroom that she now shared with her sisters, locking all three of them in. Some of her nervousness had something to do with being shut in with Winnifred. While Daria loved her sister as a family member, she didn't get along as well with Winnifred as she did with Karen. Much of the difficulty had to do with their different personalities. Winnifred loved dancing; Daria preferred to read. Daria was highly intelligent; Winnifred had little common sense. That was enough to make them clash when they had to share a room together, which sometimes happened when their father went on progress.

However, she was also shut in with Karen, and she believed that Karen would do her best to calm tempers if they both began quarreling. Karen was the big sister, the responsible one. Or at least she should have been.

This led to the second reason for Daria being so nervous. She knew that she was being shut in with her sisters because the two not only had gotten new and (according to the ladies attending Karen and Winnifred) extremely cool gowns but Winnifred also wore out her dancing shoes every night. Her father thought that if Karen alone couldn't stop Winnifred, then maybe Daria could help Karen do so.

Daria hoped that she could help Karen, especially after Francis tried to molest Winnifred and paid for it by being executed—horrifically.

Daria was glad she hadn't attended the execution. She wasn't sure she could have handled it well.

Daria lay in bed for a few moments, hidden behind the curtains of the bed that had been moved into her sisters' bedroom earlier in the day. Then she heard her sisters, who were also supposed to be in bed, moving about. That was when Karen opened the curtains. Daria sat up, looking confused. "What is going on?" she asked.

"You are about to find out where Winnifred and I have been going every night," Karen informed her.

"Really?" Daria asked, now excited.

"That's great. Father wants me to help you stop Winnifred from ruining her shoes," she added as she climbed out of bed.

"Unfortunately, if there wasn't a very good reason for me to allow Winnifred to ruin her shoes every night, I'd try a lot harder to stop her," Karen said as she took Daria's hand and led her to the chest where the gowns they wore for special occasions were kept. "However, even if I tried harder, I might have failed since Winnifred was so frustrated about not being able to dance as much as she would have liked."

This shocked Daria. Her sister wasn't trying to stop Winnifred? "Why?" she asked tentatively.

"You'll find out as soon as you see your new gown," Karen said as she opened the wardrobe and took a gown out.

Daria gasped as soon as she saw it. The gown was absolutely dazzling, sparkling like the stars in the night sky. She had never seen a gown like this one before. Then she saw the underdress and the petticoats that accompanied it, which sparkled just as much.

"Every night Winnifred and I go down through three magical groves and then across a lake to the castle where a troop of faeries live," Karen explained. "And you are going with us."

Daria was stunned. She was going to actually meet real *faeries*? The mere thought of doing so excited her. However, she was also nervous. After all, she was the expert on faeries between the three sisters. She knew faeries could be very dangerous, and she really hoped the faeries hadn't cast some sort of enchantment on her elder sisters to make them go to this faerie castle.

Karen added, "The crown prince of the faerie troop, Alberich, wanted you to come spend time in this realm. He seems to believe you could be more at home there than in the mortal realm."

"He . . . he hasn't enchanted you, has he?" asked Daria a little tentatively.

"I was wary too when he first approached me," Karen reassured her. "But he's actually looking out for Winnifred and me for different reasons. With Winnifred, you know how foolish she can be."

"I sure do," Daria agreed.

"He believes that if Winnifred marries King Henry like Father wants her to do, she will be unfaithful to him and will be executed eventually," Karen said. "He thinks it would be best for Winnifred if she also became a part of the faerie realm."

"And what about you?" Daria asked. She could believe this Alberich's claim that if Winnifred married King Henry, she would commit adultery and most likely lose her head. It probably *would* be best for Winnifred to become a part of the faerie realm.

"He knows how I feel about Mark, and he believes that if we go to his castle every night, eventually the king will have the man who solves the mystery marry one of us," Karen explained. "This may be my chance to marry Mark as part of my father's reward."

"I just hope the council allows a commoner to marry you because he solved the mystery," Daria said.

"I hope so, too, although Alberich believes it will happen," Karen noted. "And now it's time for us to get dressed up for a ball at the faerie palace. The faeries provided the gowns for us because our regular dancing gowns—and dancing shoes—aren't good enough for a ball at their palace."

"Well, the faeries really seem to be nice to us," Daria said, "at least for now. I just hope they aren't luring us into a trap of some kind."

"I don't think they are," Karen reassured her. "They may have their reasons for being nice to us, but I don't think they are going to hurt us. Alberich said that he'd hurt any faerie who tried to molest any of us."

Daria smiled, now totally reassured. "Well then, let's get dressed," she said, her concerns now gone.

*   *   *

Daria had always wondered what a trip to the faerie realm would be like. Would it be a truly beautiful place, a kind of paradise underneath the earth itself? Or would it be a place that seemed beautiful on the outside but underneath was a place of horror?

Now as she followed her sisters through a secret passageway sparkling with gems and through groves of trees with silver, golden, and diamond leaves, they arrived at the edge of a lake where three men dressed in dazzling clothes escorted the princesses into boats that took them across to the other side. Finally, she followed her sisters into a magnificent crystalline castle. Daria was awestruck.

A man more magnificently dressed than the men who escorted the princesses across the lake stood outside the entry to the main building inside the castle complex. "Welcome!" he announced. "Princess Daria, I am Crown Prince Alberich, future ruler of this troop of faeries."

Daria curtsied in her sparkling gown. "I am happy to be here," she said. "I always wondered what a trip to the faerie realm would be like."

"Well, at least in my realm, I hope you will find it a kind of paradise," Alberich said. "There are a few faerie realms that are beautiful but are ruled by terrible faeries who behave as badly in the otherworld as they'd do in yours. Also, some faeries in my realm and others deliberately spread rumors about how badly they can behave to scare people away from the mounds where they live and do just enough bad stuff to give credence to the rumors."

"As long as you have no intention of hurting my sisters or me, you won't have to worry about me finding your realm anything less than a paradise," said Daria.

"You might find it even more of a paradise if you spent time in the library in this castle," Alberich said as he led the princesses and their escorts into the main castle building.

"You have a library?" Daria asked, suddenly more excited than ever.

"I do indeed," Alberich said. "There are more books than you have ever read—or maybe ever dreamed of reading."

"I want to see this library!" Daria exclaimed.

"The library is on the second floor, along with the throne hall," Alberich said. "The third and fourth floors are the rooms where my siblings, my parents, and I sleep, along with our closest servants. The first floor consists of the ballroom and a magnificent dining room. Two of my attendants will escort Winnifred to the ballroom, and I assure you, she will be safe. I will make a severe example of any man of my retinue who tries to molest Princess Winnifred, and everybody knows it and would rather avoid facing my wrath."

Daria sighed in relief. "I do wish to see your library," she admitted, "but only for a little while. I may go downstairs later on to check on my elder sister."

"And if you do, I'll go with you," Daria heard Karen say. "While I trust Alberich more now, it's still better to be safe than sorry."

"So shall I escort you to the library?" Alberich asked, holding his arm out for Daria to take.

"I'd be delighted," Daria said, smiling as he led her to the staircase leading to the second floor. It was as crystalline as the rest of the interior, minus the gold and silver furnishings that Daria could see in the foyer.

Alberich escorted Daria up the staircase, which was a spiraling one, with Karen and her escort following. On the wall, there were pictures of landscapes, possibly of places in the faerie realm. That was when she saw one picture where a young woman was *dancing* in a lovely meadow. "Is that young woman *dancing*?" she asked.

Alberich looked and seemed amused. "Yes, she is," he said. "While your pictures are stationary and nobody moves in them, that's not the case with pictures, including faeries. Pictures of landscapes that don't have faeries in them, however, tend to be stationary. And none of the people in the pictures actually leave their pictures, although they can move around in them."

At the top of the staircase, Alberich led the two princesses down a corridor to a crystalline door with a golden knob and lock. Alberich took out a silver key, unlocked the door, and opened it, saying, "Welcome to our library."

Daria stepped inside—and gasped. The room was magnificent, more so than the library she had back at home in her world, and considerably larger than any library she had ever seen. There were silver chairs placed all around the room, along with golden bookshelves containing more books than she had ever seen. And she'd seen a lot of books not just at home but also at various ducal estates when she traveled with her father and sisters on the royal progress.

"I've never seen so many books in my life," Daria said, feeling like she had died and gone to heaven or at least a faerie paradise.

"I thought you might like it," Alberich said, smiling. "You can read as many books as you like whenever you come here."

"I'll definitely come back," Daria said. "But right now, why don't you show me the various books in the place?"

"Sure," Alberich said. "But I must warn you, some of them haven't even been written yet in your world."

Daria started, clearly surprised. "What?" she asked.

"I said some of the books I have here have yet to be written," Alberich explained. "All sorts of books too—mystery novels, romance novels, and some written collections of what some might call fairy tales."

Daria said, "I think for now I'll just stick to books that I'm familiar with, though I might make an exception for the fairy-tale collections."

"I'm not sure I can blame you for that," Alberich said. "Okay, I'll show you some books that you might be familiar with or that have subjects you would be very familiar with."

"Lead the way, Prince Alberich," Daria said.

*　　*　　*

The night passed in a wonderful whirlwind for Daria. Alberich first led her to a section of the library that had books on ballads, especially those involving magical beings. She picked out a book and began reading the first ballad in it. It didn't take her long to recognize the ballad, but at the same time, it seemed somewhat different from what she remembered.

The version she remembered told of a faerie lord who sang a magical song that lured every maiden who heard it toward him and had them go meet him in the forest. None of the maidens who went there ever returned. Finally, one princess heard the song and asked her father to let her go meet the faerie lord. He wouldn't let her because none of the maidens ever returned from there, so she asked her brother. Her brother finally agreed as long as she kept her honor safe. She put on her finest clothes, took the best steed from her father's stable, went to the faerie lord, and allowed him to take her to a field of gallows, where he announced that he was going to kill her; but because he was so impressed with her beauty, he would allow her to choose how she wanted to die.

The princess chose to let the faerie lord behead her but urged him to take his upper cloth off first so that her blood would not stain it. He agreed, laid down his sword, and began undressing, but the cloth muffled the magic of his song so that she beheaded him with his own sword. Afterward, the head spoke and urged the princess to first rub a pot of ointment taken from beneath the gallows on the faerie lord's head and then to take his horn, go into a cornfield, and blow it so his friends would hear, but she refused since he was a murderer. The princess took the head and washed it clear in a nearby well, where some of his other victims had apparently been drowned. Afterward, she returned to her father's castle, where a feast was held, and the faerie lord's head was placed on the head table.

But while the version she read in Alberich's book also told much of the same story, some details were changed. For example, when the princess, who was named Aldana, went to the faerie lord, who was named Haelwijn, he did not take her to a field of gallows but instead to his home in the forest, where he took off his sword before kissing the princess and fondling her. She was under his spell and ignored her brother's warning about guarding her honor and her father's warning about Haelwijn, but when he lowered her down onto the ground and began undressing, his upper cloth muffled his magical power, and she awoke from his spell, remembering her brother's and father's warnings. She got up; took his sword, which he carelessly left close enough for her to grab; got behind him; and when he took his cloth off, beheaded him.

After ignoring the head's advice and washing his head in a nearby well as she had done in the ballad that Daria knew, Aldana then returned home. But on the way, she met Haelwijn's mother, who asked her about her son. When Aldana revealed Haelwijn's fate and explained why she killed him, the mother revealed that Haelwijn never killed any of the maidens who came to him but instead kept them in underground chambers as concubines. Moreover, Haelwijn intended to make Aldana his lady and only used the magical song because he knew her father and brother would never let him marry her.

Aldana went home, and while there was a great feast and the head of Haelwijn was placed on the head table as noted in the version Daria read, Haelwijn's mother secretly retrieved the head. Aldana refused to marry anybody afterward both because no suitor could ever arouse such passion as Lord Haelwijn did and because she blamed herself for listening to sense and not following her heart.

Daria looked up from the book at last and said, "I never read this version of the faerie lord ballad."

"The version in this book was what really happened," Alberich explained. "Haelwijn was a faerie lord who attended one of my ancestors, and he never killed any of the maidens who came to him. I think he was a fairly decent guy who didn't want to kill any of the maidens, instead merely keeping them in underground chambers. He was looking for a maiden beautiful enough and well born enough for him to choose as his lady, and Aldana was more beautiful than any maiden in the mortal realm you live in."

"Why did people believe that he murdered the maidens who went to him?" Daria asked.

"Probably because the maidens never returned," Alberich said, shrugging. "Then as time passed, people began believing that he really *did* kill the maidens instead of merely keeping them as concubines or, had the princess stayed with him instead of beheading him, his lady. It didn't help that after Aldana beheaded Haelwijn, the maidens awoke from the spell. But when they were able to finally find their way out of the underground chambers and exit the forest, they all died within minutes of leaving."

"I didn't know that," Daria admitted. And that led to her reading other ballads in the book involving faeries, many of which were familiar to her but apparently had differences also mainly due to also being the original versions of the ballads she was familiar with.

Eventually, Karen said that she wanted to check on Winnifred, so they all went down the staircase to the first floor and, from there, went to the ballroom, where they found Winnifred dancing without a care in the world. That was when Daria learned that what they were dancing was called the waltz, a dance she had never heard of before. Alberich offered to teach her the dance, but she said she wanted to wait as she thought she was too young to try such an intimate dance.

So Daria sat in a nice chair, with Karen sitting alongside her, and they watched the dancing. Karen asked, "How do you like this place, Daria?"

"It's wondrous," Daria said. "I never imagined having the chance to read so many books. I might have to stay here just to read all the books in that library."

"I'm glad you like it here," Karen said. "This is a magnificent place, and the people here are surprisingly kind. I think Winnifred will be safe here, and I think you might be happy here as well."

"I'll wait and see, but for now, I'm more than willing to return," Daria happily told her sister.

Eventually, it was almost three, and Winnifred's shoes were worn out before the ball ended. Daria was offered a cup of water as was Karen, but Daria was told that the water in her cup contained an enchantment that would prevent her from saying anything coherent about where she had been if asked. Daria knew she was a bad liar, so she could see the reasons behind the enchantment. Moreover, she was more willing to keep the secret than she was before she came down to this castle, so she took the cup and drank the water before they all left the faerie castle.

Once the sisters were on the other side of the lake and were heading back through the groves, Winnifred squealed, "I was never really happy until coming here into the faerie realm! All that music, all that dancing!"

"And for me, all the books," Daria said.

Winnifred scowled at that, but Karen intervened, saying, "Daria's more of a bookworm than a social butterfly. You know that as well as I do, Winnifred."

"Yeah," Winnifred admitted, sighing. "But who knows? You might change while coming here."

"Maybe, but I doubt it," Daria said. "At least it's unlikely that I'll change too much."

They finally reached the secret passageway that led to their room and ascended the staircase. Once they exited the trapdoor and returned to their room, the bed that Karen and Winnifred used returned to its rightful place, and the magic clouds that had enabled them to change from their sleeping shifts to their ballroom gowns swirled around them. Once the clouds disappeared, they were back in their sleeping shifts.

Daria climbed wearily into her bed. While she was tired and would certainly sleep in, she had to admit that she had enjoyed herself at the faerie castle and could find herself becoming quite comfortable there. She just hoped that her being recruited into her sisters' activities wouldn't bring any harm to herself, her sisters, or anybody else.

Chapter 11

The king entered the royal council chamber and was pleased to see that all his councilors were ready and standing. He walked down the right side of the table, moving for the gilded throne at one end of the council chamber. "Gentlemen, you may be seated," he said. The councilors sat down, the men (all of whom were older) rustling their long court robes as they did so. The king sat down as well.

"Gentlemen, you probably know as well as I do why we are here," the king said. "A month and a half ago, my two eldest daughters began sleeping late. Moreover, their ladies discovered dazzlingly beautiful new dancing gowns in their wardrobe, along with matching underdresses, petticoats, and dancing shoes. Finally, the dancing shoes of my middle daughter, Princess Winnifred, were worn out as if she had been dancing every night, although the doors and windows were locked every night to keep the princesses in and safe. The prime minister urged me to return, and when I did and learned from him about this curious state of affairs, I asked both my daughters why this was happening, but Princess Karen said she could not tell me while Princess Winnifred refused to tell me.

"I believed that Princess Winnifred was sneaking out every night to go dancing somewhere and that Princess Karen went along to try to keep her under control but was unable to do so. Therefore, I chose to shut my youngest daughter, Princess Daria, in with them to help Princess Karen control Princess Winnifred. Yet even when I did so, Princess Winnifred's shoes were still worn out the next morning.

And more importantly, Princess Daria also got a new and dazzlingly beautiful dancing gown, underdress, petticoats, and dancing shoes, although neither her shoes nor those of Princess Karen were worn out. So I asked Daria if she knew what was happening, and she said that she could not tell me. And that was all she would say, no matter how many times I asked her. And the more I questioned her, the more stressed she became, until she began babbling. I stopped questioning her then out of concern for her."

"Does this mean that she *does* know where her sisters are going but has been prevented from saying so?" asked one of the councilors.

"I believe so," said the king. "If faeries, witches, or sorcerers *are* involved, she may have been magically prevented from telling me where her sisters, and now maybe herself, are going. If this is the case, then I must seek advice for how to discover where the princesses are going."

The councilors were silent, presumably mulling over suggestions on how to discover the truth. Finally, the prime minister stood up and said, "If I might venture a suggestion, maybe we should try marrying one of the princesses off to whoever solves the mystery."

The king frowned thoughtfully. "You mean, you wish me to send out a royal proclamation explaining that my daughters have received mysterious dancing gowns and equally mysterious dancing shoes and that one of them has been wearing out her shoes every night?" he asked. "And that whomever uncovers the secret behind the receipt of the dancing gowns and the worn-out dancing shoes will marry one of my daughters as his reward?"

"Exactly," the prime minister suggested. "You know how romantic young princes can be. I'm sure they would not hesitate to try to solve the mystery. And whoever fails to solve the mystery after three nights will be beheaded."

That suggestion alarmed the king for two reasons. First, he didn't think that failing to solve a mystery involving his daughters was a good enough reason to risk losing one's head. Second, he was very concerned about how foreign kingdoms might react to the idea of having foreign princes beheaded, even if the princes were willing to take the risk. It might lead to war.

"I'm concerned about the effect that penalizing any man who tries to solve the mystery by beheading him would have on foreign kingdoms who might send princes to solve the mystery," said the king. "What if the princes are scared away by the threat of being beheaded if they fail? And if they fail and *are* beheaded, what will the rulers of those kingdoms do? Maybe they would go to war against us."

"So what punishment would *you* recommend in case the men who try to solve the mystery fail?" asked the prime minister.

The king thought long and hard for a moment. What would be the punishment that would be the most effective while avoiding the possibility of war? Imprisonment? That might work for a time with aristocracy or gentry from Orgon, but with foreign princes, long-term or permanent imprisonment would create tension with the rulers who sent them.

Banishment? That would work with aristocracy or gentry from Orgon but not so much with foreign princes since they weren't born in Orgon. However, that didn't mean that he couldn't devise a similar punishment for the foreign princes.

That was when the king made up his mind. He stood up. "I shall make a royal proclamation and send it out through all the land as well as let the ambassadors from foreign lands know that the man who solves the mystery of where my daughters have been going every night shall win the hand of one of my daughters in marriage," the king said. "If that man weds my eldest daughter, he shall become king consort after my death. But if any man from the aristocracy or the gentry of Orgon fails, he will be banished from my kingdom forever."

"And what about any princes who might try their luck at solving the mystery?" asked the prime minister.

"If they fail, they shall be placed under house arrest for three days before being allowed to leave," the king said. "But until and unless the mystery is solved, they shall never be allowed to visit Orgon again. I believe it is a fair punishment for them. And it will ease tensions with foreign rulers who choose to send the princes here, as well as prevent war with them."

The minister of foreign relations stood up then. "An excellent and most wise suggestion, Your Majesty," he said.

"Do the rest of you agree?" the king asked. Everybody nodded. "Then draft a royal proclamation and send it out through all the land. Also, give copies to the ambassadors from foreign kingdoms who have embassies here."

"It shall be done, Your Majesty," the prime minister said, standing up as well.

"Thank you," the king said. "You are all dismissed." He turned to leave the council chamber.

*   *   *

It didn't take long for the royal proclamation to be drafted and sent out through all the land. Nor did it take long for copies to be sent to the ambassadors from foreign kingdoms that had embassies in the capital city so that the princes could try their luck if they so desired.

The princesses also soon learned of the royal proclamation, and their reactions were somewhat different depending on the princess involved. Winnifred was the angriest of the princesses. She didn't want anything to spoil the pure delight she took in slipping out of the castle and dancing the night away. Both Karen and Daria were relieved that none of the princes or members of the aristocracy who might try to figure out where they were going every night would be executed if they failed. But Daria felt she was too young to think about getting married and hoped that if someone found out the secret, the person who did so wouldn't pick her. Karen was mainly determined to keep men from discovering the truth until Mark came along since she hoped that if Mark found out the truth, he would be free to marry her as Alberich had reassured her would happen.

Then one night the princesses arrived at Alberich's castle, and he was waiting for them with news. "I have learned that a prince from the kingdom of Rhodesia will be arriving to try to solve the mystery of where you have been dancing every night," Alberich said.

"Unfortunately, he's not Mark," Karen said. "Winnifred is better off here, and Daria and I both think she should wait a little longer before she's ready for marriage. That means we'll have to make sure he doesn't follow us here into the faerie realm."

"Which is why I have something that I will give you at the end of the night," Alberich said, offering his arm to Daria. She took it, and they went into the castle together.

The rest of the night passed as it normally did for the princesses. Winnifred spent all her time on the dance floor while Daria and Karen spent part of their time in the library and the rest in the ballroom, watching the others dance. A couple of times, Karen danced with Alberich; but for the most part, she stayed with Daria.

Around three in the morning, Winnifred's shoes were all worn out, and they all had to return to the surface. That was when Alberich approached and handed Karen a philter. "This philter contains a powerful sedative that will ensure a person will sleep through the whole night," Alberich explained.

"I just hope the combination of alcohol and a sedative doesn't kill the unlucky guy who drinks it," Karen said. She would have suggested that the sedative be slipped into water except that she knew the water in the mortal world was rarely fit for anybody to drink. Alcoholic beverages such as beer and wine were used for that reason.

"It won't," Alberich said, "not if you slip just three drops into a cup of wine or a mug of beer before giving it to the prince and any future men who come to learn the secret. Pouring the whole amount in will probably kill anyone who drinks the drugged wine or beer, but three drops will just knock him out for the whole night."

"Thanks," said Karen, who took the philter. "I'll make sure not to put too much of the drug into the wine that I'll give him."

"I wouldn't mind if you did so," Winnifred said.

"But I probably would," Daria said. "And I know Karen would mind it. Sorry, Winnifred, but I'm afraid you'll have to settle for any man who tries to find out our secret just sleeping for the whole night, unless that someone is Mark."

"Especially Mark," Winnifred protested, but before she could say anything more, Karen intervened.

"Let's just get home and deal with this prince who's coming," Karen said. "I know you don't like Mark much, but we have more important things to deal with."

"Yeah," Daria agreed.

With that, the princesses said goodbye to Alberich and returned to the boats that would take them back across the lake.

While traveling through the groves, Daria whispered to Karen, "I'm concerned about Winnifred. Ever since she's begun coming here to dance every night, she's become more ruthless. I wonder if the fact that she drank faerie wine and thus belongs to the faeries has created some sort of magic that is affecting her somehow."

"Maybe, but you've drunk water that was enchanted, and you haven't become more ruthless," Karen said. "I think Winnifred is just a hedonist whose goal is immediate personal gratification. When Francis molested her, she nonetheless got a taste of pleasure. And once she got a taste of it, she didn't want to give it up. Her lack of common sense would prevent her from understanding the consequences of her actions or considering her long-term needs. Dancing while in the faerie realm probably just increased her desire for pleasure, and drinking faerie wine may have just heightened her determination to prevent anybody from standing in the way of having instant gratification. Or maybe her dancing in the faerie realm just made her more ruthless in pursuing pleasure."

They said no more until they were back in their bedchamber, where Karen put the philter under her pillow before climbing into bed. As Winnifred climbed into bed beside her, Karen reflected on what she had told Daria. She really did believe that Winnifred had become a hedonist after experiencing pleasure with Francis, even if he had molested her, and that this hedonistic tendency was only increased by spending time in the faerie realm, to the point where she wouldn't care if someone got hurt as long as she had fun. Which was all the more reason for Winnifred to stay in the faerie realm. Fortunately, her drinking faerie wine bound Winnifred to the faerie realm, so once the secret was found out Winnifred would stay in the faerie realm anyway.

But Karen was far less childish in her thinking and more willing to think about not only her long-term needs but also the needs of others. While Daria could be thoughtless, she had a strong enough morality and enough compassion that she *would* think about the needs of others as well as her own. And spending time in the faerie realm hadn't really changed them. Hopefully, it never would change Daria's moral code or sense of compassion.

CHAPTER 12

A large number of soldiers trooped through the Orgonian countryside. They were headed to Jolenz, an important fortified city. Among the soldiers was Mark.

It had been almost a year since he left the royal court and the capital city of Kelavia and went to the training camp for recruits. During his time in the training camp, he had learned how to fire a matchlock musket, a snaphance musket, and a flintlock. The matchlock muskets needed to be constantly lit, so in damp and rainy conditions, they were useless. Thus snaphance muskets were also provided, but they were very complex. Finally, the flintlock musket was a fairly recent invention, and not a lot of them were available. Overall, Mark preferred the flintlock muskets because they were easier to use than the snaphance ones and less susceptible to damp and rainy conditions than matchlocks.

Once Mark was fully trained as a musketeer, he was sent to the main army encampment. This occurred about two months after he arrived at the main encampment. When Mark arrived, he learned that King Robert had to leave the military operations to his field marshal and return to the capital because of a problem involving the princesses, which was unrevealed before the king left for the capital. This concerned Mark since the princesses involved were Karen and Winnifred, and because of his earlier intervention against Francis, he had close ties to them both, even if Princess Winnifred didn't like him.

But he had little time to worry about the princesses, for the Vindician troops were embarking on a campaign of trying to conquer fortified cities one at a time. Indeed, shortly after he arrived, a relief force had to be sent out to relieve a city that was being besieged by the Vindician troops. A scout with dark blond hair had come to warn the field marshal of the siege apparently only a day after the siege began despite the city being far enough away that the scout would probably have taken two days to arrive at the encampment.

The field marshal sent a relief force led by one of his best generals, a foreign-born mercenary from Brangavia named Nicholas, to relieve the city. Mark wasn't part of the force, but he learned later of the results. The scout accompanied the relief force there and gave them surprisingly detailed information about how to best circumvent the besiegers so that the besieged city could be relieved successfully. This apparently led to the besiegers being surprised by the relief force and, after a short battle with the troops guarding the city and the relief force, having to retreat.

There were two more incidents similar to the first successful relief of a besieged city that Nicholas led and resulted in success, and so the rumor spread that the scout who helped successfully relieve all the cities was, in fact, a faerie who had chosen to help the Orgonian troops defend their homeland. Mark wasn't sure why the faeries would want to help defend Orgon, although given the fact that King Robert was a decent ruler and man while the current king of Vindicia was supposed to be especially belligerent, maybe the faeries just didn't want a good king being conquered by a terrible one.

Mark hadn't been part of the other two relief forces, but after the scout reported to the field marshal that the city of Jolenz was being besieged, the field marshal decided it was time to send Mark out into the field, so he put Mark in the relief force for the city. The city, like the others, was an important, strategic one because if it was conquered, it would allow Vindician forces to more easily penetrate into the heartland of Orgon and thus conquer the capital.

During the time that Mark had been in the camp, a number of the unmarried men went into the village nearby, including Otto.

After a couple of months, Otto persuaded Mark to come with him into the village and have a good time. Otto first took him to the inn, where a number of the barmaids flirted with the soldiers who were present. They bustled around him and Otto once the two entered and began flirting with them.

That was when one redhead who apparently was from the village but wasn't a barmaid entered with several men, apparently her father and brothers. She went up to Mark, introduced herself as Ingrid, and began flirting with him. Mark was tempted to get involved with her, especially since she was of the same social class as he was; but as he began flirting back, an image of the princess Karen suddenly appeared in his mind, looking sadly at him. Mark suddenly stopped and hurriedly explained that he had been interested in someone else back home, though he also added that nothing had happened between him and the other girl because he felt he could never have her. Ingrid seemed to accept his explanation, though she was disappointed.

Mark spent the rest of the evening in a rather bad mood. He had gone off to the war so he wouldn't have to be around Princess Karen, and the reason why he had agreed to come with Otto into the village was so that he could find a girl of his own social class whom he could fall in love with, thus enabling him to get over the princess. But it seemed that it would take more time than he hoped to move on from Princess Karen and find someone else. And even though he returned to the village and spoke to Ingrid a few times since then, he still couldn't bring himself to flirt back with her.

But hopefully, time would pass, and he would successfully move on and find happiness with another girl. Until then, he'd have to wait. And going with Otto and other soldiers to relieve Jolenz from the Vindician soldiers was going to provide a welcome distraction from thoughts of his personal issues. That was when Mark heard from far off the sounds of artillery being fired. They must be getting close to the city.

Soon word passed through the relief army to stop. They were at the top of a hill that overlooked the city—and the besieging army from Vindicia. There were sounds coming from below of artillery and fierce fighting. Mark didn't know exactly what was going on beyond the fact that the Vindician forces were trying to attack the city, and the Orgonians were doing their best to repel the invaders, but he had no idea which side was successful.

Finally, the sounds of battle stopped, and all was calm. That was when Mark heard the voice of General Nicholas. "Attention, everyone! Cavalry, we are soon going to storm down the hillside and attack the enemy. Infantry, you are to follow us. And once you reach the base of the hill, you are to commence shooting at the besiegers. Hopefully, we will take them by surprise and ensure that the siege is relieved."

Mark was nervous as he awaited the signal for the troops to storm down. This was going to be his first time in combat. Otto had been looking forward to his first time in combat mainly because he thought it was going to be a great adventure or a chance to gain fame and glory. Mark was somewhat more realistic. It might be a chance to gain fame and glory, but it was certainly not going to be an adventure, let alone a great one. No, more likely, it would be a desperate fight between people defending their country and men seeking to invade it. He hoped he would come out of it alive.

That was when he heard the sound of the trumpet. It was time to storm down the hillside and hopefully relieve the city of Jolenz. Mark was near the back of the Orgonian relief force when the cavalry galloped down the hillside toward the Vindician troops. Thus, he had a fairly good view of the enemy forces, who apparently had been a little taken by surprise and now had to regroup to battle both the defenders from Jolenz *and* the relief force led by General Nicholas.

Mark and the other men in the infantry followed the cavalry down the hillside, their muskets ready to fire at the enemy, especially the cavalry. Mark hoped he would be able to tell the enemy apart from his fellow soldiers. It would be embarrassing to accidentally hit one of the men from his own side. He had heard from Duke Thomas that such things had happened before.

By the time Mark and the other men in the infantry reached the bottom of the hill, the cavalry had begun attacking the enemy cavalry and was giving them a good fight. However, that was when Mark saw someone from the enemy infantry take aim at Otto. Mark knew he had to prevent Otto from being shot. So he aimed his own gun at the infantryman from the Vindician force and fired. At about the same time, however, the infantryman from the enemy fired at Otto and managed to hit him in the shoulder. Mark's own shot went wide, hitting another man from the enemy infantry. It wasn't the guy he wanted to hit, but at least he got a shot in.

Otto nearly fell off of horse but managed to stay in the saddle. Mark knew Otto had to retreat to be taken care of, and he realized he and other infantrymen had to cover for him. So he signaled to some of the other men in the infantry. They understood, and they ran forward with him, firing as they ran.

But even as they ran forward, another infantryman fired at Otto; and this time, he got him in the back. He fell off his horse. Mark managed to reach Otto and, with some infantrymen providing cover, drag a badly wounded Otto off the battlefield. He could hear shooting taking place all around him, and there were some bullets that actually were rather close, but amazingly enough, he wasn't wounded.

Accompanying the troops to the site of the siege were men who had vehicles that could transport men off the battlefield and into moving hospitals called ambulances; unfortunately, injured soldiers were often picked up for treatment only after the sounds of battle had ceased, which resulted in many soldiers dying before they could be safely evacuated. This was probably because of the danger of bullets hitting the people supposed to take the soldiers away for treatment. The nurses for the Orgonian soldiers remained at the base of the hill while the soldiers went to fight the enemy.

The scout who had warned General Nicholas about the siege of Jolenz and had led the relief force to the hill overlooking the city came up and helped Mark drag Otto to the nurses who came forward with a cart. They put Otto in the cart, and two men took Otto off to the ambulance hospital. "I hope Otto will be all right for Duke Thomas's sake," Mark said, looking at the men who took Otto away.

"He is alive, thanks to you," the scout said.

"I'm glad I was able to get him off the battlefield," Mark said. "I can't believe I didn't get wounded while I was doing so. Either I had great cover from my fellow infantrymen or the soldiers from the Vindician army were remarkably inept."

"Your fellow infantrymen did provide good cover, but there were a couple of shots that probably would have hit you if you didn't have a little *special* assistance to make sure the bullets didn't hurt you," the scout said.

That was when Mark realized the truth. This scout really *was* a faerie. And he was probably there to make sure the Vindician troops didn't conquer Orgon. Still . . .

"Who sent you?" Mark asked. "And more importantly, why?"

"Crown Prince Alberich sent me," the scout said. "As for why, he is a decent faerie who does not like the Vindician ruler and wants to ensure that he does not conquer Orgon. There are very few faerie troops who like the Vindician ruler, in fact. And the list of faerie troops who don't like the Vindician ruler includes the faerie troop living under Vindicia itself."

"Is the Vindician ruler *that* bad?" Mark asked.

"I have heard rumors that Vindician king Godfrey's first son, Christopher, is leading the Vindician soldiers here in Orgon in part so that he doesn't have to deal with his father," the scout said. "Also, I have heard rumors that King Godfrey's second son, Jason, does *not* have a good relationship with his father and is becoming desperate to get away from Vindicia for good."

"Wow," Mark said. "I'm glad *my* king isn't that bad."

"No, King Robert is a decent man and a good ruler," the scout said. "We all know that."

Mark then heard the sounds of fighting gradually ceasing. The scout said, "I believe the soldiers from Vindicia have decided to retreat. I'm going to have to follow them if they do decide to leave Jolenz."

It didn't take long for Mark and the faerie scout to get confirmation that the Vindician soldiers had decided that they were better off retreating from the city. The faerie scout left as the Orgonian soldiers began celebrating their victory. Mark joined them and reported to General Nicholas that Otto had been badly wounded and that, because he had gotten Otto off the battlefield so quickly and the scout had helped him get Otto to the men who would take him to the ambulance hospital, Otto had not died from his injuries. That said, it was possible that Otto would die anyway from disease due to the wounds becoming infected or severe loss of blood or both.

"I believe that Duke Thomas will be very grateful to you for rescuing his second son," General Nicholas told Mark as the medical people came onto the battlefield to collect the other wounded soldiers, as well as the dead ones.

"How many men were wounded?" asked Mark. "Or killed?"

"I don't know," General Nicholas said. "But we will soon find out. After we have collected our dead and wounded, we shall have a great feast in the city of Jolenz to celebrate the successful relieving of the siege. I hope you will join us."

"Of course, I will," said Mark. He was relieved. His first encounter on the battlefield had been a success, with no injuries and with him having rescued the son of a duke. Even if Otto died, at least he didn't die on the battlefield.

*   *   *

Ultimately, the Orgonian troops collected one hundred men who were dead or wounded from the battlefield. Half the soldiers were already dead, the other half, much like Otto, merely wounded. Most of the casualties on the battlefield, however, belonged to Vindician soldiers, and they were collected by the defenders of Jolenz since the Vindician forces had already retreated. The dead ones were going to be buried in a mass grave with proper burial rites, while the wounded were going to be kept as prisoners of war until or unless the Vindician king would pay a ransom for them, which he would only do for the most noble of the men.

There was evidence that the Vindician soldiers had tried to dig covered trenches, also known as saps, and mines around the besieged city. General Nicholas learned from the mayor of the city that every night before the relief force arrived, various troops from inside the city itself along with some university students made sorties to destroy the sap works so that the Vindician troops wouldn't be able to cut the city off completely and starve it into surrendering before help could arrive. While the sorties had been mostly successful, the main reason for the successful relief of the city was that the relief forces arrived before the Vindician troops could totally seal themselves off from outside help that might come.

Mark, meanwhile, learned that the wounded soldiers, including Otto, were being treated in a monastery that had been converted into a hospital decades ago. The former monks were allowed to remain and were joined by former nuns, all of whom were skilled in herbal medicine just like Princess Karen. While this hospital and others in the country usually treated sick and poor people with little or no expense since King Robert had local governments provide enough money to the hospitals, there was enough room for wounded soldiers who needed treatment in this former monastery. Mark spoke to the head of the hospital and learned that Otto's condition was very serious, and it was unclear if he would recover, though at least Otto was alive for now. He also learned that a letter had been sent to Duke Thomas, who was with the field marshal, and that the duke would come as soon as possible.

Then it was time for the great feast. But as Mark entered the great hall where the feast would be served, his thoughts now turned to what he had learned from the faerie scout. He didn't know anything about international politics—after all, he was born a commoner, not a courtier. Nor did he know much about royal families or royal courts. His only experience with royal families was with the king and his daughters, and while Princess Winnifred certainly seemed to be a thorn in the side of her father and sisters, that family didn't seem to be all that dysfunctional, at least not from his brief experience with them. King Robert certainly wasn't a bad father, and Princess Karen was a concerned and loving sister to Princess Winnifred.

Actually, Mark had little experience with dysfunctional families, period. His own family had been a close-knit and loving one, and while the father of his first girlfriend, Sarah, had been a social climber of the first order, Mark hadn't heard anything about Sarah's father abusing his children other than beatings or spankings, and lots of parents beat or spanked their children if they misbehaved. So the faerie scout's revelation of the dysfunction within the Vindician king's own family astounded Mark and made him wonder what could possibly cause it, whether royal or commoner. Was it simply a pattern passed down from parent to child? Was it a matter of personal choice? And if the sons of the king of Vindicia were so dissatisfied with their father that they would want to escape, how could this relationship have become so bad?

Mark didn't know the answer to these and other questions about the Vindician king and his family. But he *did* know one thing: he was glad this kind of relationship didn't exist between the king of Orgon and his daughters.

Chapter 13

"I am surrounded by incompetents!" Prince Jason was just outside the great hall when heard his father, King Godfrey, bellow these words. Jason stopped dead still, knowing full well that it was not a good idea to come anywhere near his father when he was in one of his rages.

Jason was the second of three sons by King Godfrey and the younger of the two sons by Godfrey's first wife, who died in childbirth after giving birth to a baby girl four years after Jason's birth. (There was a stillbirth of a male child in between Jason's birth and that of his sister.) His elder brother, the crown prince, was named Christopher, while his younger half brother was named Victor and was his father's favorite. While Jason was too young to remember much about his mother and like all members of royalty he had been raised by a nurse, he *did* have some vague memories of a loving, kindly woman who was willing to spend time with him, unlike his father, who rarely visited Christopher or Jason when they were young and even now only spent time with his sons if he felt they were useful to him in some way.

King Godfrey was a monster. Jason never said it out loud, at least not in front of his father or any his father's most sycophantic followers, but he knew it to be true. The king believed that rulers should be absolutely ruthless and showed this mindset by strong-arming people for more taxes, often brutally punishing those who weren't able to pay, and brutally silencing those who dared to criticize his regime, like one nobleman who had bad-mouthed the king within earshot of him. This occurred ten years ago, when Jason was just eight years old. Moreover, he had a terrible temper, and the slightest thing (or, worse, nothing) could send the king into a deadly rage, with terrible consequences for the people who aroused his fury. One of his most sycophantic followers was actually executed for not singing the king's praises right away as the king didn't care that the follower in question had begun to go deaf.

Moreover, the king hoped that his own sons would develop the same mindset as he himself had; and when Jason and Victor were old enough to be given over to tutors, the king personally picked the tutors, hoping that they would encourage a ruthless, cruel mindset in the sons. However, Jason's tutors had secretly rebelled, teaching Jason to be a decent guy and refusing to let him mistreat his younger siblings like the king wanted him to. As a result, the king eventually executed every tutor whom Jason had.

But Jason wasn't the only one to see tutors be executed for daring to not instill the king's twisted mindset into his sons. Apparently, when Christopher and Jason's mother was still alive, Christopher was old enough to be handed over to tutors, and she advised the king to pick tutors whom she led him to believe would encourage the kind of mindset the king wanted Christopher to have but would actually instill a gentler (but firm) mindset. Jason had been told that his father was so furious when he found out that the tutors were not what he hoped they would be that he might actually have killed his wife had she not been pregnant and died in childbirth. As it was, Christopher's tutors got the brunt of the king's wrath.

That was why the king personally picked the tutors for Jason and Victor. While it didn't work on Jason, it seemed to work on Victor either because the tutors in question had become sycophantic loyalists or because Victor's mother also went along with her husband's ideas. Victor's mother, the second queen, was someone who was more interested in fashion and jewelry than in being a good mother or stepmother. That said, Jason had never known his stepmother to be abusive to him. Then again, she didn't need to be abusive, not with her husband around.

While neither Christopher nor Jason was ruthless enough to truly satisfy the king, Christopher *had* learned how to fight and was competent enough as a warrior that the king rarely picked on him. Jason, however, was a different story. He never really liked fighting and preferred reading and music, although he was an indifferent poet. This caused the king to pick on Jason mercilessly or to encourage Victor to do so if Victor was around. As a result, Jason often avoided his father's presence, spending most of his time at the castle in the library. When Jason became old enough, he would often go down to the village and spend time getting to know the people there, including one who apparently was an old beggar woman. But after Jason gave her some food and drink, he learned that she was actually a faerie named Vivian who hung around the village, and he began spending time with her. Either option was better than spending time at the castle.

Jason had enough of living in a nightmare of a kingdom, and thanks to one courtier who actually had relatives in Orgon whom he would visit every year, Jason knew of a way to get away from the abuse of his father and, to a lesser extent, Victor. Seven months ago, the courtier had returned from his yearly visit and informed Jason of the situation involving the Orgonian king's daughters, especially the middle sister, who apparently wore her shoes out every night despite being locked in with her elder and younger sister. The eldest and youngest themselves didn't really wear out their shoes, but it was believed that they were involved in their sister's escapade. That was when Jason learned that whoever could learn the secret of the princesses' escapades would marry whichever princess he preferred, and if he chose the eldest princess, he would become king consort after the king died. At the time, two princes had already come to Orgon to uncover the secret, only to fail and be under house arrest for a time before leaving Orgon and being unable to return until the secret was revealed.

Jason immediately saw that this was the way out. He could marry the eldest princess and stay in Orgon, eventually becoming king consort upon her father's death. This could help him begin a new life away from Vindicia. Unfortunately, there was one major problem—his father. King Godfrey still didn't like Jason, viewing him as a total weakling. Jason could gain his father's respect by becoming his representative when dealing with delinquent taxpayers, but the idea of strong-arming taxpayers with threats of severe violence if they didn't pay repulsed Jason. Victor might have no problem becoming the representative as he was showing signs of being much like the king, but Victor was only eleven years old. He wasn't old enough to be his father's representative.

But if he could somehow be clever enough to convince his father that becoming a suitor for the hand of the eldest princess would be more advantageous for his father in his plans to conquer Orgon than simply trying to invade the kingdom, that *would* be a way to get his father's consent to leave Vindicia. And if he somehow learned the secret of the princesses, he'd marry the eldest princess and never have to return to Vindicia ever again. Or if he *had* to return, it wouldn't be for long as he would then leave to marry the eldest princess and never come back.

So Jason bided his time. Seven months had passed, during which he learned from Vivian that a third prince had tried to uncover the secret, only to fail and have to return to his own kingdom and never return to Orgon. Jason had no intention of being the fourth one to fail, so if he tried and failed, he might just kill himself. Granted, committing suicide would be a mortal sin, but the thought of returning home to Vindicia as a failure was beginning to seem like a fate worse than death for Jason. He might just be willing to kill himself rather than return to his father and continue living in fear.

That was when Jason heard his father complain, "I can't believe that, after eighteen months of my eldest son being in Orgon, he hasn't gotten anywhere near the castle belonging to the king and has stayed on the margins of Orgon. Why can't he do anything right?"

The courtier said, "He suggested that the faerie troop connected to Orgon might be helping the Orgonians."

"He's an idiot!" the king bellowed. "I'm much more powerful than any faerie!" Jason was horrified to hear such words and was afraid that the faeries would not only punish his father severely for claiming to be more powerful than they but also punish Vindicia for it. His father might deserve punishment, but there were many innocent people in Vindicia who would be hurt if the faeries punished the whole kingdom, and Jason didn't want that.

The king added, "And why are you just standing around? Get out of my sight!"

Jason watched as the hapless courtier passed by him while fleeing the great hall, looking relieved to be leaving the king. Jason couldn't blame him. He waited for the courtier to go around the corner before peeking through the doorway that led to the great hall. The king was pacing in front of his throne, muttering what may well have been obscenities. Jason was unsure whether to enter the great hall now or leave and wait for a better opportunity.

But then the king suddenly turned toward the doorway where Jason stood. "Who's there?" he asked suddenly.

It looked like his decision was made for him. Jason sighed and stepped into the doorway. "It's just me, Your Majesty," he said.

The king frowned. "Oh, it's you," he said, almost snarling. "What do you want, you pathetic little mouse?"

This stung, but Jason did his best to ignore it. He had a goal in mind, and he couldn't let his father's insults prevent him from at least trying to achieve it. "I know you want to conquer the kingdom of Orgon but that invasion doesn't seem to be working out for you," he said. "Why not try a better solution?"

"What could possibly be better than invasion?" asked the king.

"Marriage," Jason said, "specifically marriage to the crown princess." He then proceeded to tell his father about what he had learned from the courtier about the princesses and the Orgonian king's declaration that whoever solved the mystery of where the princesses went every night would win the hand of whichever princess the successful suitor wanted. He didn't tell his father there was a third suitor who had tried and failed—the king didn't even think about the beggars in the country, let alone realize that at least one of them was a faerie in disguise.

"So if you allowed me to go to the kingdom of Orgon, I might be able to solve the mystery of where the princesses go every night—or at least where the middle princess, named Winnifred, goes every night to dance. And if that happens, I'm going to choose the eldest princess."

"And you think that will give me a means to conquer the kingdom of Orgon?" the king asked.

"Maybe," Jason said. "At least it would get someone you think of as a pathetic little mouse away from here, if I succeed in solving the mystery, of course."

The king looked very thoughtful for a long moment, and Jason looked a little nervous. Would he be able to succeed in convincing him that this would be the best solution for all concerned? Especially for him? Or would his father once again decide that war was the best solution?

*   *   *

King Godfrey thought long and hard about his pathetic son's suggestion of having Jason solve a mystery involving the princesses of Orgon and marry the eldest princess as a means of conquering the kingdom. From an early age, the king had been an aggressive man who enjoyed reading about military tactics and strategies. He learned all that he could about war. He was also impatient and hot tempered, even as a boy, so when he became king after the death of his father, he chose to exert power over the countries surrounding him through war.

His father tended to use arranged marriages as a strategy to exert influence over other countries, but Godfrey was too impatient, too quick tempered, and viewed war as the quicker route. He personally led his troops into various conflicts, spending time with his first wife and later his second wife only to ensure that he had children, preferably sons. Indeed, one of the reasons why he only had two children by his second wife was that he spent a lot of time in a costly but ultimately successful invasion of a neighboring country north of Vindicia.

He wanted his sons to share his love of fighting and even more of dominating people. This was why he was so disappointed in his first wife and then in his second son. He wasn't as disappointed in his eldest son, for while Christopher wasn't willing to treat the king's subjects the way the king felt they should be treated, Christopher was at least willing to learn how to be a good fighter and how to plan military campaigns. Jason, on the other hand, took after his mother, who preferred to read and listen to music and poetry—mere mush in the king's eyes.

But the king's favorite son was Victor, whom he'd personally named since it came from the king's favorite word, *victory*. And Victor had been carefully taught to be the kind of prince his father wanted all his sons to be, so Victor was almost as aggressive and ruthless as the king was, if less hot tempered. Victor wasn't old enough to be a soldier, but he took to the lessons on war with avidity, at least according to his tutors. The king had high hopes for Victor, dreaming of military campaigns where his son would bring victory and help conquer nations. The king was sure that Victor would help his father conquer more countries than Christopher did.

This brought the king back to the problem in front of him. He didn't like the idea that marriage would be a useful means to conquer Orgon. It was too slow, too ponderous. War was a swifter and thus a better solution. On the other hand, Christopher certainly wasn't doing a good job of invading Orgon, and his courtiers were beginning to be concerned about the money being spent on the campaign, afraid that a costly long war might drain the country's treasury. Perhaps he should at least give his worthless son a chance to prove that marrying the crown princess of Orgon would be a more effective strategy than just invasion. Perhaps if Jason actually succeeded, he'd use the opportunity to plot a swift invasion while Orgon had its defenses down, thus conquering it.

Of course, that depended on whether his pathetic little mouse of a son would actually succeed in solving this mystery. And the king didn't have much hope there. Still, maybe the chance that he could invade and conquer Orgon this way was worth the risk of failure. So the king made his decision.

"You may actually have something there," he told his second son. "How many princes have actually tried in the interim between the courtier's return to Vindicia and now?"

"I'm not sure," Jason said. "It's been eighteen months since you sent troops to invade Orgon, and the dancing apparently began soon after the invasion. It has been seven months since the courtier returned from Orgon, so there may have been a third suitor. But if there was, I doubt he was successful either."

"Well then, we'll see if your little scheme isn't so pathetic after all," the king announced. "I'll send one of my most trusted courtiers to Orgon to announce your intention to solve the mystery and win the crown princess's hand in marriage. And if it doesn't work, as I suspect it won't, no harm will be done."

"But if it does work?" Jason asked.

"Then you won't be so pathetic after all," the king said. "Now get out of my sight!"

Jason quickly left. The king smiled. He wasn't going to tell Jason what he planned if his son was successful. What he didn't know wouldn't hurt him after all. And he suspected that his son only suggested that the marriage would be a good way for the king to conquer Orgon to persuade him to let Jason marry an Orgonian princess and that Jason had other motives. If this worked, he'd finally have conquered Orgon. If not, well, at least he had a good excuse to continue the war.

* * *

It did not take long for the envoy from Vindicia to come and announce Prince Jason's intention of solving the mystery of the Orgonian princesses. Nor did it take long for the princesses to learn of it, and none of them were pleased as became apparent when they visited the faerie realm the night after they learned of Prince Jason's planned visit.

"Another guy is here to try to spoil my fun!" Princess Winnifred complained as she and her sisters were led by Prince Alberich into the crystalline castle.

"He won't be spoiling your fun, even if he was, by some chance, to succeed," Alberich reminded her. "You will remain with us no matter what."

As Winnifred sighed in relief, Princess Daria spoke up. "But I *am* very concerned. After all, this is the son of our worst enemy."

"And he might be here simply as a ploy for the king of Vindicia to try to conquer us," Princess Karen added.

"The king of Vindicia *is* planning to use the marriage as a means to lower your guard and invade Orgon without giving any fair warning," Alberich explained. "I learned that from Vivian, one of the faeries in Vindicia. However, Prince Jason only wants to get away from his father and only suggested that the marriage might be a more effective means to conquer Orgon than the current campaign as a means to persuade his father to go along with the plan. Jason doesn't really know about his father's scheme, but if he did, Vivian believes that he'd oppose it."

"Sounds like Prince Jason and his father are not on very good terms," Karen noted.

"They aren't," Alberich said bluntly. "The king is a terrible man and a very cruel ruler. The country is going down the drain due to his cruelty, and the main reason why it hasn't totally gone to pieces by now is that the king can go to war and gain glory that way, unlike other rulers who aren't madmen but are still incompetent. And Jason isn't anything like his father, which is why his father picks on him so often. The king's eldest son, Christopher, is a little closer to his father than Jason is, but the crown prince is more rational and less obsessed with war and fighting."

"I'm glad about that," Karen said. "While I feel pity for Prince Jason, having to live under a tyrant and being so desperate to get away that he is willing to take on the challenge to find out where we've been going every night, he's not Mark, and I don't want to be a pawn in his father's plans. Nor do I want the prince to be a pawn."

"There's just one problem," Daria noted. "If Prince Jason is so desperate to get away from his father's tyranny that he's willing to try to solve the mystery of where we go every night, if he fails, he might be desperate to avoid returning."

"He *is* considering killing himself if he fails," Alberich noted. "At least that is what Vivian said."

This alarmed Karen. She had been glad that her father had not wanted the unlucky suitors beheaded if they failed to solve the mystery of where she and her sisters went every night because she wasn't so ruthless that she would harm men who really did nothing to her other than try to solve a mystery that she didn't want solved at this point. And that wasn't enough of a reason to want to harm them. But now someone was coming whom she didn't want to solve the mystery, but if she ensured that he failed, he might kill himself, and she might have his death on her conscience.

"That's no big loss to me if he commits suicide," Winnifred said.

"But it *is* a mortal sin!" Daria protested.

"We have to prevent it," Karen decided. "And the best way to prevent it . . . is to keep him here, at least until his father dies and at the very longest until Mark is able to try his luck and solve the mystery."

"I can help with that," Alberich said. "No later than the third night, you must allow him to follow you here. Once he is here, I will have the faeries give a toast to his solving the mystery, and he will be given a goblet of clear water. But the water will be laced with a drug that induces amnesia. He will forget his identity, his past, everything about the upper world and will stay here until the mystery is solved."

"That is a great idea," Karen said. "I'll probably drug his drink the first night, but either the second night or the last, I won't do so, and he'll follow us down here and stay here for a while. It's better—and safer—for him."

That was when Daria said, "Speaking of Vindicia, I remember hearing reports that a princess from there named Vera married the king of Brangavia and had a daughter and a son. But as the daughter of now-queen Vera grew older, she became so beautiful that her mother became jealous of her and, in the end, tried to have her murdered with poison. But a good witch misled the queen and gave her a potion that merely put the girl in a coma. I also learned that it was rumored that the reason why Queen Vera became jealous of her own daughter was that the queen made the fatal error of suggesting that she was not only more beautiful than any mortal woman but also more beautiful than faerie women, and the faeries chose to punish her by giving her a magic mirror that told her who was the most beautiful woman of them all and by making her own daughter—I think her name was Blanche—more beautiful than the queen."

"Why don't you and your sister Karen follow me to the library and I can show you something that will prove whether the rumors about the queen were true?"

Karen had an inkling that the whole story *was* true, and that was why Alberich wanted them to go into the library—because one of the books in it would have the tale. So Karen and Daria followed Alberich into the library, where he went to one of the bookshelves and took out a book that he opened to a particular page. He said, "This is actually a book that will be written in the future by two brothers who will become academics and collectors of what you would call folklore. They will publish a book of collected folklore that will ultimately include the story of Queen Vera and Princess Blanche. Here is the tale, with some major differences from the true tale. It's called 'Little Snow White.'"

Karen saw Daria take the book and begin reading the story. At one point, Daria said, "You're right about this being very different from the original account. The villain in this isn't Snow White's biological mother. It's a stepmother."

"That's because the authors tried to tone down the story for children later on," Alberich explained. "I guess mortal parents became more concerned about what was suitable for children later in history. Anyway, by the time the story will be collected, the reasons for the queen having the magic mirror in the first place will have been dropped, so the authors won't be aware that the queen unwisely claimed to be more beautiful than faerie women and thus was given the magic mirror as an initial punishment, and then her daughter, Blanche, will become more beautiful than her as a second punishment."

"What about the witch who thwarted the queen's scheme?" Daria asked.

"As the tale is retold, the queen herself will become a witch, so there will be no need of a second witch," said Alberich.

"Well, I'm glad that Mother was never that vain," Karen commented.

"No, your mother was never that vain," Alberich reassured them. "In fact, I don't think she ever was really vain. The king of Vindicia's second wife is rather vain, but she never said that she was more beautiful than any faerie woman."

"That's not being not so vain. That's just having more common sense," Daria suggested.

"Yes," Karen agreed.

The rest of the night was spent in the usual way, reading books in the library and spending time in the ballroom. However, at one point during the dancing, Alberich said, "You are fourteen now and soon will be fifteen, Daria. Maybe you would like to learn how to waltz."

"Not yet, thanks," Daria said. "I am far more comfortable now, but I think I will wait until I'm fifteen to actually learn the waltz. I'll feel grown up enough to try it, I think."

"Very well," Alberich said, not pressing any further. Karen was relieved that Alberich had proved to be nothing less than a gentleman toward Karen and her sisters. She was now no longer afraid of this troop of faeries because of Alberich. Indeed, she now occasionally thought that if he would fall in love with Winnifred or with Daria and one of them (most likely Daria) returned his feelings, she wouldn't mind having Alberich as a brother-in-law.

But finally, Winnifred's shoes were worn out as usual, and the princesses had to leave the castle to return to the mortal realm. Once they were back across the lake, Karen led the way back to the stairs leading to their bedroom, feeling happy over the plan to save Prince Jason from possibly committing suicide and from being a pawn in his father's scheme to conquer Orgon. It might cause problems for her father when Prince Jason disappeared, but she'd cross that bridge when she came to it.

And hopefully, by the time Mark solved the mystery, the king of Vindicia would be dead, and Jason would be free of his father's tyranny. And hopefully, the new king would be a wiser—and saner—ruler than this king was. Karen hoped that everything would work out well in the end, despite the obstacles standing in the way, except for the king of Vindicia, of course, who was one of the obstacles.

CHAPTER 14

Prince Jason stepped out of the coach that had brought him to the castle and looked around. The castle was big and sturdy, maybe not quite as grand as his father's castle but close enough. Servants in royal livery moved forward, perhaps to greet him, probably to escort him to the king of Orgon.

"Welcome to the kingdom of Orgon, sir," one of the servants said.

"Thank you," Jason said, bowing. "Could you please lead me to the king of Orgon?"

The servant who greeted him took his arm and led him into the castle. "Where are we going, sir?" Jason asked.

"To the lesser audience chamber, which is just off the great hall," the servant said.

He led Jason into the great hall, which was impressive. There were banners, but instead of captured battle banners hanging from the crossbeams like at his father's castle, the banners portrayed various coats of arms, no doubt belonging to those who boasted a title and a coat of arms. He didn't know where the battle flags were, but hopefully, they were in some nice place where they could be appreciated.

The walls were coated with what appeared to be whitewashed plaster, presumably keeping out drafts and insulating the room from dampness. There were columns and a statuary, possibly painted, and walls that were definitely painted between the columns, above which was a gallery that held likenesses of various knights and ladies who looked down on him. Yes, it was very impressive, much more impressive than the great hall in Jason's own castle, which was stained with decades of smoke and soot.

The servant led Jason through the hall and into the lesser audience chamber, which may have been smaller than the great hall but was just as impressive. The room was covered in floor-to-wall hangings. Some were tapestries; others were curtained arras. The only break in the hangings was a single window, curtained and glazed. And sitting on an impressive throne was the king of Orgon.

The king was a regal figure in a purple velvet doublet, matching breeches, and a white linen shirt that could be seen underneath the doublet. He looked brave yet kind, something that could hardly be said about Jason's own father, a man to whom kindness was anathema. Yet he seemed wary probably because Jason was the son of a man who wanted to conquer the king's domains.

Escorted by the servant, Jason reached the king and watched as the servant fell immediately to one knee and made a deep bow, saying, "Your Majesty, with your royal permission, I present to you Prince Jason from the kingdom of Vindicia."

"We are always willing to receive new guests, even those from nations hostile to Orgon," the king said. "Please rise."

When the servant rose, the king turned to Jason. "I have sent for wine and cakes, so please take refreshment, Your Highness," he said. "And since you have traveled far to come here, I will have another servant bring you a seat."

"That is most kind, Your Majesty," Jason said. The servant in question gave Jason a goblet of wine and offered him some cakes. Jason took one and waited as the servant put the refreshments on a nearby sideboard before leaving and then returning with a single low chair. Jason thought about his own father and how he'd treat a visiting guest, especially one from a hostile nation. His father would probably not allow his guest to take any refreshment, demand very strict etiquette, and not offer his guest a seat. Already, Jason liked this king more than his own father.

Jason proceeded to sit down on the chair without looking, believing that the servant would put the chair under Jason to prevent any disaster from occurring. When Jason sat down, he sipped his wine and nibbled on his cake. "I appreciate the hospitality, Your Majesty," Jason began. "I believe you know the matter that brings me here."

"The matter concerning my daughters?" the king asked.

"Yes," Jason said. "I wish to solve the mystery of where they go every night and who provided them with such sumptuous gowns and shoes."

The king looked wary, and Jason wasn't sure he could blame the king. After all, Jason *was* from Vindicia, and his father was trying to conquer Orgon.

"May I ask why you wish to solve the mystery?" the king asked warily.

Jason briefly considered whether he should be honest before deciding that the best way to get the king to accept him was to be honest about his motives. "I wish to marry your eldest daughter and live here in Orgon for the rest of my life," Jason explained, "and never have to live in the same country as my father ever again."

The king looked surprised at that. "You do not like your father, Prince Jason?" he asked.

"I think it's impossible for anybody to really *like* my father," Jason said. "He is a monster. You do not have to tell him that, but it is the truth. I do not feel at home in my father's castle, and I try to spend as little time with my father as I possibly can. If I'm in the castle, you can find me in the library. But I'm often outside the castle, trying to avoid my father's presence and that of my half brother, Victor. If my father isn't telling me I'm pathetic and useless, he's encouraging Victor to taunt me."

The king looked at Jason with some sympathy. "What about your elder brother?" he asked.

"Christopher is at the head of the army that's invading your country," Jason said. "I think he agreed to lead the army to get away from our father, pressuring him to be as warlike as Father himself is. He's lucky. I'm not."

"So you want to marry one of my daughters just to start a new life in a country that isn't Vindicia," the king stated.

"That's right," Jason said. "I just want to start a new life somewhere else, anywhere else. I actually had to tell my father that marrying the crown princess might be a better way for him to conquer Orgon just so he would allow me to leave Vindicia."

The king looked thoughtful as Jason sipped more of his wine and ate some more of his cake. Finally, the king spoke. "Maybe you would like to meet my daughters," the king suggested, "especially Karen. She's the oldest one."

Jason nodded, relieved that the king was willing to accept him as a suitor. "Do you know where they are?"

"Daria—she's the youngest one—can be found in the library most of the time," the king said. "She's socially awkward and loves to read. Karen can often be found in the gardens, especially the herbal ones. She's an herbalist and can concoct very effective potions for pain relief and sleep aids. Except for an hour every day, when she is allowed to go outside with her ladies-in-waiting, Winnifred can be found in the quarters she shares with her sisters."

Jason frowned. He didn't know much about the situation involving the princesses other than what he had learned from the courtier who had gone to Orgon, and that courtier hadn't mentioned the fact that the princess Winnifred only went out of her quarters for an hour every day. Maybe the courtier's Orgonian relatives didn't know about it. "Why does Princess Winnifred have only an hour to be allowed to go outside?" Jason asked.

"Because about two years ago, the music and dance instructor for the princesses tried to seduce her," the king explained. "Winnifred is not very smart and is easily flattered, so he managed to get her to spend some time alone with him in the chapel at a manor belonging to one of my most trusted courtiers, Duke Thomas. However, an herbal gardener who worked at the estate, a young man named Mark, was awakened when they tried to enter the private garden, followed them, and saved Winnifred. I had the instructor executed for high treason as a result since Winnifred was betrothed to the king of Brangavia, and the instructor hoped to become Winnifred's lover and use the situation to gain power at the Brangavian king's court."

"In other words, the guy was a social climber," Jason concluded. "And so you're trying to protect your second daughter from being exploited by keeping her under close surveillance."

"Yes," the king explained. "Karen and Daria have more common sense, so I don't need to keep them under as close a watch as Winnifred. Come with me, and I will introduce you to my daughters before I will officially allow you to try to solve the mystery."

The king extended his hand, and Jason rose to approach him before kneeling and kissing the king's extended hand. "I am extremely grateful to you for your consent!" he exclaimed. "Since Princess Daria can be found in the library and since I'm fond of literature, I would like to go there first."

The king nodded, rose, and along with the servant whom Jason had first met escorted the prince from the lesser audience chamber and through the great hall toward a stone staircase. From Jason's first view of the castle, he had seen that it was apparently three stories high, so he assumed that the library was on either the second or the third floor.

They walked up the stone staircase, and the king stopped when they reached the second floor, thus suggesting that the library was there. Jason's suspicions were confirmed when the king led him down a long corridor to two doors. The servant opened the doors, and the king entered the room, followed by Jason.

The library was as impressive as the other rooms that Jason had been in. Three of the four walls consisted of two stories of shelved books while the fourth wall had a higher story that had shelved books and an entryway on the lower story that led to a balcony from which one could look out over the castle walls. His attention then turned to the middle of the room, where several women and a young girl who looked to be about fourteen or fifteen sat in chairs with plush seats. The women and the girl stood up as soon as they saw the king and

Jason standing in the room. The king turned to the girl and spoke to her.

"Daria, I would like you to meet Prince Jason of Vindicia," the king said as the girl curtsied. "Prince Jason, this is my youngest daughter, Princess Daria."

Jason looked at Princess Daria. Although she had black hair instead of blond like the traditional image of a princess, this girl was still quite pretty with a creamy complexion and a subtle hint of rose on her cheeks, lovely gray eyes, a small nose, and a lovely mouth. She wore a dark red dress that showed off a modestly endowed slim figure.

"It is a pleasure to meet you, Princess Daria," Jason said, bowing courteously as he spoke.

The princess curtsied, maybe a little awkwardly but not too much so. "So you're from Vindicia," she said.

Jason sighed as he was reminded of his kingdom's all-too-rocky history with this one. "It is not my fault that my father is a monstrous tyrant who only knows how to dominate people in his own kingdom and how to dominate and conquer other kingdoms," he said a little sharply. "Life there is a total misery for me, and I just want to escape it."

Princess Daria immediately looked apologetic. "I'm sorry, Prince Jason," she said. "I have a habit of being rather blunt sometimes, and I have no love for your father's kingdom either."

"Most people in my country don't love it," Jason said, relaxing a little. "Maybe I should change the subject by asking you what you were doing before I arrived."

"Reading," Princess Daria said, "at least until a few moments ago, when my ladies warned me that I might get a headache if I continued reading."

"What exactly were you reading?" Jason asked curiously.

"A chivalric romance," Princess Daria explained. "It's about this knight whose father was such a bad tyrant that his vassals rose against him and killed him but allowed the knight's mother to live. The knight was taken by a water fairy and raised on an island inhabited by women. He had many adventures, including helping rescue a queen from a king who had abducted her and taken her to his castle."

"I believe I remember reading about this knight whom you mentioned," Jason said. "Wasn't he whipped by a dwarf early on in the story?"

"He was," Daria said, showing evident interest now. "You like to read?"

"If I'm in my father's castle, you can find me in the library," Jason said. "It's better than spending time in my father's presence, although I often spend time outside the castle as well. I hear you love to read also."

"I do," Daria said, her gray eyes beginning to sparkle. "Other than my sister Karen, I believe books are my best friends."

Jason smiled, finding a kindred spirit in this princess. "Do you like philosophy?" he asked.

"Somewhat," Daria said. "I prefer reading romances, ballads, and especially folklore about faeries, but I don't mind learning philosophy. It challenges my mind."

Jason would have spoken more about philosophy except that King Robert said, "I believe you also need to meet my other two daughters, Prince Jason."

"May I come with you?" Daria asked. "My ladies probably would say that I have read enough and need some fresh air."

"If it is okay with Prince Jason, then of course, you may accompany us," the king said.

"I'd be very pleased to have her come with us," Jason said.

"Then we must go to the quarters that my daughters share as that is most likely where Winnifred will be," King Robert said. "My daughters have their quarters in the second tower."

On the way out of the library, the king explained more about his daughters' rooms. "Initially, while all three princesses had rooms in the second tower, they all had separate rooms since Karen was the crown princess, and Daria and Winnifred were very different," the king explained. "But after the scandal involving Winnifred, I had her move into Karen's room. And after they began sneaking out every night—or at least Winnifred did—I eventually had Daria moved into the same room with her sisters."

"How well do you get along with your sisters, Princess Daria?" asked Jason curiously.

"I get along quite well with Karen," Daria explained. "She cares about me and Winnifred and is very reasonable. She looks out for us when Father can't do so. It reassures me. I don't get along so well with Winnifred. I love her, but she is so foolish, and we don't have much in common. She loves dancing and music. I prefer reading. I'm an intellectual. She is a hedonist. But she's not deliberately cruel, merely thoughtless and foolish."

"That's something," Jason said. "I have a younger half brother named Victor, and he's becoming a lot like my father was at Victor's age—mean, belligerent, aggressive. I don't like him, and he doesn't like me. At least you don't have a cruel sister or half sister or a tyrant of a father."

"No, Father isn't a tyrant," Daria acknowledged. "And I'm glad about that. Your father is a tyrant?"

"Yes," Jason said. "He calls me pathetic, useless, weak. I'm not a pushover, but he wants sons who are warriors and only warriors. I prefer music and literature, and he could hardly care less about it. I also have an elder brother, Christopher, and he's more of a warrior than I am, but he is reluctant to hurt or kill anyone just to prove that he's a warrior, even if Father urges him to do so."

Daria looked at him with sympathy and then placed a hand on his arm. "You really have a terrible father," she said. "I'm glad I don't."

"Me too," both Jason and the king said at the same time. Jason looked at the king, who just shrugged.

*   *   *

Fortune must have been really smiling on Jason, for after he, the king, Princess Daria, and their attendants all left the library and went down the staircase, they encountered a group of women who were headed to the great hall. Among the women was one young blond girl of about sixteen who wore a small crown much like the one Princess Daria wore. Clearly, she was one of the princesses.

Jason's suspicions were confirmed when he heard the king say, "Prince Jason, I'd like you to meet my middle daughter, Princess Winnifred. Winnifred, this is Prince Jason from the kingdom of Vindicia."

She was rather pretty as well. Not only did she have golden blond hair but her complexion was also like wild rose petals and cream, and she had pretty blue eyes. Her face was more angular than that of her sister, who had a pleasing oval-shaped face, but her figure more than made up for her face being rather too thin and angular for him. Her square neckline was cut low enough to frame a generous bosom, and her sky blue gown showed her curvaceous figure off to her best advantage.

Princess Winnifred frowned at him maybe because he was from an enemy kingdom but extended her hand somewhat reluctantly and said rather coolly, "I am honored to meet you, Prince Jason."

"Likewise," Jason said as he bowed and kissed Princess Winnifred's hand. She snatched it away as soon as she could do so. Clearly, she did not like him. That made his choice easier if he had to choose between the three princesses since he didn't want to marry one who didn't like him.

Of course, he had to meet the third princess. "Princess Winnifred, would it be okay if I asked you if you knew where your elder sister, Princess Karen, is at the moment?" he asked.

Princess Winnifred didn't reply, but one of the ladies attending her said, "I believe that she is either in the herbal garden or in the private one."

"Then we shall all go to the gardens in the back," the king said. He led the way through the great hall and through a set of double doors in the back that led outside to a small patio overlooking the rear of the castle. The rear of the castle consisted of a series of pathways surrounded by trees and hedges that showed evidence of careful planning and design. "Where is the herbal garden?" Prince Jason asked.

"It is on the right-hand side of this part of the castle," the king said. "There is a vegetable garden that is on the left-hand side as well. The private garden is in the back and can only be opened with a key. The only people who have keys to the garden are myself and the gardener who is assigned to care for it."

He led them down the central pathway until they reached the center, where a huge fountain stood in the middle of a circle, dominating it. Then the king led the party down a path to the right, passing among rows of trees and hedges until they reached what presumably was the herbal garden.

Jason had never really seen an herbal garden back in his father's castle. His father never really liked gardens probably because they were too soothing for his belligerent ways. They had a vegetable garden and formal gardens but no herbal gardens or even a private garden. And his father and half brother rarely, if ever, frequented the formal gardens. So Jason was curious to see what an herbal garden was like.

What he saw on the other side of a small gate was an attractive circular area surrounded by various attractively colored flowering plants and containing a few small benches where people could sit if they chose to. He also saw a group of young women gathered around in a circle and one young woman of about seventeen or eighteen carrying a basket that seemed to contain what must have been freshly picked herbs, all of whom turned around to look at the king, his attendants, and Jason.

The young woman who carried the basket was the one to speak. "Hello, Father," she said. "I presume that the new suitor has just arrived."

"He has," the king said. "Karen, I'd like you to meet Prince Jason of the kingdom of Vindicia. Jason, this is my eldest daughter, Princess Karen."

Prince Jason looked at the princess. She was lovely as well with a very pleasing heart-shaped face and lovely green eyes. Tendrils of golden red hair escaped from underneath her coif. She wore a very lovely green dress and a matching green hat that perched on top of her coif, along with a gauzy veil and brown gloves.

Princess Karen handed her basket to one of her ladies-in-waiting and then curtsied. "It's an honor to meet you, Prince Jason," she said more warmly than Princess Winnifred had greeted him.

Jason bowed. "I'm very pleased to meet you, Your Highness," he said. "I hear you spend your time in the herbal garden."

"I'm an herbalist," Princess Karen explained. "My mother was one as well, and by the time I was seven, I shared her interest in botany. Before she died, she gave me her herbal medicine book, and I've studied it ever since."

Jason was reminded of his mother in that moment. He wished he'd had more time to get to know her. But she apparently shared his love of music, literature, and poetry, something that his father could hardly care less about.

"How old were you when your mother died?" he asked.

"I was eight," Princess Karen said. "Winnifred would have been six and a half years old, and Daria would have been five."

"I was four when my mother passed away," Jason said. "She died in childbirth. She apparently loved music, literature, and poetry, and I'm told that I'm a lot like her."

"You might get along well with my sister Daria," Princess Karen said. "She loves literature and listening to and reading poetry. Well, she loves listening to *good* poetry."

"I met her," Jason said. "And you're right, I do think I'd get along quite well with her. And I like listening to good poetry as well. But my father hates poetry unless it's about his favorite subject—war."

That was when the king said, "So you've now met all my daughters." Then he spoke loudly enough so that those inside the garden and outside it could hear him. "Tonight as customary whenever we have a visitor who is willing to try to figure out where my daughters have been going every night, we shall have a great feast for our guest. After the feast, he will be taken to a chamber that is part of the quarters where the princesses live and is right next to where they sleep, and the door to his chamber will be left open so that nothing might occur without his hearing it. But for now, we shall escort Prince Jason back to the castle and let him settle in."

"I will see you tonight then, Prince Jason," Princess Karen said, curtsying.

"Likewise," Jason said, bowing.

"What will you be doing in the meantime?" the king asked.

"Has Winnifred left our quarters?" the princess asked.

"Yes," the king said. "She is just outside the herbal garden as is Princess Daria."

"Then I'll probably have a couple of my ladies take the basket of herbs that I have picked into the kitchen while the rest of my ladies and I join my sisters," Princess Karen said.

"I shall take my leave of your sisters before I head inside," Jason said.

The king led Jason out of the garden, where the princesses Winnifred and Daria were waiting with their ladies-in-waiting.

"I shall see you tonight at the feast, Princess Winnifred and Princess Daria," Jason told the princesses, bowing to them.

"Very well then," Princess Winnifred said rather coldly.

"I'd be happy to discuss philosophy with you at the feast, Prince Jason," Princess Daria said, curtsying in reply.

"Or maybe we can discuss poetry," Jason said. "Your sister Karen said that you love reading good poetry. Until tonight then."

And with that, Prince Jason and the king took their leave. On the way back to the castle, the king asked, "How do you like my daughters?"

"I'm not that fond of Princess Winnifred," Jason said. "That's mainly because I don't think she likes me. If I solve the mystery, I definitely won't marry her."

The king nodded. "And what about Karen? Or Daria?"

"I like them both," Jason told the king. "I have quite a bit in common with Princess Daria, but I also think I could get along with Princess Karen. I thought I would marry Princess Karen before I came here and met your daughters, but now I think I could marry either her or Princess Daria."

"Well, there is one thing you don't know that I should tell you," the king said. "It might help you make up your mind."

"What is it?" asked Jason.

"I have reason to believe that Karen fell in love with Mark, the gardener who saved Winnifred from molestation," the king explained.

Jason was surprised to hear that. He had yet to hear of a princess who fell in love with a gardener, let alone married one. "And how does he feel about her?" he asked.

"I suspect he reciprocates, but he believes that he is too far below her in station to have a chance with her," the king explained. "He went off to war to try to forget her. So far, he is alive, and he managed to prevent the younger son of an ally of mine, Duke Thomas, from being killed while relieving a besieged city named Jolenz."

Jason contemplated the situation. If Princess Karen was in love with someone else, maybe he should step aside and court Princess Daria instead. Or maybe she would come to like him anyway.

"I'll wait and see," he concluded. "If I solve the mystery, I may have enough time to decide which one of the princesses I prefer. Also, Princess Karen might come to like me."

"That is a good idea," the king said. "You don't have to decide right away."

Jason sighed, relieved by the decision. He decided that he was going to spend time with both Princess Karen and Princess Daria and figure out which one of the two sisters he liked more. If one of the princesses fell in love with him, that would probably settle the matter, especially if only Princess Daria fell in love with him, and Princess Karen remained in love with this guy Mark. If both fell in love with him, however, that would be a very difficult decision since right now he liked both of them in different ways.

But he didn't have to decide right away after all. Hopefully, time would solve the problem for him.

CHAPTER 15

"Happy fifteenth birthday, Daria," Karen told her youngest sister.

Two days ago, the second son of the king of Vindicia, Prince Jason, had arrived in Orgon as a suitor for the hand of one of the princesses. Although the courtiers were naturally a little wary of him since his father was trying to have their kingdom conquered, he was nonetheless well received at the great feast they held that night to welcome him.

Prince Jason sat at the head table along with the king, the princesses, and the most important of their ladies-in-waiting. Since the prince had decided not to try to court Winnifred, he was seated between Daria and Karen, with Winnifred seated some distance away from them both.

As the evening meal progressed, it became apparent to Karen that while Jason was a nice, pleasant prince and while she felt she could get along well enough with him, he just didn't strike any major sparks of interest in her. On the other hand, he was getting along quite well with Daria as the two became engrossed in a discussion of poetry, good and bad, though mostly good. Karen concluded that if Prince Jason was to marry any of them, it was to be her sister Daria.

But Mark was not in a position to solve the mystery, and moreover, the king of Vindicia was still alive and would use his son's efforts as part of a plan to conquer Vindicia. She could not allow Prince Jason to be a pawn in a scheme to conquer Orgon nor to attempt to commit suicide, so the plan was to drug his drink the first night and then either the second or the third night to allow Jason to join them in the faerie realm and have him enchanted until his father was dead and Mark could solve the mystery.

So that night, once Prince Jason and the princesses were ready to go to bed, he was escorted to the antechamber just outside their bedchamber. Karen had Winnifred give him a cup of wine, in which she added three drops of the drug that Alberich had given her. She knew that wine naturally induced sleepiness—that was one reason why she might add herbal potions that calmed people down to wine—and the drug that Alberich gave her would ensure that Prince Jason would sleep throughout the night. She also knew that the drug was tasteless since it had been used on other suitors before him, and they never mentioned any odd taste in the wine.

Sure enough, Prince Jason had become very sleepy and fell fast asleep, and the girls snuck out to dance in the faerie realm or, in Daria's case, to read since she hadn't felt quite ready to dance. The next morning, Winnifred's shoes were worn to pieces as usual, while Daria's and Karen's shoes weren't nearly as worn out.

Prince Jason had been concerned but not unduly alarmed since he still had two more nights to try to solve the mystery. But Karen had to decide whether she should avoid adding the drug to the prince's bedtime drink the second night—last night—or wait until tonight to do so. What ultimately made her decide which night to avoid using the drug was Daria's reminding her that today would be her birthday and that she was feeling comfortable enough that she would probably join in the dance.

That was when Karen decided that she would have Winnifred drug Jason's drink on the second night and not tonight so that Daria would have a chance to dance with Jason. She informed her sisters of her decision, and Daria approved. Winnifred, of course, would rather have the drugged drink given tonight as well, but she was overruled. Also, she was reminded that once Prince Jason was at the faerie castle, he'd be given the enchanted drink of water, and he would stay there as a result. That made Winnifred more willing to let Jason follow them into the faerie realm.

"Thank you," Daria said, smiling. "And tonight I'm going to get a chance to dance the waltz with Jason. I danced with him the first night he came here, but we danced the traditional dances, and none of those allowed me to get anywhere near as close to Jason as I saw Winnifred and even you dance the waltz."

"No, they didn't," Winnifred said, frowning. "I much prefer the waltz to the dances we have at court."

"I wonder how Jason will react to having to dance so closely to me," Daria said. "Or how *I* will react to dancing so closely to him. That's one reason why I didn't want to dance the waltz until now."

"We'll have to explain to him all about the waltz," Karen said. "I know it was hard for me to get used to dancing so closely to a guy, especially one I wasn't in love with, but I got used to it. It might be easier for Jason if he dances with you since I think he'd get along better with you than with me. You have more in common with him than I do. Besides, while I don't know whether I struck any major sparks of interest in him, I *do* know that he struck none with me."

"Yes," Daria said. "I think Father noticed it too since he had me partner Jason that night and not you. Incidentally, Jason spoke to me just before I joined the two of you."

"What did he say?" Karen asked. She assumed he was getting very nervous. After all, tonight was the last night for him to have a chance at success, and the last thing he wanted was to return home in disgrace or maybe return home at all.

"He was becoming extremely nervous and upset," Daria said. "I think he suspects that his drink was drugged these past two nights."

"Why do you think that?" Karen asked, becoming a little nervous herself.

"Because he asked me if I had slipped a drug into his drink," Daria explained. "I told him that I didn't."

"No," Karen said. "That's because *I* slipped the drug into it, not you. And I had Winnifred give it to him."

"He seemed to accept my denial fortunately," Daria said. "But he might suspect that I know about the drug in the drink, which I do, of course."

"Yes," Winnifred said. "If it wasn't for the fact that Prince Jason's going to be enchanted anyway, I'd push for his drink to be drugged tonight."

"I know," Karen said, "just as I know you'd rather not have the secret come out. But trust me, even after the secret comes out, you're going to stay in the faerie realm and dance there forever. That's the only way to keep you safe from the consequences of your own foolishness."

"Karen doesn't need the protection," Daria added. "And I don't need as much protection as you do. But for now, Jason needs more protection than even you do."

"Yes," Karen said. "So tonight he'll follow us into the faerie realm, and he'll stay there until his father is dead and until Mark solves the mystery. Then he'll be free to leave—hopefully with you, Daria."

Daria smiled a little shyly at that. That was when Karen noticed that their ladies-in-waiting and a minstrel who had been trailing behind them at a discreet distance as they walked through the formal gardens were coming closer. "Maybe we should have the minstrel sing us a ballad," Karen said, changing the subject. Daria and Winnifred both looked confused for a moment, and then they seemed to understand, for they both nodded. Karen turned to the minstrel. "Why don't you sing us a nice ballad while most of us do embroidery and Daria does some reading along with maybe a bit of simple sewing?"

Daria looked relieved. She wasn't exactly a great weaver, not as good as her sisters and nowhere near as good as the ladies who attended all three of them. Daria could sew simple stuff, but intricate embroidery was beyond her. So when most of the ladies and her sisters did embroidery, Daria did a few easy stitches of sewing and spent the rest of her time reading.

The minstrel nodded. Karen gestured to Lily, Elke (who had obtained a place in Daria's household), and one of Winnifred's ladies-in-waiting, all of whom came up with baskets. They each took out a plush velvet cushion and placed it on the best seats for the princesses' comfort. Karen took her seat, her basket of embroidery beside her, and was followed by Winnifred, who also had a basket of embroidery, and Daria, who had a simple bit of needlework and a book in her basket. Once they took their seats, the ladies took theirs and got out their own needlework.

The minstrel struck a chord and lifted his voice in song. Karen was a little surprised that the song wasn't a ballad. Instead, it seemed to be a song that urged women not to be so upset when a man proved to be inconstant, suggesting that all men were like this. She wasn't sure whether this was meant to vilify men (after all, she didn't believe that *all* men were faithless) or to excuse them by suggesting they couldn't help being unfaithful because they were men. But when the song urged them to convert misery into a cheery and pleasant attitude, she smiled in understanding. She had to do that when Mark left for the war after all. Still smiling, she took out her needlework and began work on a piece of embroidery for a sleeve.

*   *   *

Jason was becoming desperate. This was the third night, and if he failed to uncover the secret of where the princesses went every night, he'd have to return home in disgrace. The king may have been trying to be humane (and pragmatic) when he decided not to have the failed suitors beheaded, but Jason almost wished that the king *would* behead him just so Jason wouldn't have to return home.

The first night, he was given a bedtime drink by Princess Winnifred, who was wearing a pale blue dressing robe over what was probably a shift; and after drinking it, she left him, and he was alone in the antechamber just outside the princesses' bedroom, with the door unlocked and left slightly open so that they could not slip past him without knowing it. But soon after he was left alone, he suddenly began feeling tired—no, not just tired but *exhausted*.

He tried to keep his eyes open, tried to remain awake. But it was no use. His eyelids were like leaden weights, and soon he succumbed to exhaustion and fell asleep. The next thing he knew, morning had come. Alarmed, he alerted the ladies who attended the princesses, and they woke the princesses long enough to check their shoes. That was when he saw the magnificent dresses that had apparently been given to them before the nightly escapades began. As for the shoes that accompanied the dresses, while neither Princess Karen nor Princess Daria's shoes had been significantly worn, Princess Winnifred's shoes had huge holes in them.

He'd failed. The first time, he chalked up the failure to being tired from the long journey from the port to the castle where the king and princesses lived. Since the princesses didn't come down from their quarters until it was almost noon, he spent the morning learning as much as he could about Princess Karen and Princess Daria from their father.

Once Princess Karen and Princess Daria came down, he spent a large part of the afternoon with Princess Daria in the library, discussing literature and poetry. Daria's vast knowledge of faerie lore really impressed him, and while she wasn't quite as interested in poetry unless it was part of a ballad about faeries, she was interested enough that they had a stimulating discussion of poetry.

Jason was really bonding with Daria to the extent that he was less interested in marrying her sister Karen than he had been when he first arrived. So the second night—last night—he had high hopes of succeeding where three before him had failed and getting the chance to marry one of the princesses, most likely Princess Daria. Now that he had recovered from the long journey, he was confident that he would not fall asleep.

But the same thing happened last night. He drank the bedtime drink that Princess Winnifred gave him before she retired with her sisters, and once again, he quickly became very sleepy soon afterward, trying to keep his eyes open before finally succumbing to exhaustion. And the next thing he knew, it was morning, and Princess Winnifred's shoes were once again worn out.

That was when Jason began to suspect that perhaps the princesses had drugged his drink. He didn't want to think that Daria had been the one to drug it, so he asked her. She denied it, and he thought she was probably telling the truth to an extent. But was she telling the entire truth? Did she know about the drugged drink?

He didn't want to think she knew about it, but he had to admit to himself that she probably did. That said, it was more likely that one of her sisters put a drug in his drink, probably Karen since she was the one who was interested in herbal medicine and might have known how to concoct a sleeping draft. Still, he suspected that Daria knew about the drink, and that worried him. Did she not want to marry him? He hoped that wasn't the reason behind her allowing him to be drugged.

But whatever the reason was, he was determined not to make the same mistake two nights in a row. So tonight after the princesses retired from the great hall and went upstairs, he followed them and their ladies. Once they were in their quarters, the princesses were taken inside the bedchamber, and the door was closed so that Jason could not see the princesses being undressed. One of them carried a goblet of wine that one of the princesses would give to Jason before going to bed.

Sometime later, the ladies-in-waiting exited the princesses' bedchamber. Not long thereafter, Princess Winnifred came out with the drink, most likely drugged. He accepted it, waited until the princess retired, and then looked for a place to dump the drink. The only place he could find was inside the lining of his velvet cloak, so he dumped the drink into the lining, sat down on the chair, and waited for about several minutes before pretending to snore.

Not long thereafter, he heard Princess Winnifred exclaim, "He fell asleep! He actually fell asleep!"

He heard a second voice, probably that of Princess Karen, but it was very low, so he couldn't really hear the words. Soon thereafter, he heard sounds of the princesses moving about, so he opened the door a little bit more and peeked inside.

The princesses had gone to a huge wardrobe and opened it. As they did so, a dazzling light suddenly appeared, and Jason involuntarily looked away. When the light faded, he looked back.

The princesses were now dressed in the most magnificent dresses he'd ever seen in his life. In fact, the dresses were *too* magnificent for any human hands to weave. Indeed, they made Jason's clothing, although rich enough, look rather dingy.

The princesses looked over their reflections in the mirror before Princess Karen went to her bed and clapped her hands three times. The bed immediately sank into the floor, and a trapdoor opened under it. The princesses got into a line, with Princess Karen first, Princess Winnifred second, and Princess Daria third.

Jason quickly slipped into the room and crept up behind the princesses as they descended through the opening. He followed Daria down a spiral staircase deep into the earth, trying to make as little noise as possible. After all, he didn't have an invisibility cloak, and he didn't want to be seen by them.

When he reached the bottom, he followed the princesses through an underground passageway sparkling with gems. He couldn't help but look around in amazement. Finally, he emerged into a grove of trees that surrounded a long roadway. He followed the princesses through the roadway, looking in awe at the silvery leaves shining in the darkness.

Jason was even more amazed when the roadway led him into a grove with trees that now had leaves that apparently were of the purest gold since they were reddish yellow in color and then through trees with bright, shining leaves like diamonds. He had never seen trees like these before. And to think that the princesses had probably been traveling down this road every night!

Finally, the trees ended, and Jason emerged to find himself standing near the shore of a huge lake. He saw the princesses approach three boats, each of which contained an extremely handsome young man who stepped out to help each princess aboard. Jason knew he had to follow the princesses. But he didn't want to be seen by them. It was obvious to him that they had taken great pains to conceal their activities not only from their father but also from any young man who might discover their secret after all.

That was when Jason's eyes fell onto a fourth boat a little off to the side. It didn't have anybody in it, so as soon as the other three boats set off across the lake, he ran to the fourth boat and got in it. He saw two oars for rowing purposes, so after he loosened the rope that held it to shore, he rowed behind the princesses.

It seemed to take a very long time to cross the lake, and a mist seemed to hang over it, blocking Jason's view. But finally, the mist lifted, and he saw the most dazzling palace, one that made his father's castle and the Orgonian king's look quite dingy in comparison. He was beginning to see why the princesses needed such magnificent gowns as clothing like his own probably looked even dingier in such a magnificent setting.

Jason was both amazed and excited. This trip was like nothing he'd ever experienced. And hopefully, the trip into the faerie realm would result in his successful return and claiming of a bride, probably the Princess Daria.

* * *

Jason had stopped rowing when the boats in front of him pulled up at the dock one by one. He knew he had to stay hidden if he wanted to return safely to the mortal realm without being seen by any of the princesses, especially Princess Winnifred. She was the one most likely to want to get rid of him permanently.

Thus, he watched as first Princess Karen, then Princes Winnifred, and finally Princess Daria arrived at the dock and were helped off by their escorts. When Daria was helped off, that was when the escort looked back toward Jason. His heart stopped in that instant. Had he been spotted after all? What would happen to him if he *had* been seen?

Then the escort turned away with an apparently careless shrug, and Jason relaxed. As the princesses were escorted up toward the castle, Jason slowly rowed his boat toward the dock, trying his best to avoid making any noise. Eventually, he made it to the dock and stepped off the boat. Now he tied the boat carefully before looking up to see the princesses ahead of him, going slowly up the stairway past terraced gardens that were as lovely as the castle itself.

Jason ran on tiptoes up the stairway, only stopping when he was a couple of steps behind Daria. He didn't want to tread on her gown and let her know he was following her after all. He followed the princesses up the stairway to the top of the hill where the castle stood and then into a huge courtyard where a tall blond man stood wearing the most magnificent doublet and breeches that Jason had ever seen. Glittering with gold and precious jewels of every size and color, they made Jason's doublet look even dingier.

"Welcome back, Princesses," the blond man said.

"We're happy to be here, Prince Alberich," Princess Karen said, identifying the host. He seemed to take no notice of Jason but instead turned on his heel and led the princesses and their escorts toward the main building.

Jason quietly followed, feeling a tiny bit envious over the magnificence of this Prince Alberich's outfit. The next moment, however, he realized that since the outfits of both Prince Alberich and the escorts for the princesses were almost as magnificent as the gowns for the princesses, he'd probably be less likely to be noticed since who'd notice a guy dressed in an outfit that looked so dingy when compared with such magnificent clothes?

When Jason entered into the main building, he was even more amazed at the magnificence of the interior. He looked around as he followed Prince Alberich, the escorts, and the princesses toward a pair of magnificent double doors, which opened at their approach. Once Prince Alberich, the escorts, and the princesses were all inside, Jason quietly stepped in; and when he took one look at the magnificence of the ballroom and of the clothes of the people inside, he knew that he was severely underdressed for the occasion.

Feeling rather self-conscious, he slipped into a corner and watched as Prince Alberich took Princess Karen's hand and Princess Winnifred's escort took her hand before both men led the two out onto the dance floor. Romantic, unfamiliar music began to play, and Jason watched in amazement and shock as the men on the dance floor drew the women close, clasped their arms around the waists of the women, and began turning around the dance floor.

But the biggest shock for Jason was yet to come. For as soon as the dance was over, he heard a low feminine voice say, "I was pretty shocked when I first saw this dance as well, Prince Jason."

Turning, he saw Princess Daria, giving him a smile almost as dazzling as her gown.

*　　*　　*

Before the sisters went down into the faerie realm, Karen had agreed that Daria should be the one to inform Jason of the peril he was in and to offer him a way out through enchantment. That was why Daria, as soon as she spotted him in the corner, approached him when the first dance was over.

Jason stuttered, "D-d-did you know I was behind you and your sisters?"

"I'll tell you soon enough," Daria promised, "*after* I help you learn how to dance this dance, that is, if you're willing to dance with me."

"What kind of dance *is* it?" Jason asked, extending his hand as an indication of his willingness to dance with Daria.

"It's called a waltz," Daria explained, taking Jason's hand and leading him toward the dance floor. "It's not going to be popular in the mortal world for some time, probably years after we're both gone. I watched the faeries and my sisters do it, and I have learned the steps and the timing, but I've never done it before. I may be clumsy."

Jason smiled at that. "I may be rather clumsy as well," he admitted.

They walked out onto the dance floor, and as the first strains of romantic, moody, eerie music played, Jason drew Daria in his arms; and as Daria began counting the beat for Jason, they began dancing to the music. Everything began shifting around them. Slowly, Daria stopped counting the beat as she looked up at Jason, and he looked down at her. Time seemed to slow down in that moment. She noticed how pretty his blue eyes were and wondered if he thought her own gray eyes were pretty as well.

Slowly, their awkward steps blossomed into a lovely and graceful waltz, but Daria barely noticed it. All she noticed was Jason, until she heard the music slow down. Their steps slowed and ended just as the last beat finished.

Daria heard Jason say, "At least I didn't step on your feet."

Daria chuckled a little at that and said, "No, you didn't."

They danced several more times without speaking except for Daria counting the beat. Gradually, the two became more and more confident in their dancing skill. Finally, Jason spoke. "I might not have learned this dance at court, but I learned how to dance, and I guess dancing skills never fade, even if you have to learn a different dance."

"Yes," Daria said, smiling up at him. "My sister Winnifred might not agree, but I'm kind of glad you're here dancing with me."

"I wouldn't have been able to be here if I hadn't—" Jason hesitated for a moment and then shrugged and said, "If I hadn't disposed of your drink. It was drugged, right?"

This was the time to tell him. Daria knew it now. So she took a deep breath and said, "That one wasn't. But the ones before the final drink Winnifred gave you were drugged."

* * *

Somehow Jason was no longer really surprised that the world had shifted under his feet once again. Until this moment, he had thought he had outsmarted the princesses by pouring what he thought was a drugged drink into the lining of his cloak. But if the drink had never been drugged, had he actually outsmarted himself?

"Why was the final drink that your sister Winnifred gave to me not drugged?" he asked.

Daria took a deep breath and then explained everything about how his father was going to use the arranged marriage to launch a secret attack on Orgon in an attempt to conquer it. Apparently, this Prince Alberich had allies among the faerie troop living underneath

Vindicia who told him everything about his father's plans, and he had, in turn, told the three princesses everything.

"So Prince Alberich, Karen, and I came up with a plan to both save our kingdom and prevent you from possibly committing suicide either in a determined attempt not to return to your kingdom or in an equally determined attempt to mess with your father's plans once you learned about them," Daria explained. "That plan is to submit to an enchantment that would keep you here until after your father is gone. If you stay here, enchanted, Alberich has learned that your father will travel to the troops that are currently in Orgon, relieve your brother, and lead the troops into a battle that will ultimately end with his death. And during that one, the young man whom my sister Karen loves will be wounded but not fatally. It will take him a long time to recover, however, and when he does, he will learn the secret, and you will be able to return to your home, with your father gone and your brother hopefully being wise enough to stop the invasion even before you return. And even if he doesn't, your return will end the invasion for good."

Jason reflected on all this for a moment. The faeries were acting to save Orgon and Jason himself at the same time. And Daria and Karen were the faeries' willing allies in this matter. He wasn't all that surprised to find out what his father's plans were had he succeeded, and he privately admitted that if he had found out they were before this point, he probably would have dropped the whole scheme and confronted his father possibly so his father could kill him, and Jason would finally be free, even if it was through death.

But this plan might be better for all involved. If he submitted to an enchantment and stayed in the faerie realm and if this Prince Alberich was telling the truth, he'd not only be physically safe but his father would also be killed in battle, and his brother would be king. Hopefully, his brother would be a better king than his father ever was. Moreover, until the spell was broken, he might have the chance to dance with Daria every night.

The moment that Jason had taken Daria into his arms so he could waltz with her, he felt something tingle down his spine, and he involuntarily held her a little more tightly. Then they began to waltz, and at that moment, he felt like everything was whirling around him, and he was dancing on the edge of . . . something. If he didn't look into Daria's pretty gray eyes and looked around instead, if he let her go, if he stopped dancing, he might go spinning into space.

That, more than any other motive, was what led Jason to ask, "If I submit to the enchantment, will you keep dancing with me?"

Daria smiled at that. "Of course. Every night I'll come and dance with you. You're the first male whom I've come to like enough that I'd be pleased to marry."

Jason took a breath in relief. "You'll find out my answer at the end of the night," he told her. He had a feeling that was when he'd have to choose to submit to the enchantment or not. But already, he was beginning to believe that he would. "In the meantime, why don't we dance some more?" he asked.

"I'd be happy to," Daria said, her gray eyes shining.

Jason escorted her out onto the dance floor, and the night passed in a whirlwind of excitement and happiness. He didn't speak much to Daria, but he didn't need to. The way she looked up at him, the way they danced together, the way her hand felt, so warm and soft in his own—that said far more than words ever could.

Finally, Jason heard Prince Alberich announce that Princess Winnifred's shoes were all worn out with dancing, and thus the princesses had to return home. Jason turned to Daria and asked her, "How are you feeling?"

Daria glanced down at her shoes and said, "I think they're actually rather worn, maybe not worn through like Winnifred's are but certainly worn out enough that I'm kind of glad the dancing's over."

That was when attendants came forward and began handing out goblets to the guests as Prince Alberich announced, "And while we were here, I'd like to reveal that we have a special guest who joined us for the evening. So when it's time to make a toast, we should give a toast to Prince Jason of the kingdom of Vindicia!"

That was when an attendant gave Daria a goblet and handed Jason another. Jason took a look at it and was relieved to see that it held clear water. If a mortal ate any faerie food or drank anything other than clear water, that mortal was bound to the faerie realm and would have to remain here for a certain amount of time, maybe forever.

"Does your goblet have only water in it?" Jason asked Daria.

"Of the four of us mortals, only Winnifred has wine in her goblet," Daria explained. "She belongs to the faeries. It's best for her, you see. But the rest of us have only drank clear water."

At the same time, there was an odd look in Daria's eyes as if she wanted to convey something to him but wasn't sure how to. Then she glanced at his goblet, and Jason looked at the clear water inside. When he looked up at Daria, she nodded—and then he *knew*.

The goblet might not have held wine, but the water was still enchanted. And Jason somehow realized that if he drank from it, he'd stay in this realm for an unspecified amount of time. He wouldn't return to the mortal world for a good long while. But if it gave him the chance to dance with Daria nightly during that time—and if it would ensure that, eventually, he'd be able to start a new life once his father was hopefully gone for good—then letting himself be enchanted would be worth it.

So when Prince Alberich offered the toast, "To Prince Jason!" Jason lifted his goblet, clinked it with Daria's own, steeled himself inwardly, and drank.

CHAPTER 16

Prince Christopher was surprised to see his father riding into the Vindician campsite and his half brother, Victor, right behind the king. King Godfrey had given command of the invading Vindician forces to him so he could prove himself on the battlefield, and Christopher had accepted the command mainly to get away from his father.

He had been initially successful, taking control of a town in Orgon and using it as his base of operations. However, efforts to gain more territory proved largely fruitless. The Orgonians had proved to be very efficient defenders to the point that Christopher believed that the faeries were helping the Orgonians. But whenever he tried to suggest the possibility to his father in a missive, all he got was angry denials of the possibility and an insistence that his troops or Christopher's leadership itself was incompetent.

Thus, Christopher was relieved when he learned that his brother, Prince Jason, suggested the idea of peace by an arranged marriage between Jason and one of the daughters of the king of Vindicia, preferably the eldest—if Jason could solve the mystery of where they went every night and why the shoes of one of the princesses, named Winnifred, were worn out every night. Almost two months ago, Prince Jason went to the kingdom of Orgon to solve the mystery; but two nights in a row, he fell asleep and was unable to determine where the princesses went or why Princess Winnifred's shoes were all worn out. He was then left in the antechamber outside their bedroom for the third night, as he had been for the previous two nights, but the next morning, Jason was apparently not in the antechamber, nor was he in the princesses' bedroom.

Christopher didn't know many of the details. However, he *did* know that the king of Orgon had sent out an extensive search party to find Jason. His disappearance worried Christopher since he was fond of his brother, and they were fairly close. Had Jason been abducted? If so, was someone in the castle party to the abduction?

Christopher didn't know. But maybe his father had more details. Maybe that was why he was here.

When the king and his half brother dismounted from their horses and the horses were led away, Christopher approached his father. "Do you know anything more about what happened to Jason?" he asked.

"The king of Orgon sent a messenger to the court a week ago," King Godfrey said. "The message from the king was that search parties had searched for Jason everywhere, even among the Orgonian troops, but there was no sign of him. The king also spoke to his daughters."

"And?" Christopher asked.

"And the eldest princess apparently said that the faeries had him," his father said, snorting. "She also apparently insisted that he was unharmed."

Christopher was unsure whether to be relieved or to be even more worried. He didn't know if the eldest princess was telling the truth, either about the faeries having Jason or about him being unharmed. And even if she was telling the truth about both matters, he strongly suspected that the princesses had a hand in his abduction. And if they did, why? Was it for a benevolent purpose? Or was it for a malicious one? And if it was for the latter, were the princesses willing parties to the malicious purpose, or were they under an enchantment and being controlled by the faeries?

"You sound like you don't believe the report," Christopher said cautiously.

"I don't," his father said. "I believe the king had him secretly arrested and put under guard just because he's my son."

Christopher wasn't so sure of that. He thought it more likely that the eldest princess was lying about Jason being unharmed. But he knew from past experience that it was futile to argue with his father, at least if he was convinced of something.

"Are you absolutely convinced that the king had actually imprisoned Jason and was using the faeries as a scapegoat?" he asked tentatively.

"I'm positive on it," his father said. "And that's why I'm here. I believe that you're not ruthless enough to be an effective military commander, or you're too incompetent. Therefore, I will be sending you back home, and *I* will be taking charge of the forces here."

Christopher was rather relieved. He didn't really want to be invading another kingdom, and the only reason why he was in charge of the invasion forces, other than wanting to get away from his father, was that the king had decided to stay home for once. His father was getting older, and he might have been suffering from arthritis of some kind since he'd been complaining about pain in his knees a couple of months before deciding to have Christopher be in charge of the invading army. But now his father was in charge, and Christopher could go back home, away from his father.

"What about Victor?" he asked.

"Victor has just turned twelve, and I believe it is time for him to begin his career as a soldier," the king explained.

"I hope this military campaign isn't his last one," Christopher said.

"It won't be," Victor, a blond like his father and half brother Jason, said.

"I want all the senior officers to meet with me and Victor in your tent," his father added. "We'll discuss war strategy here. And tomorrow you will be free to return home, Christopher."

Christopher sighed in relief. At least he had to endure his father's presence one day before returning home. And with any luck, his father would be just as unsuccessful at conquering Orgon as Christopher himself was.

* * *

Mark was among the infantrymen who stood in position behind trenches in front of a derelict castle near Jolenz, which had been previously occupied by the Vindician troops when they tried and failed to capture the city. It had been a little over a month since the Orgonian troops had learned from the faerie scout that King Godfrey of Vindicia had arrived to take command of the Vindician troops and had displaced Crown Prince Christopher, who had been the previous commander. During the time that the crown prince had been in command, the Vindician troops had managed to gain some territory, but it was minimal at best and never near any significant cities or towns. This was partly due to the effectiveness of the faerie scout and partly due to the crown prince not being very aggressive as a military leader.

However, King Godfrey was far more aggressive than his eldest son; and thus, General Nicholas had to prepare an aggressive strategy to prevent the king from making any more territorial gains. The faerie scout had discovered that the Vindician troops were headed toward the city of Jolenz, so General Nicholas went with the troops under his command, including Mark, to intercept King Godfrey's troops before they could reach the castle and attempt to use it for a second siege. The Orgonian troops were successful in reaching the castle first and set up a fortified camp behind it while digging trenches in front to protect it from the Vindician troops, as well as a field fortification called an abatis, which was an obstacle formed by the branches of trees laid in a row, with the sharpened tips directed toward the enemy and interlaced with wire to trip up the enemy. Repeatedly, the king of Vindicia rode out of his camp and challenged General Nicholas to come out of his fortified camp. Wisely, the general always refused.

Then the night before, the faerie scout apparently reported to General Nicholas that the supply situation for the Vindician troops was worsening and that King Godfrey was getting desperate enough that he was planning to attack the Orgonian camp the next day— today. As a result, General Nicholas apparently prepared his military strategy with his commanding officers. The plan, as Mark had learned from his superior officer, was for the infantry to fire from the trenches and make sure that the abatis would stymie the Vindician advance. The cavalry would be kept in reserve and ensure that the Vindician troops would have no chance of success.

So Mark was prepared with other infantrymen on the right wing of the Orgonian army behind the trenches, waiting for the first sign of an attack from the Vindician troops. There was a guard on the ramparts of the ruined castle who would be the lookout. A series of trumpet blasts would announce that the enemy was moving toward the castle to attack it.

Suddenly, Mark heard a series of trumpet blasts. He looked back toward the ruined castle and thought he saw the trumpeter on top of the ramparts blowing. The Vindician army must be moving forward. Hopefully, the abatis and the trenches would be sufficient to stop their advance.

He then heard the sounds of men charging up the hill toward the castle and the trenches and abatis that were waiting. Mark steeled himself. It was time to fight.

*   *   *

King Godfrey watched his infantrymen charge up the hill from his position atop his trusted steed. He had no doubt that, under his aggressive leadership, his men would easily overwhelm the Orgonian fools and take control of the castle. However, his men then encountered the abatis that was being used to defend the castle, as well as intense fire from the Orgonian defenders. The abatis stymied his men's advance, along with the defense by the Orgonians, and many of his men were being killed or merely wounded as a result.

Things were clearly *not* going the way that he hoped would happen. He had to conquer Orgon, to avenge the imprisonment of his son Jason, and to satisfy his desire for military glory. Maybe if he personally led the next wave of attack, things would go better for his men.

Much to his dismay, his trusted lieutenants all advised him to let someone else lead the second wave as he was not only the leader of the Vindician troops but also the king; and if he died, the whole invasion would probably fall into chaos. But he insisted on doing it himself, and his men finally yielded, seeing how determined he was. Accordingly, he chose to send most of the cavalry into battle, even if they had to dismount their horses to do so. He also wanted to have his son Victor be part of the second wave. But this time, the lieutenants all threatened to mutiny if he did so, insisting that they could not allow a mere boy risk death by being part of the second wave of attack, even if he was now twelve years old. So he agreed to have him be part of the cavalry reserve.

The second wave was formed, and the king personally led the charge. He was going to do his very best to lead his men through the abatis and take the castle. He took his sword and did his best to hack his way through the branches of trees that created the abatis. As he was hacking his way, however, a bullet tore into his right shoulder, and he dropped his sword. But he was unwilling to retreat and leave the battle to his second-in-command, so he picked up the sword with his left hand and did his best to continue hacking through the tree branches.

But just as he emerged from the branches to face the trenches, a second shot tore into the muscles of his right knee. He fell to the ground, and as he did so, he saw that the shooter was a young man not much older than his second son and maybe about the same age as his first one. He had to keep fighting. Even if he died, he had to keep fighting. He began crawling toward the enemy lines, yelling at his men to keep fighting, when the young infantryman from Orgon apparently fired a second time.

* * *

Mark watched as the injured soldier fell to the ground after being hit in the temple. He didn't know who this man was, but whoever he was, he was very defiant and aggressive. Another soldier emerged from the abatis right behind the first soldier. Mark took aim and fired, hitting the second soldier in the right shoulder.

As this was going on, he heard the sound of a trumpet blast. It distracted him just long enough for the second soldier to lift his musket with his left hand, aim, and fire at Mark. The bullet hit Mark just above his left shoulder. He could tell where it hit by the pain he felt.

Mark fell to the ground, deciding on the spot that it would be best to at least pretend to pass out and hoping that, if the Orgonian calvary was sent out, no horses would trample him. But as he looked at the ground he lay on, suddenly, it began to shift around him and apparently dissolve in a multitude of colors. Then he suddenly felt very lightheaded and dizzy. Mark closed his eyes and passed out for real.

* * *

This was rather strange. Mark was back in the herbal garden where he once worked, on Duke Thomas's estate. Apparently, enough time had passed that it was now night, and moonlight illuminated the garden. And there, with her back turned to him, was Princess Karen. But her back was turned only for a moment, for the next instant, she turned, smiled at him, and walked over to him.

Mark couldn't resist the temptation to take the princess into his arms and hold her very close. She looked up at him and smiled, and he found himself bending his head so he could kiss her. But the next instant, a strange multicolored light seemed to surround them both. Suddenly, he felt Princess Karen being wrenched from his embrace. Mark tried to reach her, but he was being held back by some force. As he struggled, Princess Karen's screams were in his ears.

That was when Mark's eyes flew open, and he woke up with a start, pain radiating from his left shoulder. The whole thing had just been a dream. What a relief!

Mark sighed just as a young man with fair hair came to his side. "Are you all right, sir?" the young man asked him.

"Other than this bullet in my left shoulder, I'm all right," Mark said.

"Lie back down then," the young man said. "The doctors are going to see if they can remove the bullet from your left shoulder after you're transported to the former monastery in Jolenz."

As Mark lay back down, he looked around him. He was inside a tent, most likely the tent used for temporary housing of wounded soldiers before their being taken to a monastery where monks and nuns who were trained in herbal medicine would take care of them. He could see wounded men being brought in by various officers. The battle must be over since the men would not be collected from the battlefield until after hostilities ceased.

"How . . . how long was I unconscious?" he asked.

"Not more than three hours, I believe," the young blond man said. "The battle's over, and soldiers from our side are bringing in wounded men they found on the battlefield and some dead ones too."

"How . . . how did I wind up in here?" Mark asked.

"Well, this multicolored light suddenly appeared on the pallet where you're currently resting," the young fair-haired man said. "When I checked it out, the multicolored light suddenly coalesced into a distinct figure. And when it disappeared, you were lying on the pallet. I could see that you were wounded, so I went to work cleaning the wound as best I could and bandaging it. I'm glad I was able to get to work on it right away. The wound might have become worse had you been out there while the battle was going on."

Mark thought about what the fair-haired man had said about the ground shifting and dissolving in a multitude of colors just before losing consciousness. He must have been transported to the tent by magical means, possibly by faerie magic.

"You said that the battle is over," Mark said. "How did it go for us?"

"It was a decisive victory for us," the young man treating him said. "The Orgonian cavalry apparently was able to cut down a number of the exhausted Vindician troops while others were shot down by our infantrymen. But you were one of three hundred Orgonians whom we found wounded on the battlefield, and at least seventy are dead."

"I wonder how many Vindician troops were killed or wounded," said Mark. "I know I shot at least two of them and may have killed one of those."

"You did," a vaguely familiar voice said. Looking up, Mark saw that General Nicholas had entered the tent and was now looking down on Mark.

Mark asked, "What happened after I passed out? The last thing I remember was being hit in the left shoulder by a man I wounded shortly after shooting and possibly killing this belligerent officer, falling to the ground, and then apparently being transported here. I passed out during the last part."

"Our cavalry was able to cut down many of the exhausted Vindician cavalrymen once they made it past the abatis," the field general explained. "After that second attack, we found a badly wounded Vindician cavalryman trying to drag a corpse into the abatis. When we caught up to the officer, he said that he was going to bring his ruler's body back to his countrymen, even if it killed him."

Mark was stunned by what the field general said. "The king of Vindicia is *dead*?" he asked.

"When we cut the officer down, we retrieved the corpse and took it with us behind our own lines. We then sent a messenger to the Vindician side to announce the possible death of their ruler and ask them to halt hostilities while they identified the body. They sent the youngest son of the king to identify the corpse, along with the commander of the artillery. They both confirmed that the body the cavalryman was trying to drag back was indeed that of the king of Vindicia. Also, one of the infantrymen beside you witnessed the identification and told me later that you had shot the king in the right knee and then in the temple," the field general said.

"So *I* killed the king of Vindicia?" Mark asked in understandable amazement.

"It appears that you did so," the field general confirmed. "I didn't identify you as the soldier who shot the king to his son or the commander of the Vindician artillery. But that was before I found out that you were the soldier responsible or that you had been injured. We are going to do our very best to ensure that you recover as fully as possible. A hero like you should be given the very best medical treatment possible, even if it means you have to leave the military for good."

Mark was still reeling from all that had happened. While he was thrilled that the battle had been a decisive victory for the Orgonians, the fact that he, a commoner, had shot and killed a king, even if it was in defense of his homeland, was still something that he had yet to fully accept. It would probably take time for him to do so.

"What is going to be done with the body of the former king of Vindicia?" asked Mark.

"We are going to keep his armor as a trophy, but the rest of his clothing and his gold jewelry were left on the corpse," said the field general. "Representatives for the king's second-in-command took the corpse back to their lines, and I believe they are going to take the king's corpse to be cleaned, embalmed, and then brought in solemn procession back to the capital. We are going to have some of our men follow the processional to make sure they get the corpse back to Vindician territory."

"I hope the new king doesn't hate us for killing his father," Mark said.

"I hope not either," said the field general. "But I have heard he is more reasonable than his father ever was. In the meantime, you are going to be transported to the former monastery in the city of Jolenz, where the best medical care will be given to you. And hopefully, the doctors will be able to get the bullet out of your left shoulder."

Mark smiled a little at the news. "I'm glad to hear that," he told the field general.

"We have also sent a message to the king informing him of the outcome of the battle," the field general informed him. "And the princesses will probably also learn what happened."

Mark couldn't help but wonder how Princess Karen would take the news. He knew that she was in love with him, and while he might be alive and out of danger for the most part, he was still wounded, and there was the possibility that he might become ill or that the wound would become infected. Or even both things might happen. Or had he been away for so long that she had forgotten all about him? Had absence made her heart go elsewhere?

*   *   *

"I don't understand why you're so upset, Karen," Princess Winnifred said as she and her sisters neared the end of the grove of diamond trees. "Mark is merely a commoner after all. And his interference caused Francis to be executed."

Princess Karen was beginning to lose her patience with her sister Winnifred. Ever since a messenger arrived earlier that day with news of the death of the Vindician king and the deaths and injuries of about three hundred Orgonian soldiers, she was seriously anxious since Mark, the young man she still loved and wanted to be with, had been wounded. Although the messenger believed that Mark would recover fully from his injuries, Karen was still very upset.

Both the king and Princess Daria were sympathetic toward Karen, even if Daria was sometimes awkward in showing her sympathy. But Winnifred was still fuming over Mark's interference in the amorous meeting between her and Francis and wasn't really sympathetic. Karen tried to remind herself that Winnifred lacked common sense, but her anxiety over Mark's safety was making it more difficult for her to remain patient.

"Karen loves him, Winnifred," Daria then said. "You know that as well as I do. You must understand that Mark was merely trying to protect you from a liaison that could have caused a serious scandal."

"And it could have cost you your life, Winnifred, had you married King Henry," Karen reminded her sister as they reached the end of the grove and emerged at the edge of the lake. "Adultery in a queen consort or the wife of the crown prince is considered high treason. Had Francis become your lover after you married King Henry or remained your lover after your marriage, you probably would have been executed as a traitor. And Francis was just using you for social advancement. Mark wasn't trying to ruin your fun. He was trying to *protect* you from a predator!"

This was about as close to losing her temper as Karen had probably ever come, and it seemed to work as Winnifred became extremely pale. Karen sighed and said, "I'm sorry I had to be so blunt, but your attitude toward Mark annoyed me."

Winnifred merely nodded and allowed herself to be led to the boats, which took them to Prince Alberich's castle without further incident. Once they got inside the castle and met Alberich, Karen immediately asked, "How is Mark?"

"He will recover fully from his injuries," Alberich said. "The faerie scout I sent to the Orgonian forces will be able to remove the bullet with magical means. That said, he will be laid low with a fever for a time, and there will be temporary paralysis in his left arm and hand. But within eleven months, he will be fully recovered from his injuries."

Karen felt weak with relief. "I'm glad to hear that," she said. "I still love him, even though it's been so long since I saw him. I wonder if he still feels the same way."

"He does," Alberich reassured her. "Now let's forget all about this unfortunate situation for a time and enjoy ourselves with the dance."

Karen agreed, took Alberich's arm, and let him lead her into the ballroom, where the evening passed as it usually did, with Karen dancing a relatively limited number of dances before sitting down on a chair in the ballroom and watching the other dances. At one point, Karen noticed Daria dancing with Jason and was reminded of the death of the king of Vindicia. When Alberich came off the dance floor to check up on Karen, she asked him, "What will happen now that the king of Vindicia is dead? Will the new king try to invade us?"

"I doubt it," Alberich said. "He won't have any dealings with you until Jason is released from the enchantment, but he won't invade. From what I've heard, the new king would rather avoid going to war unless he feels he absolutely has to, and this was a rather unnecessary and cost-draining invasion."

Karen sighed in relief. "I'm glad about that," she said. "Now I just have to wait until Mark recovers fully from his injury."

Alberich nodded. "Then the final act will begin," he said.

CHAPTER 17

Mark took the ax that his father handed him with his left hand, hoping that the paralysis that had affected his left arm and hand was finally gone. It had been a little over eleven months since he had been wounded during the battle that ended the life of the king of Vindicia. The best doctors had tried to get the bullet out but had been unable to. Fortunately, however, the faerie scout who had been part of the Orgonian troops was able to remove the bullet. The doctors predicted a full recovery since the bullet was now out, which meant that he could eventually wear iron armor again.

But they also predicted that the recovery would be very slow, and they were right. Mark developed a fever soon after the battle, and while he ultimately recovered from it, he was left weak for a time. More troubling was he had paralysis in his left arm and hand. The faerie scout and the doctors both agreed that the paralysis would be temporary but also noted that it would take some time for the paralysis to pass. The doctors advised a regime of exercise to prevent his left arm and hand from becoming totally useless, and Mark faithfully followed it both before being released from the monastery where he was recovering and afterward when he went home.

While the recovery process was slow and frustrating, Mark knew he had been rather lucky, all things considered. All he had to do was to think of others who were injured or killed on the battlefield to realize how fortunate he was. For example, Otto had been gravely wounded, and he came down with a bad fever. The combination had broken Otto's health, and he had died about a year after.

Much to Mark's relief, in recent days, feeling had come back to his left arm and hand, and this led him to hope that both arm and hand would function normally again. But he couldn't be sure until or unless he was able to use his left arm and hand as well as he had before the injury. And this was the test.

When Mark held the ax in his left hand, he had to put his right hand on his wrist for support, but his left hand was able to hold the ax without him dropping it as had happened a number of times before. "Looks like you're finally back to normal," Mark's father said, smiling.

"Just about," Mark said, relief evident in his face and voice. "I'm glad about it too."

"I'm just glad you survived the war," his father said. "You could easily have been killed or been so badly wounded that you eventually died."

"Like Otto," Mark said sadly. "At least I managed to get him off the battlefield so he didn't die there."

"The king was quite willing to honor you once you were strong enough to travel to the capital," Mark's father said. "He invited you to a ceremony where he planned to honor the war heroes who fought bravely against the Vindician troops."

"I know," Mark admitted. "But my left arm and hand were still paralyzed, and I wanted to wait until I was fully recovered before being honored. Now if he's got another ceremony planned to honor the soldiers, I'll attend. Maybe the princesses will attend as well."

"Maybe," said Mark's father, "which reminds me, I told you that six princes have already tried to solve the mystery of where the princesses went every night, and they all apparently failed, although one of them, the middle son of the king of Vindicia, remains missing."

"Probably the faeries got him," Mark said.

"You could solve the mystery," Mark's father suggested. "Whoever succeeds in solving the mystery will be able to marry one of the princesses. And I've heard you murmur in your sleep about one of the princesses, enough to make me suspect you might be in love with one of them."

Mark looked away to hide his embarrassment and frustration. Was everybody going to torment him by suggesting that he might be able to marry a girl he knew that he can never have? "You know as well as I do that I'm still a commoner by birth, even if I became a gentleman due to being honored by the king," Mark pointed out. "I still think there are too many obstacles in my way."

Mark's father sighed. "You may have a point," he admitted. "I've got to go bake some more bread. At least you're almost fully recovered, if not entirely so."

He went inside, and Mark sat on the stump of a tree. He was relieved that his arm was just about fully healed from the wound he suffered. But he was no longer a soldier since the new king of Vindicia had chosen not to continue the invasion and recalled all the Vindician soldiers. And he was no longer a gardener but now a gentleman. He knew how to be a gardener, and he learned how to be a soldier. And as a soldier, he wasn't really idle. Being a gentleman, on the other hand, was a recipe for idleness, and that was something Mark neither knew how to handle nor really wanted to. *So what happens now?* Mark thought. Where was he going to?

Finally, he looked up and saw an old woman walking slowly down the road with great difficulty. Mark got up and asked, "Are you all right?"

"Not really," she said. "I'm an old beggar woman with no place to go, and few people will help me out. Right now, I'm tired, and I'm very hungry."

Mark felt pity for the old woman. "I'll go see if I can get you a loaf of bread prepared by my father," he said. "He's a baker."

Mark went inside and found his father, who was preparing bread. "There is an old beggar woman who is tired and very hungry outside," Mark explained. "I'd like to get her a loaf of bread and give her a sip of water or maybe beer, if the water's not clean enough."

"The water's pretty clean," Mark's father said as he picked up a loaf of bread and handed it to his son.

"Thanks," Mark said. He then got some water and went out to give the old beggar woman the bread and water. The old woman accepted both gratefully, sitting on the stump as she ate. Meanwhile, Mark managed to locate a stool and pulled it over to sit with the old woman.

When she was finally finished, she said, "I'm very grateful to you for your kindness, sir."

"You're welcome," Mark said. "I'm happy to be useful to someone. I'm a gentleman now, but I'm not used to being idle. I was a gardener before becoming a gentleman and then was a soldier until I was injured while defending my country from an invasion. Now I don't know what I should do."

"I have an idea about what you should do," the old beggar woman said.

"What?" Mark asked curiously.

"Solve a mystery," the beggar woman suggested. "I've traveled around the country, begging for food, and I have heard a lot about the princesses."

Mark sighed. "So have I," he said. "But I'm a commoner by birth, even if the king made me a gentleman because I prevented a social climber from taking advantage of the princess Winnifred."

"Do you have feelings for the princess Winnifred?" the beggar woman asked.

Mark snorted. "Her?" he asked. "Not likely. She's too flighty for me. No, I'm not in love with the princess Winnifred. I'm in love with her elder sister, Princess Karen. And she returns my feelings for her. But she's still the crown princess, and I'm still a commoner by birth. I don't think the councilors will allow the king to let her marry me."

"You may be surprised," the beggar woman suggested. "I know that Duke Thomas was against you being a suitable consort for Princess Karen, but your rescuing his younger son, Otto, and preventing Otto from dying on the battlefield apparently changed his mind enough that he wouldn't mind if you solved the mystery and married the princess. And I think the others would be aware of your service to the king and would not mind either."

Suspicions arose in Mark's mind. "How do you know all this?" he asked.

"Because I am not what I appear to be," the old beggar woman said, and for a brief moment, the disguise dropped, and Mark saw an incredibly beautiful blond woman not much older than himself. The next moment, she was the old beggar woman. But he now knew who she really was—a faerie.

"Prince Alberich, crown prince of the faeries, is aware that you and Princess Karen are in love," the disguised faerie informed Mark. "He is willing to help you. In fact, the whole mystery was planned by him to ensure that, eventually, you would be able to get together with Princess Karen."

Mark's mind was reeling from this revelation at first. But then he remembered the faerie scout who had joined the Orgonian troops and the faerie magic that had transported him away from the battlefield after he'd been wounded and that had gotten the bullet out of his shoulder. Mark now knew that the faeries had been watching out for him and had been protecting him because of Princess Karen.

"So if I solve the mystery, I'll be able to marry Princess Karen?" he asked, torn between hope and fear.

"You will," the faerie reassured him. "We'll help ensure it."

"How will I be able to find out where the princesses have been going every night?" Mark asked, becoming more eager now.

"Once you arrive at the castle, I believe that Princess Winnifred will do her best to steal a drug slipped into wine that has been brought to each suitor when they arrived to try their luck," the disguised faerie explained. "She does not like you due to your being responsible for discovering her amorous meeting with the music and dance teacher and thus contributing to his being executed."

"But I was just trying to save Princess Winnifred and protect her," he insisted.

"You were," the faerie said. "But she has a childish mindset, especially when it comes to pleasure. She doesn't like anything getting in the way of her having fun, even if it won't. She may try to drug your drink, unless Princess Karen finds her and stops her.

So you must not drink the wine that will be brought to you during the three nights you will be at the castle, and you must pretend to be sound asleep to fool Princess Winnifred, if nobody else."

Then she took a small package out from underneath her beggar's cloak and gave it to Mark. "Open it," she suggested.

Mark did and found a cloak inside the package.

"Once you have pretended to be sound asleep, the princesses will ready themselves for their departure to wherever they go," she explained. "You must put this cloak on. Once you do, you will become invisible and will be able to follow the princesses without being discovered."

"And I will be able to solve the mystery and will be rewarded with Princess Karen's hand," Mark said, "unless she's forgotten all about me."

"She hasn't," the faerie reassured him. "She was very upset when she learned about your being wounded and was relieved to learn you would be all right. She wants to marry you, and we want to help you do so. So overcome your fears and accept your destiny."

With that, she got up, curtsied, and promptly vanished into thin air.

Mark got up and stared at the spot where the disguised faerie had stood for a moment. Then he looked at the cloak, which was still in his hand. It had all been real.

And since what he had experienced was real and not just a dream, he now knew what he had to do. He had to follow the faerie's instructions to the letter and just have faith that he would be rewarded with the hand of Princess Karen after all.

No more time for giving in to fear. He had to take the chance.

CHAPTER 18

King Robert was sitting in his suite of rooms inside the castle, feeling extremely frustrated. It had been nearly three years since his daughters Karen and Winnifred had obtained dazzling new gowns and matching dancing shoes, and Winnifred began wearing out the shoes every night. Then his youngest daughter, Daria, also obtained a dazzling new gown and matching dancing shoes shortly after she was moved into her sisters' bedchamber; and while her shoes initially didn't show signs of being worn out, eventually, they too did. Only Princess Karen's shoes resisted being totally worn out.

Six princes had come to try to solve the mystery, but five had clearly failed and were briefly put under house arrest before being allowed to leave and unable to return as long as the mystery remained. The sixth, Prince Jason of Vindicia, mysteriously disappeared after two nights of failure, and he could not be found anywhere in the kingdom. Karen had insisted that the faeries had Prince Jason and that he was unharmed, but this only increased the king's concerns. If what Karen said was true and Prince Jason *had* been taken by the faeries, this meant that his daughters might have been involved in his disappearance. And the idea of his daughters being in league with the faeries was very unsettling, given the reputation of faeries for being tricksters or careless with humans at best and otherworldly nightmares at worst.

His thoughts were interrupted by the arrival of a page who looked to be about twelve years old. "Yes?" he asked.

"There is a young man here who wishes to see you," the page said. "He apparently is a gentleman, and he claims to have met you before."

"What is his name?" the king asked, mildly curious.

"Mark," the page said. With that, the king was suddenly reminded of the young gardener-turned-gentleman who had saved his middle daughter from a social-climbing predator and later become a soldier.

"I think I do know the young man in question," the king said. "Please have him come to the lesser audience chamber. I will speak with him there."

"As you wish," the page said, bowing as he departed. The king made his way to the lesser audience chamber, accompanied by one attendant, and sat down on the throne. He asked the attendant to bring some wine and cakes for himself and for his guest, and the attendant departed.

Soon the page announced the guest. When the guest entered the room, the king could see that it was indeed the young man who had provided such useful service to the king in the past. "Welcome, Mark," the king said as he rose from his throne.

"Thank you, Your Majesty," Mark said, bowing down on one knee in front of the king. While this was clearly the same Mark that the king remembered from the time when Francis tried to seduce Princess Winnifred, he also looked somewhat different from before he had gone off to war and been wounded in combat. There was something in his expression that looked different from before.

The king's thoughts were interrupted by the attendant, who had come with the wine and cakes that had been requested. The king took some wine and a cake and offered some to Mark. While Mark refused the cakes, he did accept the wine. The page had left briefly but now returned with a chair that Mark sat on.

"I am sorry that I was unable to give you some form of honor for your service during the invasion of Orgon by Vindicia," the king said. "Since you have come here, however, I can rectify the situation."

"Thank you, but that is not why I am here," Mark told the king.

"Then why are you here?" the king asked.

"I have heard of the mystery involving your daughters, sire," Mark explained.

"I'm sure you have," the king said. "First Winnifred and then Daria began wearing out the shoes that came with their new gowns. Only Karen hasn't worn her shoes out yet. Six princes have tried, and at least five of them have failed."

"I wish to try my luck in solving the mystery," said Mark, "that is, if you will allow a commoner such as me to choose one of your daughters for my wife if I succeed in solving the mystery for you."

"I would be more than happy to allow you to marry one of my daughters, especially if you choose Karen," the king said with delight. "She is still in love with you, I believe, and I also believe that the council will be more willing to accept you as a possible suitor for my daughters once I inform them, including Duke Thomas. He is grateful to you for ensuring that his son Otto did not die on the battlefield, even if Otto never recovered."

"Thank you," Mark said, looking up and smiling. "The main reason why I decided to come here and solve the mystery is that I have been encouraged by someone who apparently has knowledge about such things to overcome my fears about my suitability and attempt to marry the young woman I love."

"In that case, I will go announce your arrival as a suitor to my daughters," King Robert said, delighted. "Princess Daria is probably in the library, but I will have to find out if my other two daughters are in the quarters that they share together or if just Princess Winnifred is there and Princess Karen is somewhere else, most likely in the herbal garden, the formal gardens, or even the private garden. You will have to come with me."

"Very well," Mark agreed. "When shall we do so?"

"Let's do so right now," the king said, standing up. "Come, Mark, and we'll go announce the news to my daughters." And turning, he led the way out of the lesser audience chamber.

*　*　*

Karen was on her way to the herbal garden, accompanied by her ladies-in-waiting. It had been a decent day once she finally got out of bed after a night of dancing, wandering around in the gardens, and chatting with the faeries at Prince Alberich's court, as well as Alberich himself. She and her sisters ate their meal in their quarters as usual, and then Winnifred stayed in their quarters, still allowed to go outside, while Daria went to the library with her ladies-in-waiting as usual, and Karen chose to do some sewing with her own ladies before heading to the herbal garden to pick herbs and to relax.

She always liked relaxing in the herbal garden when she wasn't busy picking herbs. The scents were familiar and, perhaps for that reason, calming to her, especially now since she knew Mark was coming back into the picture and with it the end of her time spent nightly in the faerie kingdom. It was a little sad, oddly enough. But almost three years of spending her nights in the faerie kingdom was a long time, and there were some nice things about Alberich's kingdom, such as the gardens, especially the herbal garden. There were a lot of herbs that had incredible healing properties, and already, she was studying them to find out if she could use any of them for herbal medicine now that Daria and Winnifred were busy dancing, and Karen didn't need to watch over them as much. Maybe once the nightly dancing was over for her and probably Daria, she could ask Alberich whether she could at least continue studying the herbs in the faerie herbal garden.

Then she heard footsteps on the path behind her and heard her father call for her. Karen turned around to find her father with Daria, a disgruntled Winnifred, their ladies-in-waiting . . . and Mark. He seemed a bit nervous, and Karen felt the need to reassure him. But before she could do so, her father said, "Karen, you remember Mark, the young former gardener who saved Winnifred from scandal."

Karen smiled warmly as she said, "I do, indeed."

Then turning to Mark, she said, "I'm so relieved that you're okay, Mark. Is your left arm functioning normally?"

"As normally as possible, considering that I was shot and had to exercise it so it wouldn't wither away," Mark said in a somewhat dry tone. Karen found herself chuckling at that. At least he developed a nice sense of humor about the whole situation.

"I'm here to inform you that Mark has come to the castle with the intention of solving the mystery of where the three of you have been going every night," the king announced, apparently not just to Karen but also to Daria and Winnifred. Winnifred looked sullen unsurprisingly. Karen wanted to reassure Winnifred that, even though the mystery was going to be solved, Winnifred herself would remain with the faeries, but that would be revealing too much.

"Where are you currently going, Karen?" her father continued.

"To the herbal garden," Karen explained.

"Mark, why don't you go with my eldest daughter and her ladies-in-waiting?" her father suggested. "The rest of us will return to the castle."

Mark looked even more nervous, but before he could say anything, Karen said, "I'd be delighted to have you join us, Mark. You've never seen the herbal garden at the castle. It's very lovely, and since you once were an herbal gardener, you should find it interesting."

"All right," Mark said, joining Karen and her ladies as they continued on their way to the herbal garden. Karen took a somewhat uncomfortable Mark's arm, and they led the way, with the ladies following them. Occasionally, Karen glanced back and thought that she saw her ladies whispering among themselves, but she wasn't sure if they were plotting something or if they were just gossiping.

Finally, they arrived at the herbal garden. A lady opened the gate, and they all entered. Karen led the way, pointing out various herbs to Mark, who seemed to recognize most of them. Finally, they reached the middle of the garden, where some benches sat.

One lady moved forward to place a cushion on one of the benches, and Karen sat down, with Mark sitting beside her but keeping a slight distance away from her. Karen then took a good look at Mark. He didn't seem to have changed all that much in about three years. He was still as tall as he had been, and he still had a little beard. He was a little leaner than he was before but not terribly thin. Nonetheless, there was a distinct change that was hard to place yet unmistakable.

"You seem changed," she told him after a moment.

"War changes people," Mark replied rather bluntly.

He sighed and added, "I'm sorry, but it's true. War isn't really glorious like some would believe."

"Like the former king of Vindicia, I suspect," Karen said. "He probably thought war was great."

"I'm sure," Mark agreed, sighing again. "But I saw men fall on the battlefield. Some died. Others were merely wounded, including me."

"I was really worried when I found out about your injury," Karen admitted. "I'm glad that it wasn't as bad as it could have been—no, not just glad, *relieved*. I'm very relieved."

Mark looked closely at her, and Karen found herself looking back into his dark eyes. There was still warmth in them, but she thought she could see a darkness that wasn't just due to the color of his eyes. He had been scarred and not just physically.

Impulsively, Karen moved closer and took hold of Mark's hand before he could draw back from her. Then she stood up, drawing Mark along with her. Finally, when they were standing up, Karen moved closer and touched Mark's shoulders in a comforting gesture.

Immediately, Mark's arms came around Karen, and he drew her close, shaking as he embraced her. Karen rested her head against his shoulder and put her arms around his neck, lifting one hand to gently stroke his dark hair. She felt sympathy for Mark. He clearly had gone through a rough time, even if his injury had turned out not to be so bad and even though he got out with his sanity intact.

Mark's shaking gradually ceased, and Karen heard him confess, "After Otto's being so badly wounded, I began having nightmares, not every night but often enough. I would dream that I saw him fatally wounded in front of me. And after I was wounded myself, I would sometimes dream of the battle that led to my being hurt, only it would always end with a soldier aiming a musket at my head."

Naturally, this horrified Karen. So she simply pressed closer to him and said, "I'm sorry you had to go through all that. At least it's over now."

"Yes," he agreed. "Thank you for comforting me."

"You're more than welcome, Mark," Karen said, drawing back just enough so she could look up at him.

At the same time, he looked down at her. And in that instant, she found herself looking deep into Mark's eyes. She saw the warmth gradually change into passion. Karen's heart began beating faster. She could see that he still felt the same way about her that he felt so long before.

And as if in confirmation, Mark said, "I wanted to forget you, Karen. I tried to forget you. From time to time, I tried to take interest in other girls who showed an interest in me. But every time, I would see your lovely face, and I would wind up pulling back. I can't help it. I'm still in love with you, Karen."

"And I'm still in love with you, Mark," Karen said. What she didn't tell him—and wouldn't until they were in the faerie realm—was that her love for him might well be the reason why she didn't dance so much that she wore her shoes out. She didn't want to dance too often with men whom she wasn't interested in, even Prince Alberich.

Karen gently touched Mark's face, and he smiled and bent his head down to kiss her. She closed her eyes. Then she heard the gate slam open and Winnifred's angry voice calling for her.

"Thanks a lot, Winnifred," Karen muttered under her breath as Mark immediately drew away from her. Karen turned to see her ladies, along with Winnifred and her ladies, coming forward. Only then did Karen realize that her ladies had withdrawn while she and Mark were talking. Most likely, it was to give the two of them privacy. Karen appreciated the kindness of her ladies and thus was very annoyed by Winnifred's attitude toward Mark.

"Hello, Winnifred," Karen said, trying her best to conceal her annoyance toward her sister. It wasn't very easy, but she had to do so. "What did you want?"

"Mainly to get *him* to return to the castle," Winnifred said.

"I'd better go now," Mark said. "But before I go, how are you doing, Winnifred?"

"Very well," Winnifred said. "I'm having so much fun."

She would have said more, but Mark prevented her by turning to Karen instead and saying, "I'm happy to see you again, Karen. And this is a very lovely herbal garden."

"I'm glad you like it," Karen said. "You return to the castle, Mark. I need to pick some herbs. But once I do, I'll see you inside the castle."

"Farewell for now, Your Highness," Mark said as he turned to leave.

"Farewell, Mark," Karen replied and watched as he turned to leave with Winnifred and her ladies.

Once they were gone, Lily sighed and said, "I'm sorry Winnifred interrupted you. We were trying to give you and Mark some privacy. I told the other ladies how you felt about him."

"I'm glad you did so," Karen said. "But Winnifred hates Mark. I fear she hasn't forgiven him for his role in getting Francis executed."

"But Mark was only trying to protect Winnifred," Lily protested.

"You and I both know that," Karen agreed. "But Winnifred is too immature to recognize it or accept it. She's such a fool."

And Karen knew that Winnifred's foolishness was why she was better off with the faeries. But Karen had to live her own life within the strictures of being the crown princess and heir to the throne. And that meant she couldn't stay in the faerie realm forever, just long enough for Mark to spend time with her there and free Jason from the spell. And then hopefully, everyone would earn a happy ending, including Winnifred.

CHAPTER 19

The end of the ballad signaled the end of the formal dinner, so Mark stood up along with the king, his daughters, and their attendants. Everyone else stood up as Mark followed the royal family and their attendants out of the great hall.

Once outside, Princess Daria announced that she would not be going to the library tonight as she had a headache. Instead, she would retire early. Princess Karen volunteered to concoct an herbal remedy for her headache while Mark followed the other princesses and their ladies to their quarters.

They entered the second tower, where the living quarters for the princesses were situated. Mark had learned that the three princesses once had separate rooms but that Winnifred was moved from her bedchamber to Karen's after the scandal with Francis while Daria was moved in with her sisters after the nightly escapades began. Now the ladies who attended the princesses all slept in the two bedchambers that the princesses once had or slept in dormitory-sized bedchambers on the floors below and above. Mark followed the ladies up a long spiraling staircase to a second-floor landing where the rooms for the princesses were located. When Mark followed them through the doorway, he looked around in awe and wonder.

As a commoner, Mark was very accustomed to living and sleeping in humble surroundings. Even during the brief time between his becoming a gentleman and his departure for the wars, he had slept in a dormitory-type setting with other gentlemen that, while comfortable enough, was hardly luxurious or elegant. So naturally, he was awestruck by the beauty and elegance of the antechamber he found himself inside. On the ceiling was a painting devoted to a Mother Earth goddess while the walls were covered with a lovely green damask, and paintings of the princesses in hunting garb were hung on the walls. The chairs were also covered with green damask, and the furnishings were elegant but not ostentatiously so. On the other side of the room near a white-paneled door, Mark saw a portable bed, simple but elegant.

"That is where you will sleep," one of the ladies-in-waiting informed Mark. "On the other side is the bedroom for the princesses. You are to observe where the princesses go and where they—or at least Princesses Daria and Winnifred—dance. The door between this chamber and the bedroom will be left partially open while the door leading to a cabinet area will be locked so that they can't do anything or go anywhere without you hearing them.

"Thank you for telling me this," Mark said as Karen came in with her ladies-in-waiting and gave Princess Daria an herbal remedy, which the youngest princess gratefully accepted and drank. Mark could see that Karen was protective not only of her sister Winnifred but of Daria as well. This only endeared her to Mark.

"I'm going to rest for a bit inside," Princess Daria said as she exited the antechamber through the door near his bed. Her ladies-in-waiting took their leave and exited also.

"The rest of us will do some sewing," Karen informed Mark. "Do you know how to play music?"

"I'm afraid I never learned how to play musical instruments," Mark told her. "But I do know some peasant songs."

"Maybe you can sing some for us until you go to bed," Karen suggested.

"And when we're all ready to go to bed, I'll give you a cup of wine," Princess Winnifred added.

Mark knew what that meant: Princess Winnifred was going to drug him. Well, he knew how to outwit her, thanks to the faerie who had visited him.

For some time, the princesses and their ladies sewed, and Mark sang some peasant songs. He noted that Princess Winnifred didn't like the songs, but Karen showed some interest. He wasn't sure if the interest was just polite or real e, but he was grateful that she wasn't being condescending to him.

Sometime later, Princess Winnifred loudly announced that she was tired of sewing and ready to retire. Mark waited as the princesses were escorted into their rooms and prepared for bed. Afterward, the ladies left the bedchamber and then the antechamber.

That was when Princess Winnifred came out, wearing a pale blue robe covering a pale blue shift. She had a cup of wine ready for him and handed it to him. Mark took it, waited for the princess to return to her bedchamber, and then quickly poured the drink into the bed before getting in it to go to sleep.

When he thought sufficient time had passed, Mark began to snore as if he was fast asleep. He heard Princess Winnifred laugh at that. "It would have been better for himself had he never come here," she said. "Actually, it would have been better had he never come into my life, period."

"Karen would not agree," he heard Daria say.

Mark could hear movement inside the room. He didn't dare get up and watch the princesses yet, so he kept snoring. Finally, he heard a tapping sound and reached under the bed, where he kept the bundle that contained his invisibility cloak. He quietly got up and went to the door, peeking inside.

The princesses wore the most magnificent dresses he had ever seen. Karen wore a golden gown that shone so brilliantly that it nearly hurt his eyes. Princess Winnifred wore a silvery gown that glimmered like the moon. And Princess Daria wore a gown that dazzled like the stars. They stood in front of some kind of opening in the floor.

"I'll go first," he heard Karen say.

Mark knew what he had to do. He took the invisibility cloak out of his bundle and swung it around his shoulders. Once he had the invisibility cloak on, he hurried to follow the princesses, knowing that they would lead him to the heart of the mystery.

Mark managed to get behind Princess Daria and follow her down just as the trapdoor began to close. Unfortunately, he hurried so fast to get behind her that he accidentally trod on her gown. Princess Daria gasped and said, "Something's pulling at my dress."

Mark froze for one instant and then heard Princess Winnifred laugh and say, "Don't be silly, Daria. You probably just snagged your gown on a shard of crystal that poked up through the staircase."

"She's probably right," Mark heard Karen say. "Relax, Daria. Everything will be all right."

Princess Daria seemed to relax enough to follow her sisters down a beautiful crystalline staircase, but as Mark followed, he could see Daria occasionally peek behind her as if to see if there really was someone following her. Mark was awestruck by the beauty of the staircase, and when he reached the bottom, he was even more awestruck at the passageway in front of him and the princesses. It was crystalline as well and shone in the darkness, almost blinding him.

Mark followed the princesses through the passageway, emerging to find an avenue of trees with silvery leaves, shining and glistening in the dark. As they went along, Mark couldn't help but look at the leaves with an awestruck expression. His awe and wonder increased as he followed the princesses through avenues of trees with gold and then diamonds for leaves. The last avenue of trees were especially magnificent in Mark's eyes since they reminded him of the crystalline staircase and passageway.

Finally, the princesses emerged from the avenue of trees as did Mark. And when he did, he found himself standing near the edge of a great lake that seemed to stretch out across the horizon. At the edge of the lake were three men who were dressed magnificently in doublets smothered with silver and precious gems of every kind.

"Good evening, Princesses," one of the men said, stepping forward. "The faeries are expecting you, of course."

"And I'm expecting a wonderful night of dancing," Mark heard Princess Winnifred say eagerly as she took the arm of the man who had stepped forward. Mark saw the other two men step forward and escort the princesses to three boats that he saw on the shore.

Mark knew he had to get onto one of the boats, or else, he'd be left behind with no way to get to the other side and discover exactly where the princesses were going, though by now he figured out that they would be with faeries and would be dancing. So he ran on his tiptoes toward the boats, and right after Princess Karen was being helped into a boat, he got in as well.

The boat carrying Princess Karen was the first to leave the shore, followed by the boats carrying Princess Winnifred and Princess Daria. But Mark soon noticed that although the boat carrying Princess Karen was the first to leave, it soon fell behind the other two boats. "I don't understand," Mark heard the man escorting Princess Karen say. "The boat is heavier tonight than it usually is. I might have to row with all my strength just to make it across, although I might use some magic to help."

That was when Mark saw Karen look right over to where Mark was sitting, beside her. For one long moment, Mark's heart almost stopped. Then he heard Karen say, "It doesn't really matter. It's such a lovely night. I don't mind falling a little bit behind. And it's rather warm anyway."

"You're right," Karen's escort said, and soon the boat sped up slightly, enough to have them not fall too far behind the other boats. Mark looked behind him, and already, the shore was incredibly far behind him.

Eventually, Mark saw on the other side of the lake a dazzling castle, huge and shining like a diamond in the night. From it came the joyous sounds of trumpets and kettledrums. In front of the castle was a long road that wound through what seemed to be gardens before stopping near a dock that shone like silver.

Princess Winnifred's boat was the first to reach the dock, and her escort helped her out of the boat. Then Princess Daria's boat reached the dock, and her escort helped her out. Finally, Princess Karen's boat pulled up, and her escort did the same. As the princesses and their escorts began walking up the road to the castle, Mark quietly got out of the boat and followed them, making sure he remained invisible and silent.

Eventually, they reached what appeared to be a gatehouse and passed through it into a shining courtyard where a man stood, more magnificently dressed than the escorts for the princesses. Not only was his doublet smothered with precious gems of every kind but his breeches were smothered in gold and silver embroidery as well. And on his head, he wore a golden crown magnificently studded with precious gems such as rubies, sapphires, and diamonds.

Mark glanced down at his own outfit, which was mercifully hidden behind his invisibility cloak. He was wearing a purple doublet with gold and silver cloth, a white shirt made of the finest silk, and dark blue breeches. They were the finest clothes that could be provided for him, royal garments, but they looked positively dowdy next to the magnificent clothes that the escorts, the princesses, and this man wore.

"Welcome, Princesses!" the crowned man greeted them. "My subjects are waiting for you inside."

"And I'm ready to begin dancing, Prince Alberich." Mark heard Princess Winnifred say.

"It'll soon be King Alberich as my parents are almost ready to retire behind the Golden Curtain and leave me in charge," this prince said. With that, he led the way inside, with Mark trying to follow while looking around him in awe at the magnificent furnishings in the palace. This clearly was a palace fit for faeries.

Prince Alberich led the way through the castle to a set of double doors that opened at his approach. Mark followed the princesses inside and stared in awe at what was a magnificent ballroom and at the magnificently dressed people inside. Mark felt so embarrassed by the contrast between his own clothes, opulent though they were, and those of the faeries inside that he retreated into a corner, deciding just to watch.

At least he now knew where the princesses went every night. And maybe he could find out why they were coming here.

* * *

Karen looked around the ballroom, looking for any sign of Mark's presence. But she couldn't detect anything. Still, she knew that he had to be present.

Earlier, right after the ladies-in-waiting left the bedchamber, Winnifred showed the bottle of the drug that the faeries had provided, which was used to drug the drinks of any suitors who came to the castle. Winnifred revealed that she had gotten hold of it as soon as she learned that Mark had arrived to try his luck at solving the mystery and made it clear that she was going to use it. However, this didn't faze Karen since she knew that Alberich had sent a faerie to encourage Mark to come to the castle and win Karen's hand in marriage who had warned him about the drugged drink, so Karen was convinced that Mark wouldn't drink it. But Daria hadn't been informed about it since Winnifred so disliked Mark, so Daria protested, and Karen had to calm things down before Winnifred went out to give Mark the drink.

Then while they were descending the staircase, Daria cried out that she felt something trod on her gown. Karen was sure Mark had accidentally trod on it while trying to keep up with them as they descended to the faerie realm, but she couldn't reassure Daria in front of Winnifred. Fortunately, Winnifred ignored the obvious implication and suggested that Daria merely snagged her gown on a shard of crystal from the staircase.

And then once they got to the lake and got in the boats that took them to the castle on the other side, Karen's boat had fallen behind, and her escort noted how much heavier the boat was this time. That was when Karen tried to look beside her to see if she could see Mark, but he was clearly invisible to her eyes. Still, she knew he was there in the boat with her.

As she reflected on it, that was when Alberich joined her. Seeing what she was doing, he said quietly, "He's right over there, Princess Karen." He pointed to a corner of the ballroom that seemed to be empty. But then Alberich took some dust and sprinkled it over her eyes.

Karen blinked automatically, and when she stopped, she looked back into the corner and could clearly see Mark wearing a silvery cloak and looking very uncomfortable as if he was embarrassed to be here.

"He seems rather embarrassed to be here," Alberich whispered.

"It might just be because of his outfit," Karen replied. "It's opulent enough, but there was a reason why we needed new gowns to come here after all."

"Yes, our outfits are far more opulent than your fanciest clothes ever will be," Alberich agreed.

"Thank you for showing me where he was," Karen whispered to Alberich. "And please, either tomorrow night or the third night, get him some more appropriate clothes."

"I will," Alberich promised.

"And please privately inform Daria that Mark is here," Karen added. "I'd like her to know. Winnifred doesn't need to know until the third night."

"No, she doesn't," Alberich said, nodding.

He left, and Karen looked back at Mark. He really *did* seem embarrassed. Poor guy. At least Karen knew what to do and what to say to him.

So she walked over to the corner where he stood. He clearly saw her coming, but he looked confused as if he wasn't sure what he should do. Fortunately, he didn't have to do anything. For as soon as Karen reached him, she said, "I'm glad you're here, Mark. And I don't mind that you're not exactly dressed for a ball at the faerie palace. I'm not too fussy."

Mark stared at Karen in what appeared to be total shock. Then he blurted out, "How . . . how did you know I followed you here?"

"I suspected that you were following us when Daria felt something on the train of her gown," Karen explained, which caused Mark to flush and look down, seemingly embarrassed.

"I'm sorry about that," he said, looking down. "I just didn't want to be left aboveground while you traveled down that staircase."

"I believe you," Karen said. "And then when we all arrived at the lake and I got into the boat that would take me to the castle, it fell behind, and my escort noted how heavy it was tonight, and I realized you were in the boat. But I couldn't see you until Prince Alberich sprinkled golden dust in my eyes, which presumably allowed me to see someone who was invisible. He could see you."

"Did you know that a faerie gave me this invisibility cloak?" Mark asked.

"I did," Karen admitted. "Prince Alberich told me. But I couldn't tell Daria the truth because Winnifred needed to be kept in the dark for the time being. Prince Alberich will tell her before we leave here tonight. But Winnifred won't know until the third night."

"And apparently, Prince Alberich approves of me," Mark added. "I'm surprised that a faerie would take such interest in the affairs of mere mortals."

Karen smiled at that. "I'm a little surprised myself," she admitted. "But not all faeries are truly malicious toward humans. In fact, I've learned that most faeries aren't truly malicious toward us. Most of the time, they either have a rather . . . *odd* sense of morality or they just want to be left alone or they only behave badly if you offend them. Prince Alberich is pretty well disposed toward mortals, unless they offend him. And I'm not willing to offend him."

"Neither am I," Mark said. And Karen was sure he meant it.

"And he's well disposed toward humans who are good people," Karen added. "And he knows that you're a good guy. He saw what you did to stop Francis from taking advantage of Winnifred. That's why he's trying to help us get together. He has no problems with people who come from different classes falling in love and getting married as long as both people are good at heart."

Mark seemed both surprised and relieved to hear this. "So he's just playing matchmaker because he thinks we're good people," he concluded. "If this is true, then I was really wrong to believe that I could never be with you."

Karen stepped closer and took his hand. "You *can* be with me," she assured him, "especially now that you know where we have been going every night."

"That reminds me," Mark said. "Have you been going down here every night just to ensure that, someday, we could be together?"

"That was part of it, but it wasn't the only reason," Karen explained. "If Winnifred married King Henry of Brangavia or any other human ruler, she would yield to the temptation of having an affair, and that would get her executed. Here, she won't be in any danger of that. Initially, I think Prince Alberich was also thinking that Daria might stay here because she's very awkward in social situations, and living here might be better for her. But with Prince Jason entering the picture and their having quite a few things in common, he's willing to let her return to the mortal world when our secret's revealed. But the main reasons are to help you and me and to protect Winnifred."

"So Princess Winnifred is going to stay behind in the faerie realm?" Mark asked.

"Yes," Karen confirmed. "She'll be safe here. And Prince Jason is enchanted now, but once the secret's revealed, he'll be freed from the spell and can leave."

"Why was Prince Jason enchanted?" Mark asked.

"Because his father was planning on using Jason's attempt to get out of Vindicia as a means to conquer Orgon," Karen explained, "and because you were still part of the Orgonian army. Also, Prince Jason was thinking about committing suicide if he failed to discover our secret, and neither Daria nor I wanted that to happen."

"What did Princess Winnifred think?" asked Mark.

"She didn't care," Karen said. "Even before Francis gave her a taste of intimate pleasure and before she began coming down here, she rarely considered her own long-term needs, let alone the needs of others, short term or long term. And she wants desperately to ensure that she gets to dance here every night, so she's the most determined to prevent anybody, other than us, of course, from coming down here and ruining her pleasure."

Mark then turned to look at the faeries, Winnifred, Daria, and Prince Jason, all of whom were dancing. "What kind of dance is this?" Mark asked.

"The faeries call it a waltz," Karen said. "It's very different from the dances we perform at court."

Mark nodded. "It's kind of similar to the gliding dance I performed for you the night you arrived at Duke Thomas's manor," he said.

"Maybe you'd like to watch how the waltz is done so that you can do it with me once you have memorized the steps to some extent," Karen suggested.

"But I'm invisible!" Mark protested.

"Only to Winnifred, Daria—unless she gets the dust that I got in her eyes—and perhaps Prince Jason," Karen reassured him, "not to any of the faeries, not really. And I doubt Winnifred will notice."

The music ended at that moment, and Prince Alberich approached Karen and Mark. "I have informed Princess Daria," Prince Alberich told Karen. "And she can see Mark now."

Karen sighed in relief. "I'm glad to hear that," she said. "Maybe you can show Mark how to dance the waltz."

"By having you dance it with me and having him watch?" Prince Alberich asked. "I'd be happy to as long as he knows that there's nothing between us, romantically speaking."

"I'm relieved," Karen heard Mark say. Then Prince Alberich took her hand and led her onto the dance floor.

* * *

Mark's eyes followed Karen as Prince Alberich led her out onto the dance floor. The faerie prince drew Karen into his arms, and as a graceful melody began to play, they began turning and spinning around the dance floor. Despite the fact that Prince Alberich had taken pains to reassure Mark that Karen wasn't romantically involved with the prince, Mark couldn't help but envy him as he expertly swept Karen around the dance floor. But Mark did note that Prince Alberich kept a fairly respectable gap between himself and Karen whenever they danced close enough for body contact.

Karen was a fine dancer, and she clearly had experience with dancing this type of dance. Never had Mark seen a girl dance so gracefully. He couldn't keep his eyes off her, even when there were other couples whirling past him.

As for the dance itself, it *was* rather similar to the gliding dances he used to do when he danced with Sarah before her father moved himself and her to the court in his constant effort to gain acceptance by the nobility and gentry and to the first dance he did at the duke's manor for the royal party. But it was more complex and graceful, of course. Still, despite the increased complexity, he thought he could pick up the steps fairly well.

When the dance ended, Prince Alberich bowed to Karen, who curtsied back. Then they did another waltz, only this time Mark paid more attention to the steps rather than to the dancers. The steps were similar enough to the ones he did with Sarah and the one he did with Elke, as his partner, that he believed, once Prince Alberich hopefully stopped dancing with Karen, Mark could do them himself as Karen's new partner.

The second waltz ended, and after the second bow and curtsy, Karen seemed to whisper something to Prince Alberich, who nodded and then escorted her over to Mark. "Princess Karen wants to know whether you know the steps well enough to be able to dance the waltz with her," Prince Alberich said.

Mark's heart began pounding, and for one moment, he felt only panic. Despite the similarity between the gliding dances he had done in the past and the waltz Karen did with Prince Alberich, he was still a commoner, and both Prince Alberich and Karen were royalty. But then he reminded himself that the two had denied any personal involvement beyond being conspirators in the dancing scheme. He also remembered how shy he'd been when he realized he was falling for Sarah, and that was during one of the dances he did with her. When he mentioned his interest to his father, his father had said that if Sarah felt the same way, he should go for a relationship with her, and he told him, "A faint heart never won a fair maiden."

While Mark's following the advice hadn't worked out quite so well that time, it was less because Sarah wasn't interested and more because of her father being such a social climber. But this was different. Even if Karen was way beyond his reach under normal circumstances despite their mutual feelings, this wasn't a normal situation. This was the faerie realm. And in the faerie realm, maybe dreams could come true.

So Mark took a deep breath, smiled at Prince Alberich and Karen, and said, "If you're ready to dance the next dance with me, Karen, I'd be happy to be your partner since I believe I can pick up the steps fairly well. I've done this type of dance before, although the steps weren't nearly as complex."

"I believe you," Karen said.

"So may I have the next dance?" Mark asked, bowing.

Karen said in pure delight as she curtsied, "Oh yes, please."

He took her extended hand and led her out onto the dance floor. Once there, he put his free arm around her waist, and she put her free hand on his shoulder as he pulled her close enough that he could feel her slender body against his own. A beautiful, lyrical yet wistful tune began to play as Mark looked down at Karen. She smiled encouragingly, and he began moving to the music, slowly at first and then gradually faster, losing himself in the light in her eyes, the grace of the dance, and the wonder of this moment.

* * *

Prince Alberich smiled as he watched as Mark and Karen turned around the dance floor. They were perfect for each other; he could see that now. All they needed was a little help, and he was happy to provide the nudges needed to ultimately get them together.

He briefly turned his attention to Daria, dancing with an enchanted Jason, and smiled. Hopefully, there would be another romance that would blossom and end well along with this one. He never thought he'd find pleasure in being a matchmaker, but it seemed that he was doing just that.

Then he turned his attention to Winnifred, dancing with one of the many gentleman attendants at the faerie court. He didn't mind that Winnifred danced with a brand-new partner every time. Most, if not all, faeries had open relationships as long as there was no cheating, abuse, predation, exploitation, or entitlement. And faeries had no double standards.

He then turned his attention back to Mark and Karen and saw to his satisfaction that Mark was handling the waltz quite well. Peasant dances apparently lent themselves well to the waltz, unlike court dances in the mortal world, despite the fact that court dances were more graceful than peasant dancing. Mark and Karen were at the far end of the ballroom when the song finally ended. They stood very close together, and Alberich decided to give them some privacy by focusing on the other dancers.

Everything was proceeding quite well. Two more nights, and then he'd free Jason from his enchantment, explain everything to the king of Orgon, and keep Winnifred in the faerie realm forever while Karen would be united with Mark, and (hopefully) a real romance would blossom between Jason and Daria.

*   *   *

Ever since Karen had first begun dancing the waltz, she'd wondered what it would be like to dance it with Mark. What would it be like to dance in his arms? Would he be as fine a dancer as he was in the peasant dances she'd seen him do at the manor? Or would he be clumsy and stumbling about?

And now she was dancing in his arms, and it was perhaps even better than she hoped. While Mark was tentative at first, gradually, he moved faster and more expertly, the slightly awkward steps turning into very graceful ones to match her own. This was why she'd gone down into the faerie realm every night, other than to protect her sisters, of course. It was to have this moment with Mark, swirling around the dance floor in a romantic waltz.

Gradually, their steps slowed as the music wound to an end; but even when they stopped, Mark still held Karen in his arms. She smiled happily up at him. "Thank you," she said softly.

"You're welcome," Mark said just as softly, looking down at her with wonder in his eyes.

In that moment, Karen knew that she wanted him to kiss her. She also feared that he might be reluctant to do so. Thus, she lifted one hand to gently touch Mark's face as a subtle encouragement. Mark's eyes darkened slightly, and then he gradually bent his head down toward hers. His breath warmly caressed Karen's face, and then his lips were on hers.

Karen closed her eyes as she slid her arms around his neck and lifted one hand so it would rest in his dark hair. He responded by pulling her closer, crushing the skirts of her gown against his firm body, and resting one hand against her waist while gently stroking her back with his other hand. Slowly, the kiss deepened.

She didn't know how long the kiss lasted. Was it just a few moments? Was it a few hours? But finally, it ended, and she felt Mark draw back. Opening her eyes, she saw him lift his head to look down at her. For one long moment, they looked at each other.

That was when Karen whispered, "I'm so glad you joined me here, Mark."

And to her utter delight, she heard Mark say, "Actually, so am I, Karen."

*   *   *

The rest of the night passed in a wonderful blur for Mark. While he'd kissed Sarah during his brief courtship of her, the kisses had never been quite as sweet as the one he'd just shared with Karen. He'd never dreamed that a kiss could be that sweet, but it was incredibly so for him. Perhaps it was just being here in the faerie realm, a place where nothing seemed impossible, that made the kiss so sweet. Or maybe it was the fact that, despite his fears, he was actually in a position to be with the girl he loved and marry her.

Whatever the reason, this led to the most wonderful night Mark had ever had as he continued to dance every waltz he could with Karen. The only times they weren't on the dance floor were when one or both of them became thirsty and sat down to drink clear water from cups that were given to them by attendants. During the times that the two sat down, Mark talked quietly with Karen about the faerie palace and the gardens surrounding them. Mark wasn't surprised to find out that there was an herbal garden or that there might be herbs down here that could treat incurable diseases such as cancer. They also talked about his time in the Orgonian army.

"I'm glad you weren't so badly wounded that you could never fully recover," Karen said.

"So am I," he agreed. "Otto wasn't so lucky, though at least he survived for a time after being wounded."

"I feel sorrow that he never truly recovered, but I never really loved him, nor was I ever in love with him, so I couldn't feel any real grief," Karen admitted. "I would've been grief stricken had you died from your injury, Mark."

They continued to dance and talk until finally, close to three in the morning, Karen looked down at her shoes after Prince Alberich announced that the princesses had to leave because Winnifred had holes in her shoes again. "They're almost worn through!" she exclaimed after she took one off so she could examine it. "This is the first time I ever came close to wearing my shoes out!"

"How long did you dance the other times you came down here?" Mark asked.

"No more than seven waltzes," she said. "The rest of the time, I either sat in the ballroom, spent time in the library with Daria until Prince Jason came down here, or spent time in the gardens."

"So you never really wanted to dance with another faerie?" Mark asked.

"Not as much as I wanted to dance with you," Karen reassured him.

The faerie who rowed her to the faerie palace then came up and said, "It's time for you to depart, Your Highness. And I suppose your stowaway friend will be joining us for the return trip."

"Yes, but don't tell Winnifred, please," Karen said, "not yet at least."

That was when Mark realized that the faeries really were aware that he was present among them, but he said nothing. Instead, he followed the princesses and their escorts through the castle and back to the boats resting on the lake. Mark waited until he saw which boat Karen was getting into, and then he got in beside her.

The faeries rowed the princesses back across the lake, and as he did so, Mark whispered to Karen, "I was going to get a token from the groves as we passed through them, but after accidentally stepping onto Daria's gown, I was afraid of scaring her further. I doubt your father will accept my story without any physical evidence after all."

"I'll chat with my sisters and try my best to conceal the sound of you getting a twig from a tree in one of the groves," she told him, "or maybe from one in all three groves."

"I think I'll settle for one tonight, one tomorrow night, and one for the third night," he said. "This was such a magical night, and it's such a beautiful place."

And so once they got off the boats and said farewell to their escorts, the princesses went through the groves of trees. Mark waited until they got to the grove of trees with silver leaves and then reached out, grabbed hold of a twig, and tried to take it as quietly as possible. Unfortunately, the twig cracked as he pulled it off the tree.

Mark hid the twig as quickly as he could, his heart beating fast. Fortunately, he heard Winnifred say, "The guns must be firing to salute us as we leave this wonderful realm."

"You're probably right," Karen said, and the princesses continued on their way.

When they went through the passageway and reached the stairs, Mark knew he had to get to his bed before they came up. Fortunately, his shoes weren't worn out, so he ran up as quickly and quietly as he possibly could. He emerged from the trapdoor, rushed to his cot, took off the invisibility cloak, and concealed it with him as he lay down and began snoring loudly enough for all to hear.

He then heard Winnifred laugh before saying, "He's still asleep, and we are safe."

But then Mark really did begin to feel tired, and he tried to keep his eyes open so that he wouldn't fall asleep in his clothes. He needed to wait until the princesses had gotten into their beds and were fast asleep before he could get into his nightclothes. But weariness overcame him, and he fell fast asleep for real.

Chapter 20

It was the third night—the last night before Mark absolutely had to reveal the truth about the dancing princesses. While he knew that after the first night he could have gone to the king and just revealed everything then, he hadn't wanted to. As he had told Karen, that night was a magical night, and the faerie realm was so beautiful. He was lured by the magical beauty of this realm, enough that he didn't want to give it up until he had to reveal the secret.

So the second night, he again disposed of the drink that Winnifred had given him when her back was turned, pretended to fall fast asleep, and followed the princesses down into the crystalline stairs into the faerie realm. They passed through the first grove, but since he had already taken a twig with silver leaves, he didn't do so this time. Instead, he waited until they reached the grove where all the trees had golden leaves, and then he heard Karen begin talking loudly to Winnifred. He used the conversation to snag a twig with golden leaves from the grove and hide it before they passed through the third grove and finally made their way to the lake, where the faerie escorts waited for them.

After crossing the lake in the boat that Karen was in and reaching the faerie castle, the rest of the night passed more or less as the first night had. Mark spent all his time with Karen, usually dancing the waltz, although whenever they needed to rest the two sat down and quietly talked. At three o'clock, the shoes belonging to the princesses were worn through, and they all had to leave. And as before, once they reached the crystalline staircase, Mark quickly went up the stairs, got to his cot, took off and concealed his invisibility cloak, and lay down so that, once the princesses emerged, he seemed to still be fast asleep. While he knew that Daria knew the truth, thanks to her coming up to them at one point during the dancing and quietly greeting him, he knew that Winnifred was still unaware of it and had to be kept in the dark—until tonight, when he would dance in the faerie realm with Karen for the last time before he had to reveal the truth to her father.

When the princesses retired to their quarters, Mark went into the antechamber just outside their bedchamber; and to his surprise and shock, he saw the most magnificent outfit laid out for him. The shirt seemed to glow like moonbeams, and the doublet shone like the sun, so much so that it almost hurt his eyes. And his breeches were dazzling, shining like starlight.

He quickly concealed his outfit beneath the covers of his cot and waited until the princesses were ready to go to bed. They all came in to say good night to him, and Winnifred handed him a cup of wine that he strongly suspected was drugged. He waited until they went into their bedroom and then dumped the drink before quickly changing his clothes. Then he got into his bed and waited until the ladies-in-waiting left the bedchamber before he began to snore loudly.

He heard Winnifred laugh and say, "He'll probably be exiled after tonight. Good riddance."

He continued snoring before he heard the door open, and the bright light of the gowns could be seen, even with his eyes closed. He heard Winnifred then say, "He's still asleep. Let's go."

When he heard the door close, he quickly put on the invisibility cloak, got out of bed, and opened the door. He saw the trapdoor open as before and the princesses proceed down through it. And as before, he followed them down through the opening, down the staircase, and through the passage until they reached the first avenue of trees. This time, he waited until they reached the avenue of trees with diamonds for leaves before taking a twig and concealing it underneath his cloak, along with the twigs he'd obtained from his earlier trips.

When they reached the lake and the boats, with their faerie escorts waiting, Mark once again got into the boat that Karen got in and sat alongside her. He reached out and whispered, "I'm here." And then he touched her hand.

Karen smiled and said, "I thought you might have joined us again."

"This is the last night before I have to reveal the truth to the others," he said, sighing. "I have to admit, I could have told your father before now, but I wanted to wait until the last possible moment."

"The faerie realm is that alluring?" Karen asked. "I can understand. It's so beautiful that it's hard to give it up. At least Winnifred will enjoy it for the rest of her life, and maybe you and I can enjoy it from time to time, maybe Daria too, if she and Jason stay with our father once he's disenchanted."

Mark smiled back and said, "Maybe."

Eventually, they reached the other side of the lake, and Mark followed the princesses to the castle, where Prince Alberich was waiting for them. He greeted the princesses, pretended not to be aware that Mark was also there, and led them all inside to the ballroom.

Once they were all inside the ballroom, Prince Alberich suddenly spoke. "I have a special announcement to make for everybody," he began, "well, mainly for Princess Winnifred. For the past couple of nights, we have had a special guest among us, unseen by those who have not had their eyes opened. His presence will not affect Princess Winnifred's fate, but it will affect the fates of others who have visited this realm. I wish him to reveal himself so we can treat him like a truly honored guest."

Mark was nervous, but then he saw Karen smile at him and give him an encouraging nod. Taking a deep breath, Mark loosened the invisibility cloak and let it fall off his shoulders, revealing himself. He could see Princess Winnifred glare at him, but before she could say anything, Karen spoke. Her voice was firm as she said, "You may dislike him, Winnifred, but I'm in love with him. And if I have to be a gardener's wife so I can be with him, then so be it. And since it has been agreed on that you would remain here in the faerie realm forever, his discovery of our secret won't affect your fate at all."

Winnifred looked at Karen and then at Mark, and then she shrugged and went off to begin dancing. Mark took Karen's hand and led her out onto the dance floor.

"Sorry about that," Karen said, sighing. "I may have to be proper since I am the crown princess, but that doesn't mean that I'm a pushover. And Winnifred's attitude was getting on my last nerve."

"I think I can understand," Mark told her, smiling. "At least I never tried to win *her* heart. And I won't have to deal with her too often once I reveal the secret to your father."

Once on the dance floor, Mark drew Karen into his arms, and they waited for the music to begin.

* * *

Many hours later, Karen heard Prince Alberich say, "I believe that Princess Winnifred has worn her shoes out." And she knew that she had to look at her own shoes. When she looked down, she saw that holes had begun to form in her own shoes, signifying that she too had to stop dancing and return home.

So she turned to Mark and asked, "How are your own shoes? Mine have begun to wear out."

Mark looked down and said, "Mine aren't in too bad shape, but they are beginning to show definite signs of wear."

"Mine have worn out as well," Daria said, coming up to them, accompanied by an enchanted Jason.

She then sighed as she added, "I suppose we should go home now and end the fantasy. But it was so much fun while it lasted."

At that point, they saw Prince Alberich signal to a faerie attendant, who left the ballroom. He soon returned with a bejeweled cup that he handed to Prince Alberich. "This cup contains water that has been enchanted. Whoever drinks this water will be enchanted into forgetting his life above," Prince Alberich began, and for a moment,

Karen's heart stopped. Was he going to renege on the bargain? Was he going to keep Mark here forever as well as Jason? If so, she would be really mad at him and at herself for trusting a faerie.

"However, if the water is poured out onto the ballroom floor, anybody who has been enchanted by this water will be freed and will be able to return home," Prince Alberich continued, and with that, he took the cup and poured the water in it onto the ballroom floor.

Karen sighed in relief, and at that moment, she heard a man groan. Turning, she saw that Daria was looking at Jason, who had placed a hand to his head and was beginning to shake it as if he was coming out of a long sleep.

Prince Alberich then stepped forward toward Karen and Mark and extended the cup toward them. "You may have it, Mark, as a sign that you have won," he told the stunned young man.

Mark looked stunned, slowly extended his hand, and took the cup from the faerie prince. "Thank you," he said evenly.

"And you have been freed from the enchantment, Prince Jason," Prince Alberich continued, turning to him. "Since you have been enchanted for so long, I should inform you that your father is now dead and that your brother is now king of Vindicia. The man whom we allowed to discover this realm and thus free you is the one who killed your father in battle."

Jason looked stunned for a moment and then turned to look at Mark, whom Prince Alberich had pointed out. "You're the one who killed my father?" he asked.

"Yes, but I did not know the man whom I killed was the king until much later," Karen heard Mark assure Jason.

Jason frowned. "He was a terrible man, but he was my father, so I can't be delighted by his death," he admitted. "Still, I bear you no grudge since my father was a tyrant. And even when I was enchanted, at least I was free from his tyranny. Prince Alberich, what kind of king is my brother?"

"I have heard reports from the faeries who live underneath his realm that he is trying to be a better ruler than his father was," Prince Alberich said.

"He has stopped the war between Orgon and Vindicia," Karen said. "My father told us so himself. The invasion was costing a great deal of money. However, your father had recalled all the members of the Vindician embassy before his death, and your brother has allowed only a couple of men to return to the embassy. If you come back to my father's castle with my sisters, Mark, and me and explain with us what had happened, it's possible that your brother will restore diplomatic relations with us as a result of your safe return."

"The same Mark whom you apparently fell in love with?" Jason asked with a slight twinkle in his eyes. Karen nodded and looked down, feeling the blood rushing to her cheeks.

She then heard Jason say, "In that instance, as long as your sister Daria isn't going to stay here in the faerie realm, I'll be happy to return with you."

"Only Princess Winnifred will stay behind," Prince Alberich said. "The other two sisters are free to return home, and I'm sure Princess Karen will be betrothed to Mark very soon. And I will return with all of you to explain to the king what happened."

"Then I suppose we must go," Karen said, looking back up and extending her hand to Mark, who took it. Jason took Daria's hand while Prince Alberich took Winnifred's before leading them all out of the ballroom in preparation for the long trip back home.

As they walked through the castle, Karen took a good look around. The faerie castle had been such a lovely place, and it was a shame that she would probably never get to do any more dancing here. If she ever returned to the faerie realm, it would probably be to get herbs for medicinal purposes and not to do any dancing.

Still, she had her duty, and she had to return to become queen regnant after her father died and rule Orgon as best as she could. And her time dancing in the faerie realm had enabled her to ensure that she would marry the man she loved. So even if her time dancing there was over, at least it had been fun. And at least Winnifred was safe.

The six eventually exited the castle and walked the long way to the dock, where the boats sat waiting. Mark and Karen got into the first boat, Prince Alberich and Winnifred got into the second one, and Daria and Jason got into the last. The men rowed the boats all the way back to the other side, and then all six made their way through the three groves and through the secret passageway before reaching the crystalline staircase.

Prince Alberich said, "Once we exit through the trapdoor, you must summon the king to the princesses' quarters, Mark. We will be in the living room, and we will explain all that happened."

Karen saw Mark bow and say, "Very well, Your Highness."

And with that, they all prepared to exit the faerie realm and face the king.

*　　*　　*

King Robert yawned as he left his bedchamber fully clothed and met up with his attendants. It had only been moments since his manservant woke him up to inform him that Mark had important information concerning the princesses and that he had to meet Mark in the quarters that were reserved for them. The king fervently hoped that Mark's message meant that he had solved the mystery of where they went every night, so he had his manservant pick a good outfit out for him and wait with the other attendants while the king dressed himself.

Now the king left his quarters with his attendants and walked all the way to the tower where the princesses and their ladies had their rooms. On the way, he asked, "What time is it?"

"I think it's past three in the morning," the king's manservant said.

"If my daughters were up this late, no wonder they were so tired every morning," the king muttered. "I've never been up this late."

Finally, the king and his attendants reached his daughters' quarters and entered in the living room. There, he came on a most amazing and dazzling sight. First, he saw his daughters sitting together, dressed in the most magnificent gowns he had ever seen. Indeed, his daughter Karen's gown was so dazzling that it almost hurt his eyes. Then he looked to the side and saw three men standing nearby. The first was a man shining brilliantly and dressed in a doublet and breeches that were practically smothered in jewelry. He wore a magnificent crown on his head. Next to him was a second man who also wore the most magnificent outfit. It took him a while to realize that this was, in fact, Mark. The last man he recognized as Prince Jason.

"Prince Jason of Vindicia!" the king said in surprise and delight. "Are you unharmed?"

"Yes," Prince Jason said. "I have been treated very well, other than being enchanted."

"I believe I should explain everything to you," said the first man. "I am Crown Prince Alberich of the faerie troop that lives underneath Orgon. Prince Jason has been with us until tonight. We kept him in my realm because we were trying to protect him from his father and prevent him from committing suicide, which he was considering doing if he failed, and after learning that his father was going to use Jason's actions as an excuse to invade Orgon when your guard was down. We did not harm him."

"I am glad to hear that," said King Robert. Then he realized that Karen had told the truth about Prince Jason and that this meant she had been in league with the faeries.

So he turned to Karen and said, "You were in league with the faeries then. You and Winnifred were in league with them from the start. And you must have recruited Daria after I placed her with you."

Karen nodded. "We were," she admitted. "That's where we were every night, with them."

Mark then spoke up. "Every night a trapdoor would open in their bedroom, and they would travel down a crystalline spiral staircase and through a crystalline secret passage into a grove of trees with leaves of silver," he said. He took out a branch and held it up to the king, who could see that the leaves on it were like silver.

"Then they went through a grove of trees with leaves made of the purest gold." And as he said it, he held up a second twig with leaves that looked just like they were made of pure gold. "And finally, they went through a grove of trees with leaves that were made of diamonds." And Mark showed them a third twig with leaves that really shone like diamonds.

"After that, faerie escorts rowed us across a great lake to Prince Alberich's faerie castle," Daria added.

"It's so beautiful. That's why we all got these outfits," she added, looking down at her own sparkling gown. "The faeries dress so magnificently that the fancy gowns we had would be rather dingy in comparison."

"And here's proof that they really spent time at that castle," Mark added as he held up a bejeweled cup and handed it to King Robert.

"There were two reasons why I invited Princess Karen and Princess Winnifred to dance with us," Prince Alberich added. "I knew about Princess Karen falling in love with Mark, and I wanted to help them get together. I thought that this mystery would be the best way to ultimately make that happen. And with Princess Winnifred, I wanted to protect her. I knew that if she married the king of Brangavia, she would yield to the temptation to have an affair and would ultimately lose her head—literally. But if she stayed in the faerie realm, no harm would come to her, and she wouldn't lose her life."

The king was surprised to hear this. "I didn't think that faeries would care about humans to any real extent," he admitted.

"We're almost as diverse as you mortals are," Prince Alberich explained. "Only a few of us act viciously without any sort of provocation. They're what you'd call the criminal type of faeries. Some of us just don't have the same kind of morality that you do. If we kidnap children, it's usually not for a terrible purpose, at least not by our standards. It's either to just have some friends to play with or because we know that mortal boys and girls grow up, grow old, and die, and we don't want to see it happen. Others of us are positively good by your standards and ours. I'm in that category. But even faeries such as I can become quite savage if provoked. Your daughters know this and are very careful not to provoke me, especially your eldest and youngest daughters."

King Robert was pleased to hear that Karen and Daria were especially careful not to provoke the faerie prince. It was proof that they were wise enough not to get themselves in serious trouble. Sadly, he knew all too well that his daughter Winnifred wasn't anywhere near wise enough. Maybe this Prince Alberich was right. Maybe the faerie realm really *would* be safer for her than the mortal one.

"So my daughter Winnifred belongs to your people now?" the king asked the faerie prince.

"She does," Prince Alberich confirmed. "She has drunk faerie wine and thus belongs to us. Your other two daughters didn't drink any faerie wine. I was thinking of giving Princess Daria some, but that was before Prince Jason entered the picture. She is free to choose whether to join us or to stay in the mortal realm and marry Prince Jason or any other prince who might want to marry her. And Princess Karen, of course, is free to remain in the mortal realm if she so chooses."

King Robert suspected that he knew what his daughter Karen would choose, especially since Mark had discovered the secret of the dancing princesses. So he turned to Mark and said, "You have solved the mystery of where my daughters went every night. As promised, you may choose to marry whichever one of my daughters you prefer."

"My mind is already made up," Mark said. "If Karen will have me, I choose her."

And with that, he held out his hand to Karen, who began to blush as she extended her own hand. "I'd be delighted to be your wife, Mark," she said as he took her hand in his.

King Robert smiled. He was happy for his daughter and knew she'd be in good hands with Mark. And now it was time to settle his daughter Daria's fate. "Daria, you may choose either to remain in the faerie realm or return to us and marry whomever you prefer as long as it's a man who will be good to you."

"I wish to know what will happen to Prince Jason first before I make my decision," Daria said.

"Since my father is dead, I will not return to the faerie realm," Prince Jason said. "I wish to return home for a few months and see how my brother has been running Vindicia before I decide whether to stay there or come here to Orgon. But regardless of whether I choose to stay in Vindicia or in Orgon, I am free from my father, so I have no reason to remain in the faerie realm."

"Then I choose to remain with you, Father," Daria said. "And maybe I can have a relationship with you that isn't affected by enchantment, Jason."

"I'd like that," Prince Jason admitted, smiling at Daria.

"Then it's settled," Prince Alberich said. "Winnifred will come back with me to the faerie realm, while her sisters will remain with you. However, I will allow you at least one day to say your farewells to her."

"We'll take three days so I can announce her impending departure to the court," King Robert said. "After that, she can go with you."

"Very well," said Prince Alberich, bowing.

He turned to Winnifred and said, "In three days' time, you will be with the faeries forever."

Then he turned to the king and said, "I suspect that the preparations for your eldest daughter's wedding will take much longer than three days. So on the day that your daughter Karen is wed, I offer an invitation to have as many members of your court come to my realm, where I will have a magnificent wedding feast prepared for you."

"I hope I can attend the wedding and take part in the feast," Prince Jason suddenly said.

"If your brother will allow you to come, then you can come," the king said, and Prince Alberich nodded in confirmation. Then the faerie prince vanished.

King Robert turned to those who were left and said, "I believe I should call a special meeting to announce that you have solved the mystery, Mark. And when morning comes, I will invite those members of the Vindician embassy who are present to the castle and reveal that you are safe and sound, Prince Jason."

"I will write them a note that you can have sent to them when you send the invitation," Jason said.

King Robert nodded and said, "It is time for us to face the councilors. Come."

And with that, he led the way out of the princesses' quarters to the great hall and hopefully to a great future.

CHAPTER 21

It was past sunset as Mark entered the chapel in the castle magnificently dressed in a doublet made of golden cloth that shone like the sun, breeches made of a silvery cloth that glimmered like moonbeams, and a cape that seemed to be studded with sparkles like the stars in the sky. There were several times in the past month where he wondered if everything that happened was a marvelous dream. After the king called the councilors to a special meeting and began by announcing that he had discovered where the princesses had been every night, he then called both Karen and Mark himself to explain everything. He did most of the explaining, with Karen being the one to reveal the fate of Prince Jason of Vindicia, who was then presented to the council and confirmed Karen's explanation of the events that led to his enchantment and then his subsequent disenchantment.

King Robert then announced his intention to betroth Karen to Mark as his reward for successfully solving the mystery. The councilors all agreed, even Duke Thomas, although the duke did suggest that Mark receive a title of nobility to ensure that his marriage to Karen would be seen as suitable. The king agreed and ennobled Mark but didn't give him an estate to rule since he would soon marry Karen and not really need one. He also announced the impending departure of Winnifred to live with the faeries.

Later that morning, Mark stood alongside Karen as the king received the ambassador from Vindicia and revealed that Prince Jason had been found and that he was fine. He presented the prince to the ambassador and explained the circumstances behind Jason's disappearance. Mark later learned that the ambassador had immediately moved to contact King Christopher, who immediately came to Orgon to see if his brother had really been found and was safe and sound. When King Christopher saw his brother and learned the whole story of Jason's disappearance, he was so relieved that his brother was fine that he decided to open a new era of diplomatic relations with Orgon. And later that morning, Mark and Karen were officially betrothed.

As promised, Winnifred returned to the faeries after three days spent saying her goodbyes, and she never looked back. King Christopher allowed Prince Jason to stay in Orgon so he could spend time with Daria and develop a relationship with her that was unaffected by enchantment. During the month that passed, Jason and Daria apparently discovered that they had a lot in common; and thus, Mark believed that once he was married to Karen, Jason and Daria would be betrothed and eventually would wed as well.

And preparations for the wedding continued both publicly and privately. Because the wedding feast would not be held in the great hall as most royal wedding feasts did but instead in the faerie realm, a small but select number of guests were invited to be present not only for the wedding ceremony itself but also for the feasting afterward. King Robert coordinated the details with Prince Alberich. Ultimately, thirty guests were invited to attend the wedding itself, with Jason and Daria two of the thirty. The bishop who would be officiating the wedding was invited to attend the wedding feast afterward, but he declined, even though Prince Alberich promised to transport food and wine from the mortal realm to his for the benefit of the human guests so they would not risk eating any faerie food or wine and thus have to stay in there for a certain amount of time.

Meanwhile, Mark was sure that Karen was a virgin since she was a princess, and virginity was a lot more important for aristocratic and royal families than for commoners. Mark himself had engaged in sexual contact with Sarah but had not progressed to coitus, interrupted or otherwise, when Sarah's father ended his relationship. And Mark didn't want to have problems with intercourse on the wedding night because of lack of experience in sexual matters. So with her father's permission as well as Karen's agreement, he often went to her bedchamber and engaged in sexual contact with her, though he planned to wait until the wedding night for full coitus.

As Mark took his place and waited for the king and Karen to appear, he glanced at the guests who were present for the wedding ceremony. They were all wearing what was probably their very best outfits, although nowhere near as splendid as his own since it had been provided by the faeries. Along with the outfit was a letter from them that stated that they had given clothes to Jason and Daria that would look like splendid normal mortal outfits during the wedding itself, but once everyone attending the wedding feast went downstairs, Jason and Daria's outfits would transform to ones more suited for the faerie realm.

Mark did not have to wait long. Trumpets could be heard, and soon the king and Karen appeared in the entryway to the chapel. Mark's heart nearly stopped as he looked at her. She was wearing the gown she'd been given when she went dancing every night at Prince Alberich's castle. Her long golden red hair was worn loose and tumbled down past her shoulders, and on top of her head was a small crown of gold studded with precious jewels; she wore a shining diamond necklace around her neck, and she carried a sprig of rosemary, which represented love, fidelity, and fertility, the latter being very important for a royal couple as Mark well knew by now.

Karen joined Mark at the front of the altar and extended her hand to him. He took it, smiled happily at her, and turned to face the bishop, who promptly began the wedding ceremony. When Mark wasn't answering the questions of the bishop, he was gazing at Karen, who gazed back at him with an equally happy smile.

After both Mark and Karen said that they knew of no impediment that would make their marriage invalid, the king gave Mark a ring. Mark looked at it and saw a motto inscribed on it. It said, "My heart is his alone." Mark smiled at the motto before putting it on Karen's ring finger. Then he took Karen into his arms and kissed her before the king announced that it was now time to depart for the wedding feast.

* * *

Prince Alberich certainly knew how to provide convenient access to the faerie world. That was what Karen thought when she and Mark followed her father out of the chapel, followed by Daria, Jason, and the other wedding guests, and saw a trapdoor open in front of her father. He looked askance, so Karen had to give him a nod when he turned to look at her so he could descend through the opening into the faerie realm.

And just as before, when she descended through the opening, there was a crystalline spiral staircase that glowed in the gloom of the dark ground. Whereas she and her sisters had to travel through a secret passage to get to the avenue of trees with silvery leaves, this time when she reached the bottom, the avenue of trees was directly in front of her. She took Mark's hand as the two followed her father through the avenue of trees.

At one point before they reached the avenue of trees with golden leaves, she looked back and saw that both Jason and Daria's clothes had transformed from normal-looking outfits into ones appropriate for a banquet and for dancing in the faerie realm. Jason's doublet, breeches, and cape shone like moonbeams while Daria's gown now sparkled like starlight.

After passing through the three avenues of trees, she once again saw the great lake where faerie escorts were waiting for the wedding party in front of a number of boats. One of the escorts said, "Prince Mark, you will row Princess Karen across the lake. And, Prince Jason, you will row Princess Daria across. We will row the others."

"Thank you," Karen heard Mark say.

As they approached one of the boats, Mark turned to Karen and said, "I don't think I would ever have thought in my wildest dreams that I'd be addressed as a prince."

"You earned it," Karen reassured him. "You saved my sister Winnifred from molestation. You also discovered the means by which we were leaving our room every night, although Prince Alberich and I allowed you to do so. But saving my sister helped you win my heart."

Mark smiled and said, "I'm glad about that." He helped Karen into one of the boats. Once she was inside, he got into the boat and began rowing it away from shore.

Karen looked out over the vast expense of water and smiled. Even if she visited the faerie realm after this time, this was probably the last time she'd visit the castle in this way. Future trips, if there were any, would probably be for herbal plants to use in herbal medicines, and she didn't need grand entrances to obtain those. Most likely, she would be provided with other quicker means for entrance into Prince Alberich's realm.

Finally, her boat arrived at the dock on the other side. Once they arrived, Mark stepped out of the boat and helped Karen out of it, and then they waited until everyone arrived before making the long trip up to the great crystalline castle.

Prince Alberich was standing in the entryway to the castle. He looked magnificent as always and said, "Welcome, Prince Mark, Princess Karen, King Robert, Princess Daria, Prince Jason, and other members of the wedding party. I will explain to you what will happen once we enter the banquet hall, which is close to the ballroom. I have managed to obtain food and wine from the mortal realm for my mortal guests. The guests of mine who are faeries, which now includes Princess Winnifred, will have food from my realm to eat and faerie wine to drink. King Robert, once the last of the food has been cleared away, you, two of your attendants, and two of mine will escort Prince Mark and Princess Karen to private rooms in this castle so that they can be put to bed."

Karen knew what that meant—the bedding ceremony. But Mark might not since he was a commoner by birth. So she asked, "May I explain privately to Mark what this means?"

"Because he's a commoner by birth?" Prince Alberich said, his eyes twinkling slightly. "Of course."

"Actually, commoners have bedding ceremonies as do the aristocracy and royalty," Mark said, "though I doubt they are as private for royalty."

"Normally, I don't believe royal bedding ceremonies are as private as commoner ones, but we'll try to establish more privacy for your sake, Prince Mark," Prince Alberich said. "After you two are properly dressed for the bedding ceremony and you are together in the bedchamber we've prepared for you, we will give you a concoction of wine and spices that is supposed to be beneficial to your health, and we will leave you alone to consummate your marriage. My attendants may come in later that evening to ask you how you are doing, but if you're . . . *enjoying* yourself, they won't even bother asking. They'll just leave you alone. And we'll have faerie music playing outside from attendants who have been told not to come in. You will stay the night here and be allowed to leave tomorrow morning as will the rest of your wedding party."

"Thank you," Karen heard Mark say in obvious relief. "We've been . . . practicing how to consummate the marriage, but we actually haven't done so."

But Karen had a question of her own. "Prince Alberich, tomorrow morning before we leave, may Mark and I be allowed to tour your herbal garden?"

"Of course," Prince Alberich said. "And you can return any time you need to for medicinal herbs that can help cure illnesses that are terminal in the mortal world."

"That reminds me," Karen heard Daria say. "I love your library. While I won't be spending time in the faerie realm forever, maybe you can allow me to come back here from time to time and read the books in your library, at least until I hopefully am betrothed to Jason and eventually marry him."

"My brother and I have agreed that once the wedding ceremony is over, I will return to Vindicia," Jason explained. "But before then, Daria and I might be betrothed."

"I'd be willing to let you spend time in my library," Prince Alberich said. "And while the ruler of the faerie troop that is connected to Vindicia isn't as friendly to mortals as I am, he's becoming friendlier since the former king died in battle. He might allow you both to spend time in his library, which is just as huge."

"I hope he does," Karen heard Jason say.

"Before we go in for the feast, I have a wedding gift for the two of you," Prince Alberich said, turning back to Karen and Mark. "And I did have to ask for permission from the Creator Deity to give my gift since it involves stuff that is in the future."

Karen nodded at Mark, not wanting him to feel like she was dominating him. After all, Mark was a man, and most men in her experience didn't want to feel like a woman was dominating him, especially if the woman in question had a higher rank. "We'd both be happy to have the wedding gift," Mark said.

Prince Alberich waved his hands in the air and then placed one hand on Karen's head and the other on Mark's. "The two of you will have a long and happy marriage and have three gallant sons and two lovely daughters, all of whom will live long enough to become adults," he said. "After you become queen regnant and king consort, you will rule happily over the land of Orgon till the end of your days, winning the respect and devotion of your subjects."

"Now *that* is the best wedding present anybody could ever give," Karen heard her father say.

"Thank you," Prince Alberich said, bowing. "Shall we enter?"

"Of course," the king said.

Prince Alberich led the wedding party to the banquet hall and threw open the doors to a flourish of trumpets and kettledrums as he announced, "The wedding party for Prince Mark and Princess Karen have now arrived!" Karen saw all the faeries whom she had encountered over her time dancing in the faerie realm. And she saw Winnifred wearing a magnificent gown and looking happier than ever.

While there may be ups and downs after the wedding feast and her return to Orgon—Karen was a realist after all—as she looked at Mark, Karen knew that, in the end, she and Mark were going to live happily ever after.

The End

Lightning Source UK Ltd.
Milton Keynes UK
UKHW011842060921
390144UK00008B/527/J